M.J. FARRELL

is the pseudonym for Molly Keane. She was born in Co. Kildare, Ireland, in 1904 into 'a rather serious Hunting and Fishing and Church-going family' who gave her little education at the hands of governesses. Her father originally came from a Somerset family and her mother, a poetess, was the author of 'The Songs of the Glens of Antrim'. Molly Keane's interests when young were 'hunting and horses and having a good time': she began writing only as a means of supplementing her dress allowance, and chose the pseudonym M.J. Farrell 'to hide my literary side from my sporting friends'. She wrote her first novel, *The Knight of the Cheerful Countenance*, at the age of seventeen.

Molly Keane published ten novels between 1928 and 1952: *Young Entry* (1928), *Taking Chances* (1929), *Mad Puppetstown* (1931), *Conversation Piece* (1932), *Devoted Ladies* (1934), *Full House* (1935), *The Rising Tide* (1937), *Two Days in Aragon* (1941), *Loving Without Tears* (1951) and *Treasure Hunt* (1952). She was also a successful playwright, of whom James Agate said 'I would back this impish writer to hold her own against Noel Coward himself.' Her plays, with John Perry, always directed by John Gielgud, include *Spring Meeting* (1938), *Ducks and Drakes* (1942), *Treasure Hunt* (1949) and *Dazzling Prospect* (1961).

The tragic death of her husband at the age of thirty-six stopped her writing for many years. It was not until 1981 that another novel— *Good Behaviour*—was published, this time under her real name. Molly Keane has two daughters and lives in Co. Waterford. Her latest novel, *Time After Time*, was published in 1983.

Virago publish *Devoted Ladies*, *The Rising Tide*, *Two Days in Aragon*, and *Mad Puppetstown*. *Full House*, *Taking Chances* and *Young Entry* are forthcoming.

D1292246

TWO DAYS IN ARAGON

M.J. FARRELL

With a New Introduction by
POLLY DEVLIN

PENGUIN BOOKS – VIRAGO PRESS

PENGUIN BOOKS
Viking Penguin Inc., 40 West 23rd Street,
New York, New York 10010, U.S.A.
Penguin Books Ltd, Harmondsworth,
Middlesex, England
Penguin Books Australia Ltd, Ringwood,
Victoria, Australia
Penguin Books Canada Limited, 2801 John Street,
Markham, Ontario, Canada L3R 1B4
Penguin Books (N.Z.) Ltd, 182–190 Wairau Road,
Auckland 10, New Zealand

First published in Great Britain by Collins 1941
This edition first published in Great Britain by Virago Press Ltd 1985
Published in Penguin Books 1986

ISBN 0 14 016.122 8

Printed in Great Britain by
Cox and Wyman at Reading, Berkshire
Set in Baskerville

INTRODUCTION

Two Days in Aragon was Molly Keane's ninth novel and is perhaps her most ambitious. Written in 1941 when the passage of time and events had cast the traumatic and dreadful events of the Irish Civil Wars of the 1920s into a new perspective, the book, on one level, is a threnody, or lamentation, for the great houses of Ireland and the end of a way of life. On another, it is a celebration of those same houses, and the life that was lived in them—and there too on different levels—by the Anglo-Irish and their Catholic servants alike; but it is also, and most satisfactorily I think, a special kind of record of the social system that pertained among the Ascendancy in the South of Ireland and a close look at those golden beehives that such "big" houses were. This social system, based on the existence of a separate, large and ostensibly powerful Ascendancy finally perished in the time of the Troubles, but it had begun to crumble with the demise of Landlordism many years before, and in the destruction or abandonment of many of the great houses its epitaph was composed.

Yet if it seems merely a shocking act of vandalism that such beautiful monuments should have been put to the torch, one must remember that to the mass of the Irish, whose forbears had been dispossessed to make way for the great demesnes over which these houses presided, they were more than great buildings. It was not easy for the Irish to perceive them as beautiful artefacts, ornaments to the countryside. They were establishments, symbols, more like Residencies than residences, and as such, when the smouldering resentments of centuries flamed into open rebellion, became targets for the flame—in every sense. And the simile of the Residency can be carried further since the English Government regarded the Irish uprising of 1916 ("The Easter Rising") as mutiny and executed nearly all its leaders.

The ways of life conducted within these Anglo-Irish houses were alien to the Irish way of life. It was not merely a question of class differences, although it was certainly that too. There was no question of anyone from the Anglo-Irish side crossing the great social divide that lay between what are sometimes called "the races". The Anglo-Irish had allegiance to the British Crown; England was their mother country, though Ireland may have been their native land: and it was English manners, mores, modes that pertained among them. Perhaps most of all the dividing line was religion: the Anglo-Irish were to a man Protestant— Catholicism or Romanism was "common". "Even so late as 1932 an Irish Peer who showed leanings towards Rome was taken by his father to look at the Sunday congregation streaming out of the Catholic church on the estate and asked how he could ally himself with them." (Terence de Vere White, *The Anglo-Irish*, Gollancz 1972). There is hostility there, and there always was hostility, though it was cloaked on one side by patronage, on the other by subservience or evasion. The way of life in the "big houses" was superimposed on the other way of life in Ireland—that of the vast majority of the population who were Catholics, spoke English as a foreign tongue and whose accent was called a brogue (the other meaning of which, interestingly enough, was a cheat), and who led lives that were more impenetrable, secret and unknowable than those of their Ascendancy masters. What is extraordinary is that so many of the Anglo-Irish, whilst recognising the irredeemable spaces between them and the mass of the people, did not

admit to their otherness. Stephen Gwynn, an ardent Irish
nationalist, born in a rectory, and who felt himself to be Irish
to the backbone, wrote "The new nationalism describes me
and the likes of me as Anglo-Irish. So all my life I have been
spiritually hyphenated without knowing it." It's as good a
description as any, and that other hyphen joining the
separate existences of the Anglo-Irish and the Irish on Irish
soil was wiped out in the Troubles and their aftermath.

Molly Keane, almost inadvertently one might suppose,
and one would be quite wrong to do so (for she is artful in her
modesty), has preserved as much of the minutiae of the last
days of the Irish Raj as any writer with more pretension to
posterity. She did not mean to be a writer, never mind a
social historian, and claims not to have set out to do anything
other than to escape the bonds of her extraordinary
upbringing in a large house in County Wexford where her
parents lived in a way that was both eccentric yet typical of
the gentry of that time. They ignored their children for the
most part save for insisting on their skill in horsemanship,
which was an essential accomplishment.

Molly Keane—or Skrine, her maiden name—was
educated in fits and starts by a series of governesses, and in
the gaps in between them, by her mother, whom she now
recalls as a remarkable linguist and musician, and who
under the pseudonym Moira O'Neill was a successful
rhymster writing about the countryside and people of
Ireland with charm and sentimentaiity. "She made no
attempt to pass any of her interests or accomplishments on to
her children. I now think what an interesting woman she
must have been. But I chiefly remember being alone as a
child—my elder sister was away at a High School in Oxford
and my brothers were at school in England. I never *did* go to
school there."

When she was older there was an attempt to formalise her

education and she went to a French school in Bray, outside Dublin, until a doctor diagnosed incipient T.B., in those days a killing disease. She was sentenced to bed for an indefinite period and out of sheer boredom started to write; or that, at least, is one of the legends. The other is that she wrote, in desperation, to earn pin money to supplement her tiny dress allowance. From the beginning she used a pseudonym, M.J. Farrell. Like mother, like daughter, though her mother never recognised it.

Startled though she was, to discover herself a writer, once started Molly Keane never looked back, and over three decades, in intense and painful bouts of writing, crammed into a few months taken off from her precious hunting, she wrote eleven novels and four plays (in collaboration with John Perry) which were great successes in the West End. Margaret Rutherford made her name in one and John Gielgud directed all four. Her last play *Dazzling Prospect*, produced in 1961, at a time when the spate of Angry Young Men plays had changed the conventions of West End theatre, was a failure.

Sarah Miles, straight out of RADA, had her first professional role in it and she once ruefully remembered, "Never was there a less apt title than *Dazzling Prospect*. It marked one of the last times that people actually threw spoiled fruit at actors in a West End production." Times had changed. As they had for M.J. Farrell whose beloved husband Bobbie Keane died suddenly, tragically aged only thirty-six. She stopped writing; not till the 1980's did she resurrect herself as a writer, this time under her own name, with the novels *Good Behaviour*, a wild success, and *Time After Time*, a dazzling *tour de force*. (She tells a good story of how, at a dinner party in her honour in Paris, the guests expressed their horror of Jasper the hero of the book "Quel bête" they said, and congratulated her on her ferocious imagination at conjuring up such a horror. "But Jasper" she said, smiling gently, "c'est moi.")

Two Days in Aragon was one of the last books to be written in her great creative period between the wars. It was written after her marriage to Bobbie Keane "a witty, happy man who loved old furniture, me, his daughters, good food and talk". *Two Days in Aragon* sets out to be more deliberately serious than her other books and though it is occasionally portentous and sentimental it is also sympathetic to the Irish cause. It also tackles head on what is either implicit in her earlier work or avoided: the enormous, vexed problem that was Ireland's turbulent relationship with England which was coming to a horrid head in the times of which she was writing. These years of rebellion and fighting are known as the Troubles, though god knows the troubles had been going on for centuries, but by 1920 the fighting was "a dreary record of reprisals and counter reprisals, burnings, murders and outrages, not between armies but between expert gunmen on both sides" (Edmund Curtis, *A History of Ireland*, Methuen 1961). The gunman became the new symbol for Ireland.

Molly Keane wrote *Two Days in Aragon* partly for her beloved husband who, she said, was far more open-minded than she, and saw things more clearly at the time they were happening. But the book was also written as a kind of atonement for her contemporaneous attitude, her condemnations and her lack of understanding. An understandable lack of understanding and one shared by so many of her class, epitomised by the attitude of her mother, who, Molly Keane once surmised, "would have dismissed Yeats as just another Irish patriot. She couldn't think that the English had ever done anything wrong whereas of course they had behaved appallingly for generation after generation."

As an artist, Molly Keane saw both sides of the tragic Irish question. She perceived, too, that the young Irishmen her friends thought of simply as murderers and fanatics, were fighting for their basic right to be self-governing. She gives excuses for their behaviour though they believed that they had reasons, moral imperatives, which, were they not to be fulfilled, would constitute treachery not only to their country but to themselves as Irishmen. This was something outside her experience but she accommodated it. Indeed throughout the book one gets the feeling of the author giving her imagination a specific imaginative wrench, jolting it to sympathy and forgiveness.

Two Days in Aragon is a precise title. The novel relates the tragic sequence of events over the last two days of Aragon, a great house by a large river in County Westmeath. Molly Keane took the name from a mountain—Araglin—near where she lived, but its name inevitably invokes the close connections that have always existed between Spain and Ireland; a strange empathy based as much on emotional affinities as on their shared, rabidly Catholic history and heritage.

Aragon is a spectacularly beautiful house, an amalgam of houses Molly Keane knew and loved, many of which were destroyed in the Troubles, and she delivers it marvellously, lying golden and rich in its demesne and valley, its inhabitants living apparently effortlessly in a way that, though long doomed, is still flourishing. Her details are so engaging; the things people eat (she describes the meals with a delicious relish that bespeaks a great cook) the way the house is furnished: the joy of cupboards full of fine linen, the sprawl of a house that is clean and grand and spacious. And, as in all the houses in her books, history and portent hang heavy in all the rooms. "The past doesn't dwell in people's minds now in the way that it did" she says, and it's a sentiment she voices strongly in *Two Days in Aragon*.

What was there then in the air of the houses that is not now?
Was it more stirred by the emotions of the past than now,
when the life of the present is gay and firm in the ether with the
radio ministering to the loneliest? Radio has stirred away the
hauntings and stillness in the old rooms. The waves of the past
cannot lap and lap, quietly encroaching onto the solid sands of
now. Houses and memories have less power to injure, less
power to assuage.

In all her books houses play an *active* part—she treats them as
though they had an actual awful power for good or ill.
Aragon's power appears benign but occasionally Molly
Keane twitches aside the serene veil and shows the
malevolence that has accumulated behind the aftermath of
evil done there, as in the discovery of a torture chamber built
by a sadistic forbear of the Foxes, the family who have
always lived in the house.

Mrs Fox, fluffy-headed, childish and widowed since her
husband died after a hunting accident, and her two children
Sylvia and Grania, are the owners of the house, but at the
pivot of the novel is its true inheritor Nan O'Neill. Molly
Keane has drawn in Nan O'Neill a powerful portrait of a
powerful woman, standing at the centre of the book as she
does of Aragon. Our first glimpse of her is as solid and sure as
a figure in Chardin or a Brueghel painting as she emerges
from the shadows of Aragon into the reader's vision in a blue
blouse and full black skirt and white apron, "its sure
soothing shape as sure a shape as a sail". Nan O'Neill is a
melodramatic figure, histrionic, obsessive and compulsive.
As its housekeeper, guardian and protector she is the living
embodiment of Aragon, which she literally worships.
Aragon is her temple, her shrine, and the people who live in
it are sacred to her, except for Miss Pigeon, an ancient Fox
aunt and scapegoat for Nan's complex pent-up virulence
and cruelties. Not surprising, since the same blood that

flowed in the veins of the builder of the torture chamber flows in Nan's veins. For she is the illegitimate daughter of the father of Hugh Fox, dead father of Sylvia and Grania, and is therefore a cousin.

Molly Keane is firing on all barrels in her outrageous portrait of Miss Pigeon, who is in fact the kind of eccentric gentlewoman who used to lurk, backwatered in the great houses, not just of Ireland, but all over Europe from Sicily to Scotland. "It was extraordinary how many old aunts there were everywhere in all the houses, getting dottier all the time, utterly arrogant and absolutely certain of their right to *be* there. They were there because they never married—there was a great shortage of men. The arrogance they were born with. I took such things for granted then, as one took so much—the whole of life is so different. None of the owners of these houses worked—they never thought of working. They had their horses, a pack of hounds, shooting, fishing—it was a hard day's work just keeping up with those things—and one needed so much less money. When I think of how Bobbie [Keane] and I lived at Belleville, I really believe that you would need at least twenty times the income now." Belleville was the beautiful house near the Blackwater river where Molly Keane and her husband spent their happy married life. Belleville was not the model for Aragon, though the Blackwater is the same river that Aragon looks down on. She remembers that "everything went up and down the river, starting with the Phoenicians—little steamers and boats plying between Youghal and Cappoquin. My father-in-law started up a boat service—the boat was called 'The Happy Harry'. Of course the service *cost* money rather than made it and during the Troubles the Republicans took the boat over—I suppose they thought it was bringing soldiers in. It got caught between the two warring parties and was sunk. That kind of thing is what happened to many houses—

Woodrooff for example [where Molly Keane spent a
formative time away from her parents] was only burnt down
because it was on a strategic point between Clare and
Clonmel and was caught in the crossfire.''

Aragon as painted by Molly Keane is a representative of
these great houses, lived in by people who felt themselves at
one with the country, who counted themselves Irish, who
were looked after by Irish servants, but who might have
come from a different planet as regards how the Irish viewed
and regarded them. In *Two Days in Aragon* Molly Keane
inclined to the view that these houses had come to the end of
their useful lives, that their span was over, and that their
burning was a cremation. Just as many people, looking back,
see the 1914 War as inevitable in a way, if only to put an end
to a way of life that was inappropriate to the twentieth
century, so it appears that the demise of Aragon—and all
such houses—was historically inevitable. Ireland after the
signing of the Treaty and for many years after it, might be
likened to China in the throes of the Cultural Revolution,
save that the killing was done. The way of life that loomed
ahead had no place in it for gracious living.

The burning of their houses was an enormous shock to the
Anglo-Irish who believed themselves to be Irish and believed
too that they commanded the loyalty of those who lived
around them and worked for them. They deceived
themselves. There was loyalty and love, certainly, but of a
kind, and it was ambivalent. The Conquered Celt has never
been straightforward in his dealing with those who consider
themselves to be socially superior. This attitude is perhaps
best summed up in David Thomson's great book *Woodbrook*
in which he speaks about the servants of an Irish house,
''They secretly cherished hatred for the major, their present
landlord and employer, whom in day to day relationships
they loved—cherished this hatred because of his ancestors

and theirs and because it might help their advancement."

Nan of Aragon is not of this ilk . . . her devotion to the house and its family is total. She serves it like a slave, proud of her chains, and though she herself is a Fox she regards the family as so far removed from her that an alliance is unthinkable. Indeed the leap that Grania, the younger of the two Fox daughters, makes in taking a native Irishman for her lover is almost unimaginably daring and damning. The appalled exclamation in *Two Days in Aragon* "that a Fox, a daughter of Aragon, should carry on an affair with an O'Neill from the mountain, was as wrong, Grania knew, to Nan as the love of black and white people seemed to her" is utterly in context with such an atmosphere. And even though this particular O'Neill is Nan's own son, she is as shocked as though she has discovered some arcane form of miscegnation. "A person like that, what can anybody nice think of you if this gets known—it's a deeply terrible shocking thing, my child, to let a man like that touch you, and of course if anybody gets to know you have then it's too dreadful, it's too dreadful then." This is to do with class. Distinctions were absolute and constituted even more of a chasm in Ireland than pertained in England.

Molly Keane has an acute ear for Irishisms, things that Irish people said that were often treasured up by those who heard them and recounted at dinner for fond patronising amusement. But hers are classic and funny and make absolute sense in their paradox, as in Nan's comment as she looks in horror at a ferret. "Everyone has their favourite animal that they hate."

Molly Keane herself seems an amalgam of Grania and Sylvia. Grania is the wild, poetic creature who makes the leap over convention and Sylvia the cool, swift elder sister, sharp as a lemon, willingly locked into a conventional way of life that could as easily be lived in England as in Ireland.

Grania, silly, artless, without a grain of common sense, is fired by ignorant, useless bravery. She is culpably innocent; a girl who causes trouble because she ignores convention and because she cannot help it. She is open-hearted and uncalculatingly gullible, a fat little slut who is a great hand at curling her hair but not too good at washing—the reverse of the impeccable, shining Sylvia, street-wise, elegant, calculating, who knows the cost of everything and finds out the price of love.

Yet it is not golden Grania, who would have died for love, who comes nearest to death, but Sylvia, and that because of the code by which she lives, a code which is so much a part of her existence that it impels her to the impossible. Sylvia, the perfect little deputy mistress of Aragon, as one day she plans to be the perfect Lady Purvis in Norfolk, is an unlikeable, though admirable character. Just once does she become human, when she makes that remarkable pact of love with the other side, the enemy. As a result her perfectly ordered life, rigid in its perfection, can never be the same again, nor can her belief in the correctness of things, in good behaviour. Even her attitude towards the man who is to be her husband will be coloured by her secret, shocking knowledge that the call of man to woman is beyond class divide, though it is she who is the cruellest snob in the book.

In *Two Days in Aragon* Molly Keane looks at the rights and wrongs of a series of traumatic events in the course of two days of Irish history in an Irish house. In doing so she has made a miniature of something very large and sad, the history of Ireland and the people who lived there and loved her. It is a fictional account of bitter events and sad truths. Elizabeth Bowen, her great friend and owner of Bowen's Court, a house in spirit much like the one called Aragon, concluded sadly at the end of her own Anglo-Irish family history, ''The stretches of the past I have to cover have been on the whole painful. My family got their position and drew their power from a situation that shows an inherent wrong. In the grip of that situation England and Ireland each turned to the other a closed, harsh, distorted face, a face their lovers would hardly know." Molly Keane saw both faces very clearly on both days in Aragon.

Polly Devlin, Somerset, 1985

I

GRANIA FOX was eighteen. She was alone in a wood she knew very well, far beyond the house and above the river. She was waiting. But she never projected herself from one moment into the next, from one day into another, because she had no imagination.

Now she took in through her body the streaming pallor of the spring light spread across the wide shallow valley beneath the woods ; the river without any glare on its smooth, lit flowing ; the fields, warm and living as flesh under the sun ; the smells of honey and gum from the blue larches and the gorse. She knew of a little dog's hunting lust, and ditches of primroses dry for sitting down, sheltered for love. She had a bunch of primroses, their pink stalks damp in her hand, fisted as in childhood to hold them—their scent was dry as powder—the lightest most affecting scent. Where was her dog now ? Where was Soo, her little black bitch?

" Soo, Soo, Soo, naughty one, Soo ! "

A little black deer came flying through its forest of game, a little black unicorn without its horn ; flying back from its other life, its great and wild life where it was a terror and a menace to the wood things, the birdies, the bunnies, the mice, the moles ; back to her slave-love life —eyes shining, unknowing of Grania. A spring into her arms, into her heart, but Grania has no claim on her now. A kiss for a wild hunter and freedom of woods and coverts till the hunter grows weary, and then come back, my little Pompey, my slave love.

Grania had no repose. She flew about doing things all the time. Now she thought she had time to get some watercress before her lover came to her. In the ditch just outside the wood there was plenty of watercress, excellent watercress, growing cleanly and richly in the steep dark ditch. She had better get some watercress.

Grania was a fat little blonde with pretty bones under her flesh ; rather a slut, and inclined to wear party shoes with old tweeds. She would be in her bath, and forget to wash very much, but she was a great hand at curling up her blonde hair, of which she was very vain. Three of the most marriageable young men in the County West-common had asked her to marry them ; but they had no skill for love-making so she refused them all, and returned to Foley O'Neill, who embraced her in woods and other out-of-the-way places, whereas the eligible young men seldom did more than hold her hand before they pro-posed. Foley O'Neill did not propose. He was so much her social inferior. A fantastic reason perhaps, but good enough for him, as he did not really want to marry her.

This evening Grania did not see him until he was beside her, she was so occupied with her watercress. He smiled and said to her in that quiet voice, neither quite of the common people nor quite of Grania's people.

" Aren't you going to talk to me at all to-day ? "

" How long have you been here ? "

" Hours and hours——"

" And hours—What a lie ! I must get this bit of cress. Wait a minute."

Instead of saying, " I can't wait," or " It's not a lie," he got down in the ditch too and picked cress neatly and seriously beside her. He could put love away while it was closer than at present.

Foley had always been a person of importance. When he was four years old his father died and his mother left the mountain farm and went back to Aragon, where she had been nurse to the Fox's before she married—there was Fox blood in her and she could not leave the place. Dymphnia O'Neill was her name, but they called her Nan at Aragon.

Foley's Aunt Gipsy, his father's sister, looked after him through his childhood, flattering and coaxing him as

" the young Master," " the young Boss." Aunt Gipsy managed the farm in a sort of a way under Nan's direction from Aragon.

Nan had always hated the poor twist of mountainy farm she had married into. But when she lived there she had worked and striven on it with all her power, civilising it a little more every year.

Nan never wanted her son to be a farmer. She spent far beyond her means on his education. From his youngest days she had horses in her mind for him—such horses were his life and his trade now. He was brave, hardworking and lucky, and, insofar as maybe in this precarious way of living, he now made a success of horse dealing.

Foley loved and feared his mother. He would discuss the twists of people's characters and circumstances with her if he wished to get the better of them in a deal. His respect for her opinion was strong. He was very much afraid of her knowing about this love affair with Grania, which she would have condemned utterly.

" Where's that silly little dog of yours to-day ? " Foley thought they had picked enough watercress for the present. They sat together on the bank.

" Hunting. She's not silly." Grania always rose in defence of her dog—her beautiful little black bitch.

" Silly and useless. She hasn't even got a tail."

" Oh, how dare you ! She's not meant to have one. Who ever saw a Schipperke with a tail. Don't be silly."

" Well, what is she good for ? "

" Good for love—they're love dogs."

" No good. They're a rotten breed of dog."

" They're the Barge dogs of Holland. You know, they pull the barges up and down the canals."

" You're telling lies," he picked up her hand and bit her wrist gently. Deeply. Real pain.

" Oh, Foley, poor Grania."

" You're telling lies and you have to be punished." The shadows of leaves were flickering across her fat white neck, trembling at a certain depth within her eyes.

He said, " I've got a present for you."

" What is it ? " She tried to keep her voice steady. But this was too much—this breaking off from love. She had no experience.

" A new ferret. It's in the car."

His triangular blue eyes held hers. He was speaking across his pause in love-making.

She answered with difficulty. " Oh, how lovely. Shall we go and talk to him ? "

He laughed, putting his arms round her.

" Do you think we need him now ? "

" No——No——"

It's not me. It's not myself. Grania was transcended, purged of all fret, or small unhappy thought, running home through the woods to her house built above the river. Soo ran beside her, leaping for the ferret that dangled horrid and malign from her hand. Across the valley the woods reached strange evening heights and deeps of shadows. Near her path were little pale blue mosses and water-green patches of bracken. Love sang at her heart no more. She had made a moment's peace with love, and now she was planning how to get a box arranged for this ferret before dinner.

II

DOWN on the dark kept paths nearer the house Grania
met her Aunt Pigeon. Aunt Pigeon was old. She was an
invalid they said. She had her own bedroom and sitting-
room, and Nan Foley looked after her. She had been tall
and fat once but now she looked to be a small old woman,
the flesh all fallen from her elegant bones—her body
huddled together and dressed in absurdly old clothes.

"We really must get Aunt Pigeon a new dress,"
Grania's mother had been saying distractedly for the last
ten years. With her voice she had a way of making
almost anything seem impossible of accomplishment ; " I
must rush to the garden for one instant and try to plant
this primrose before it quite dies." Everything was like
that. " I wonder if that tiresome child ought to have a
tonic ? Cod liver oil ? Do try to remind me, darling, if
you possibly can."

Certainly there had never been a new dress for Aunt
Pigeon. It was too difficult. She was wearing a waisted
black jacket this evening, sticking out over her thin
behind and trimmed with braid. She had a yellow-brown
skunk fur on her shoulders with topaz yellow eyes, and an
elaborate fastening system. The long skirt nearly covered
those thick boots that Nan Foley bought in the village,
and which were so heavy on her exquisitely made but
perfectly flat little feet—and then you had to lace them
up. It was a terrible business every morning, every
morning of your life. Aunt Pigeon's face was as white as
a sheep's face. Her eyes still held a little of the blue
they had been, so she always liked to wear a blue scarf
or a bit of blue trimming somewhere to bring out their
colour. To Grania and Sylvia she was part of life. They
could never remember a time when they had not known
she was more childish than themselves. They were not
particularly kind to her. Darling Nan looked after her,

and they knew she did not like Nan. Poor Nan had some
terrible times with her ; for instance, when she would not
sleep in bed on account of catching leprosy. The only way
to avoid leprosy was to sleep on the stairs. She took
terrible fancies when she got a glass of port, Nan said, oh
terrible. Such talk of Heathen Gods then, you couldn't
believe it ; and saucers of milk for the fairies tripping
you up wherever you went. Since earliest days the children
could remember finding those little offerings, hidden
under leaves, left behind stones or in nooks of trees for
her Diblins, as she called them. Dolls' saucers of curds
and jam, scraps of buttered toast from breakfast, sometimes the children ate them, sometimes the dogs. Aunt
Pigeon wagged her head solemnly when she could
remember where she had put the saucers and saw them
emptied.

Finding her this evening in the darkness of the towering
rhododendron, among the glossy darkness of the laurel
leaves, Grania had a chill moment before the customary
way of seeing Aunt Pigeon came back to her, and she was
blinded again by custom to that moment's vision of a
different creature ; alive, rather wild, strong in its desires.
Aunt Pigeon was putting something away in her pocket
which she wore hung on a tape round her waist. Complicated explorations were in progress among skirt and
petticoat, a prolonged grope for what she called her
sporran.

" I keep everything most precious just here," she would
say, patting the hiding-place with a calm and unem-
barrassed gesture. " You'd be surprised how many people
have been after this little pattern of mine. You'd be
amazed. It's so nice for when I travel. Oh, and such a
comfort to think there's one place nobody can pry into."

To-day Grania detected a good deal of bustle and confusion as Aunt Pigeon stowed away some treasure. It
might be an old ring or a letter or some morsel for the
Diblins, over which she had been brooding by herself
among the dark evergreens.

" What have you got in your sporran to-night, Aunt Pigeon ? " she asked. Aloof, benignant, patronising, she spoke from the distance of a world away—from her different star.

" Hush." Aunt Pigeon came nearer and whispered. " It's a surprise for my Diblins."

" What is it ? "

" I've been bird's nesting," Aunt Pigeon said in a tough buccaneering tone of voice. " Three Thrushes' eggs and two Blackbirds', what d'you think o' that ? "

" But did you take the eggs away ? "

" Safe in my sporran."

" And take care they don't hatch there."

" Ah, they may hatch and flutter their wings, they can't get out of my sporran."

" But the poor big Birdies ? "

" Oh, they can lay more eggs."

" Hard on them."

" Fun for them. It's nature."

" And Aunt Pigeon won't take any more eggs ? "

" Aunt Pigeon will come creeping—creeping up to their nests." She gave an imitation of herself that was a little frightening, moving without a sound on the soft path. " Pigeon will find a brown nest in the silver holly, she will put her hand into it, quiet as a mouse. Oh, it's so smooth and hot in there, and three warm little eggs all ready for her. She can't see them, no ! but she can touch them——"

" Only three ? "

" Much better three, better for eating, my darling. If there were four those nasty little birds might be hatching up in them."

" Oh, Aunt Pigeon, do put them back."

" Nothing ever gets out of my sporran."

" Think of the birds, they'll be in such a state."

" Let them cry. Let them cry. We all have a cross to bear. We can't all expect the best of everything."

III

NAN FOLEY was coming down the path from the house.
She had not yet plunged into the shades and thicknesses
of the laurel and the common rhododendron. She was
walking in the sun through the flame and salmon and
honey-yellow of the azaleas and the great house was long
and pale behind her. Straight behind her were the big
pillars of the carriage porch. They made a powerful
frame behind her, if you had been coming towards her
it would have seemed a gorgeous descent. For Nan Foley
was a beautiful woman, and as strong as one of the pillars
of the Corinthian porch. She was tall, with such wide
shoulders that her hips seemed neat and narrow. She had
a wide forehead and her grey hair curled strongly on her
head. The bones round her eyes were of that full exciting
shape which age makes more true and regular. The skin
was thick and healthy still, and hardly lined for a woman
of fifty (in 1920 she must have been fifty at least). She
wore a blue blouse with her full black skirt and a great white
apron, white as an advertisement for soap ; its pure
soothing shape was as sure a shape as a sail seen on the sea.

She turned to her left out of the bright sun, and started
walking down some steps cut in the side of the hill, they
led to the lower path through the rhododendrons where
Grania and Aunt Pigeon were talking. Nan had not
heard them, but some sensible instinct always led her
directly to her charge's most frequented places. As she
walked along she paused now and then to pull out a weed
or twist back an encroaching bough. The actions were
strong and neat and calculated to a nicety. She accomplished each little effort with a minimum outlay of
strength.

"Ah, now I have you," she exclaimed gaily as she
turned into the straight dark path and bore down on
Aunt Pigeon and Grania. "Now I have you located,

imagine ! And do you know how long it is past your
time for supper ? "

" I know you want to pack me off to bed. You needn't
tell me that, Nan."

" No, dear, no, but it's time for you to come in all the
same."

Nan gave Grania a glance while she spoke, a glance of
confidence, suggesting that they were two sensible people
who must indulge the tiresome whims of a spoilt child.
They two were of another life entirely, the sane life,
outside poor Miss Pigeon's.

" Do go in, Aunt Pidgie," Grania said, returning Nan's
look with a knowing smile. " I'm sure Nan has a lovely
supper ready for you."

" What's for the dining-room dinner ? " Aunt Pigeon
asked eagerly.

" Clear soup."

" Strong clear soup ? "

" Made of the best of shin beef and reduced to pure
goodness."

" Ah, that will do their insides good. After that ? "

" Salmon, and lettuce hearts."

" A nice salmon ? "

" Lepping fresh from the sea, imagine."

" And then ? "

" The shoulder of lamb and the first green peas."

" Was it a black-faced lamb ? "

" I believe so."

" Are they those nasty tasteless Pilot peas ? "

" No, the juicy Little Marvel."

" And a little butter and mint with them, of course ? "

" Of course, yes."

" And the sweet—— Don't tell me, I'll guess—
bottled plums ? "

" No."

" Rhubarb fool ? "

" No."

" Don't tell me, don't tell me ! Jam puffs and cream ? "

" You're getting warmer."

" Is it a gooseberry tart from the early bush on the left-hand side of the asparagus bed ? "

" It is."

" Ah, ah, I knew I'd get it right. Oh, that sounds a very nice dinner." The voice changed. The life in it when she had questioned Nan about the dining-room dinner died, and she said in a voice like the small voice of the smallest bear.

" But what's for my supper ? "

" Oh, a delicious little supper. Come in now and see."

" I'm coming, I'm coming. Oh, the hill is so steep and my feet are so tired."

Nan gave Aunt Pigeon one of those strong commanding looks of hers, a look that would have put life back in the dead by its compulsion to action.

" No delay now, Miss Pigeon, or I'll let the Diblins in to eat your supper."

" No, Nan, no. I'll leave them each a little piece, but not all Nan, please not all my supper."

She started pegging away up the warm path towards the house at an absurd rate ; such was her haste that she almost forgot to use her stick as she bundled out of sight round the corner past which Nan had come to find her.

As she disappeared Nan burst into a laugh of indulgent annoyance, the sort of laugh with which one admits a misdemeanour in an old dog.

" Well, isn't she a caution ? Now Miss Grania it's time you were in too. The dressing-gong sounded as I came out. Oh, goodness, child, what's that awful thing in your hand ? "

" It's a ferret, Nanny darling. Can you get me a box to put it in ? "

" O Jesu ! Ferrets of all things. I imagine they give me the oh's—keep away from me with it, will you now, will you, will you, Miss Grania."

" I can't put it in among the others yet. It's a stranger to them, so do find me a cosy box for the night ; one we can close up, Nan, mind. I wouldn't lose it for the world."

"Where did you get it?—the dirty thing—keep off from me like a good child."

"I got it, I got it from a tinker on the hill."

Grania had no intention of telling Foley's mother where the love gift came from. Nan would be on to this affair if she got so much as a breath, as a hint, as a whisper on the breeze, and the strength of her disapproval, Grania truly felt, would be well matched by the strength and weight of her opposition in the matter. For a Fox, a daughter of Aragon, to carry on an affair with an O'Neill from the Mountain was as wrong, Grania knew, to Nan as the love of black and white people seemed to her. But her secret, her joy and her thrilling refuge, were still her unshared delights. Her foot was set now in a strange country, and its ways were before her. She was not going to share her speculations or tell her present joy.

"God forgive me, I hate them. I think everyone has their favourite animal that they hate—look at the spot on its back—I thought it was only Foley had the breed of the white ferrets with the spot on them."

Grania held the ferret up, its horrid little hands hung down, its neck lifted and twisted a little as it peered about it with red eyes. Soo, who had been sitting trembling with disgust, made a spring towards it. It was the diversion Grania had played for. Screams from Nan. Screams from Soo. Screams from Grania, and awful hissings from the ferret, mingled under the dark thin boughs of the laurels and rhododendrons.

"Indeed, Soo, I wouldn't blame you, Petty. Who's a love? Who's a little wee? Who didn't like a dirty ferret? Come to me, love. Kiss for Nanny? Now, pet! Now! I'll go on and get the box for you, Miss Grania."

Nan went striding away carrying Soo in her arms as if she was a baby, and for the moment the ferret's resemblance to Foley's breed seemed to be forgotten. Grania was glad to be alone again. She went slowly with a delicious weariness up the path, and when she got back into the sunlight she felt overcome by her own well-being and happiness.

The scent of azaleas caught in the back of her nose like a fog of honey and pepper. The harsh almost animal breath that is behind its scent was not here yet, only the wild pungent sweet of its earliest flowers. Great groups almost grown to the size of trees flowered along the wide grass borders of the avenue towards the house. They were above the trees that dropped down the steep bank of the valley. Rooks were flying to and from their nests in the tree tops below. Above the house again, the hill climbed up nursing the sun in its hollows and elbows, sheltering the rare trees, and the rhododendrons, and tender magnolias, and camellias that flowered so freely along the side of this valley.

Aragon stood high above a tidal river. So high and so near that there was only a narrow kind of garden between house and water. It was almost a hanging garden, as Spanish as the strange name Aragon. There was a path under the long line of windows, then a wide short flight of steps with little stone foxes, flying along, stretched brushes out in the air behind them, at the top and the bottom of the steps. Below the steps there were no flower-beds, but a narrow piece of dark grass, and another path, and a very low wall built above the drop to the river. If you sat on the wall you looked down into a grove of ilex and beech and cherry trees. You looked down into the highest places of the trees familiarly from above. Into rooks' nests and into the stone pine where herons built, you might sit and stare, and breathe up the fogged white scent of Portugal laurel flowers on the heavy river air.

Directly underneath the house and this grove, the river swelled and shrank with the tides. You could look deep into the river bed, and up its slow turns towards the mountains and down its straighter way to the sea. Small ships could come up above Aragon, and it was nice to watch them go up and down on the tides.

You sat on the wall above the steep fall of ground as on a balcony. Leaning, you looked down the full river, and across the shining country of fields and woods and mountains. You looked directly down on wet trees and on the bright backs of flying birds—they seemed to be swimming across the air below.

The house itself was long and pale, but it did not share in the coldness and obscure gloom proper to so many beautiful houses of the Georgian age in Ireland. Perhaps because of the deep shelter that surrounded it there was a calm and a kindness about its lines ; lines that had all the strict flow and balance of their period. Beauty so correct and satisfactory since then there has never been ; nor so much dignity with so little heaviness. The great stone carriage porch of Aragon was not pompous ; the balustrade round the roof edge, with its cut stone urns at regular intervals, had the severity belonging rightly to decoration.

Above the house, and above the wall of the castle that had been here before the house, the pleasure grounds were made. There you went up and down half-circular flights of steps and breathed the hushed air in grassy spaces. You walked among towering rhododendrons, great red castles of flower, and saw the air blue in the bamboos and eucalyptus, and golden in the sticky apricot of azaleas. It was the quietest, most solemn garden. The parliaments of rooks in the woods below, only an echo here, a ring for the circle of quiet.

IV

" OH, GRANIA, my dear child, you naughty thing, why are you so late ? Where have you been dear, really ? It's five minutes to dinner, and have I got time to run out and give my Canary Birds a drop of water before the gong sounds ? "

Grania's mother met her in the hall. She was little and pretty and distracted, always on the point of doing some tremendous thing and never having time to accomplish it. Her two passions in life were cards and her garden, and she would sacrifice any one or anything for either. She was a bad gardener and a bad gambler. Yet no disasters ever disgusted her of her two pursuits. Of course, plants were difficult and would sometimes refuse to grow ; if cards would not always come your way, what of it ? Next time would be different.

Grania and Sylvia were fond of their mother in an unpositive kind of way, but Nan Foley adored and served her with a sort of passion.

" Oh, Mummy, I won't really truly be a moment, not a second."

" Well, not too quick perhaps, darling, or I shan't have time for my watering. I'll just rush——"

They ran away from each other, Mrs. Fox still talking, and flying out of doors in her mauve tulle teagown with all the bows, her bronze beaded evening shoes hurrying comfortably along towards the newly planted primulas.

Grania went bundling up the wide staircase to her bedroom.

As she reached the landing one of the tall lightly-curved mahogany doors opened and Sylvia came out.

" My dear Grania, how late, aren't you ? And, oh, my dear, how you do smell." She nipped her thin nose between finger and thumb and continued to talk, holding her skirt away from Grania with the other hand. " You smell of musk and, oh, every conceivable awfulness. Put a drop of something in your bath, but not my Rose Geranium."

" I wouldn't touch your filthy Rose Geranium."

" Then who, one rather wonders, half-emptied the bottle ? " Sylvia let go her nose and the question at the same instant.

" I suppose you mean I did."

" Perhaps—perhaps not."

" You don't believe me ? "

" Did I say so ? "

" As good as."

" Oh, my dear child," Sylvia laughed her cold non-plussing little laugh, " have it your own way, and use the rest too if it's going to mask this very curious smell."

" Shut up, shut up, shut up."

" Certainly, certainly, certainly."

Grania opened and slammed the door of her bedroom. In three words Sylvia could stir hatred and passion in her so that she sweated and cried with rage. Now she tore off her clothes, all her peace forgotten, and rushed to the bathroom determined to pour the rest of the Rose Geranium down the drain, only to find that Sylvia had removed the bottle and left a small tin of Jeyes Fluid in its place.

Neatly and arrogantly Sylvia walked down the stairs ; unstirred by her little contest with Grania ; cool and charming in her pale grey dress ; a string of river pearls round her neck ; a string of pearls which she had collected singly since childhood, to which she still added and substituted better for less perfect little pearls with untiring interest. The poachers on the river would bring her the odd mussel pearls they found, and for these she would drive the shrewdest and most good-humoured bargains. She would often go pearl fishing herself, compelling any biddable girl friend to fish with her, and long and cold and unsuccessful these outings usually were. But Sylvia

had the gift of making any labour she undertook a sort of
excitement, more important than a game, more enthral-
ling than a party—there was a fire somewhere within her
cool artistry, a thin scented flame, sharp as a frosty star.

She went into the drawing-room now and sat down to
wait for dinner, for her Mother and for Grania. With a
nice calculation of their probable lateness she decided
that she would just have time to finish the wing of a swan
in the exquisite and elaborate piece of tapestry work on
which she was working. Head bent to lifted hands she
sat in the full spring light, her needle digging and darting
with such skill and certainty that she seemed to be drawing
the very bones behind the feathers in her work.

The drawing-room at Aragon was a particularly
beautiful room—in a long and very fully curved wall tall
windows looked out over the river below. The river light
swelled up to the windows in great swimming reflections
on the air.

In winter time this light was as cold as the water.
Although it was too wide a light for melancholy or petty
depression, it was empty, it retreated to darkness and the
water. But in summer and in springtime there was
another quality in its taking of this beautiful room. A
possession of light, of soft airs familiar with the room
for many years. There was a very old paper on the walls,
a dark rococo design striping them formally, dark and
gold against white. It was not a pretty paper, but it was
peculiar and valuable. A carpet had once been woven to
follow the circle of the room. It gave you the feeling of a
large pale pond with wreaths of faint ghostly flowers on
its round margins. Two knife-thin marble mantelpieces
stood one to each side of the inside wall, a high mahogany
door marking the centre between them. Thin buff marble
was inlaid in their pillars. Delicate plaques and swinging
wreaths decorated them. Portraits of ancestors in dresses
and coats of maroon and pink and plum and pale pearly
green, were hung, far too high, on the walls ; over doors
and above mirrors, squeezed upwards and closer together

as the generations progressed onwards. There was a quantity of china in the room, most of it Dresden and not all particularly good, little flowers curling as tight as cauliflowers and plentiful as gravel thrown on cement on many of the pieces. But there was a pair of fine horses, pallid yet fierce, standing on one of the mantelpieces.

It was a difficult room in which to arrange furniture. The largest tables looked islanded and isolated, and smaller ones were like desolate sea anemones stuck here and there in space. Even the grand piano (in 1920 still magnificently shawled and bephotographed) had a pathetic spinet-like appearance. The room indeed was made for parties only, parties in the grand manner. It was in no sense of the word a sitting-room and refused to allow its grandeur to be in any way cajoled or modernised. The Bucks and Belles of Ireland had danced here, the windows open to the river and candles burning in the darkly bright clusters of the chandeliers and wall brackets. There had been plenty of the best claret drunk at Aragon in those days ; routs and card parties with lands all gone on the throw of the dice, at the same tables where now they played a silly game of the moment called " Put and Take," and Mrs. Fox sat late into the night when she could get people to play bridge with her.

To-night ten minutes after the gong had rung, Mrs. Fox came bundling in from the garden, some of her bows a little moist and drabbled, and those bronze shoes rather dirty where their sharp curved heels had dug their half-moons in the grass.

" Oh, Frazer," she said in the most abject way to the butler, who was standing rather reprovingly in the hall. " Oh, Frazer, how naughty of me, I am sorry. I had intended to be really punctual to-night. Are the young ladies down yet ? "

" Miss Sylvia is down since five minutes to eight, Madam."

" Oh, you must really give Miss Grania a good scolding for me. She's never in time for anything. There you are, precious," as Grania came hurrying down stairs. " Come on—let's get into the dining-room, and Sylvia'll think we were in time. She's just too punctual for anything. Just go in and tell her we're finishing our soup, Frazer."

Frazer came quietly up to Sylvia as she was clipping off the thread at the completion of her swan's wing. He stood behind her for a just perceptible pause before he spoke.

" Mrs. Fox and Miss Grania, Miss, have just this moment gone into the dining-room. Excuse me, Miss Sylvia, but I fancy a little joke is intended—the idea being that they have finished their soup, Miss."

" Thank you, Frazer." Sylvia rose neatly and briskly. As she walked through the room she paused to alter, to its distinct improvement, the position of a bowl of roses. She crumpled up the wrapping torn off a newspaper and threw it in a waste basket as she passed by a writing table. Frazer followed her into the dining-room, knowing that she would get the better of her mother and Grania without giving him away over the soup joke.

" So sorry," Sylvia said as she came into the dining-room and went across to her chair. " Very stupid of me." Frazer pulled back her chair and she sat down. " Where have you got to ? Soup over ? Please go straight on, Frazer. I don't want any soup, thank you."

Frazer looked towards Mrs. Fox with tolerant compassion and mild inquiry as to whether the joke was to proceed. An access of dignity suddenly succeeded her childish nonsense.

" I'll have some more soup, please, Frazer." She turned to Grania, " Have a little more, dear, too, just to keep me company."

Sylvia was always driving them into such undignified corners.

Dinner proceeded as described by Nan to Aunt Pigeon. Grania and her mother ate with pleasure, commenting on the new peas, the crispness of the lettuce hearts, the goodness of the salmon. Sylvia ate very little and very neatly but her enjoyment was higher and stricter than theirs, although she said nothing about the food and its cooking. Actually she had visited the peas daily for the last fortnight, and compelled the gardener to pick them before they reached maturity. She had obtained, after an endless correspondence, the seed of this lettuce from France, and had ordained the butchery of the black-faced lamb. She spared herself comment on any of these subjects.

For what was Sylvia saving up ? That was the question. Towards what end was that store of secret energy directed. When would the expense of spirit begin ? And if she found no object, either man or thing, on which to expend herself, what then ? And where would it drive her ?

Of course Sylvia had her admirers among the young soldiers who were quartered in the garrison town. Why not. She rode well, played tennis well, and though she had not Grania's blonde, untidy beauty, she had a birdlike tidy prettiness which was very attractive. Also with a competent restraint she seldom made intelligent remark except now and then on the subject of horses. But that was allowed, it was admirable. But beyond this Sylvia had her love—her love was still untold. Schooled and strict and clear as an unpicked lemon among its leaves, her love was there for her to take some day.

No one knew yet but he and she, and they, in knowing themselves exactly matched, kept silence still with one another, because of the life and strength of their secret. They would play the exquisite game out, meeting and parting without a word of love spoken ; keeping each a cool length of distance from the other, crossing the distance with a glance, contradicting the glance with a word, a pause, a carefree sentence to show how far was the mind from this deeper look given. They had their own language, their own subjects in common ; their fishing, their horses, their dogs. And each collected glass and knew enough of the subject to venture to back his knowledge by buying. Glass and horses are curious bonds, but through such things they spoke to one another.

There was no reason why they should not have been engaged and married six months ago, but they had not, and in this kept distance and brittle restraint had grown the fonder. His name was Michael Purvis, and he came from Norfolk. He would leave the army when his father died. He would be rich and a good match for Miss Fox of Aragon. Sylvia only waited for her hour.

" Who is coming to play tennis to-morrow ? " Sylvia asked her mother, and listened attentively to her reply, sorting, planning, piecing out her own intentions in regard to the party, should he be there.

" Colonel and Mrs. Ingram."

" Bridge for you."

" Well dear, yes, but do you mind ? "

Grania said, " Darling, you won't take Tony Craye to make a fourth, now angel, promise."

Sylvia said, " Of course she will—anyhow he's not a very exciting tennis player."

" He's just my form."

" Oh, you can manage a rabbity game without him." Sylvia said gently.

" Grania's tennis is never going to improve, poor pet, if she's always put with the duds."

" I don't want to improve."

" She likes flopping about and screaming."

" I don't scream. You shut up."

" Oh, all right. We'll give her Tony, Mummy."

" Yes, darling, of course I will. I'll try out that new Major Radley for bridge."

" He looked a dreary old heap. Michael Purvis likes bridge."

" Oh, I don't know if he's coming. I said, just any of the Boys——"

They came in dozens every Sunday afternoon to Aragon, the soldiers from the barracks. They were institutions, those tennis parties that ended in supper, and cars that wouldn't start pushed down the avenue late into the night. They had been going on as long as

any one could remember. All the Aunts, except Aunt
Pigeon (and there had been six Miss Foxs in the previous
generation) had married into smart cavalry regiments on
the strength of these parties. Cider cup and moonlight
on the river succeeding long long games of tennis, played
out in sweeping strokes from the base line, and underhand
serves from the elegant spoon-like racquets.

But enough of easy jeering at the first tennis players.
They got their men, and they kept these men either with
skill, or tenacity, or because of a curious ignorant charm
which they had, a reserve, a dignity, a power to ignore . . .

They still came to Aragon, the successors of these
officers, although in 1920 the roads in the South of Ireland
were hardly the most sensible places for Ireland's enemies
on Sunday or any other afternoons.

Dinner at Aragon came to its decorous end. Coffee
with sugar candy and cream was handed in the drawing-
room, and then Grania and Sylvia and Viola sat reading
and sewing by the green-shaded gas light. The windows
were still open, and the full evening tide swelled the river
to greater, fuller widths below.

Grania put down her paper soon, and went across to
the window. She knelt on a stool leaning out, her fat
white arms cold and dented on the window ledge. She
kept very still, holding in her mind the troubled and secret
delight that belonged to her. She was frightened by the
thought of all that was happening to her, and the in-
exorable calm flowing of the river gave her a false sense
of strength and peace. Of all people, she longed to discuss
the matter most with Nan, Nan who was so strong, so wise,
so gay in her councils, but of all people alive she could
less let Nan know than any other. Foley was afraid of
her too, exceedingly afraid of her sensible anger.

But Foley did not know this little fearfulness that was
not sure at all which was now on Grania's mind. She
had not told him. She could not say anything yet. She
must wait another week at least before she told him what
she feared. Or did she fear ? There was a warmth and

an importance about her suspicion. Like all women when they think themselves with child Grania saw all things in focus only to this tremendous happening. The idea would grow to a certainty of importance when she was alone. Sometimes it frightened her. But her love was so ignorant, her trust so complete, that she only put off the time for telling Foley because she promised herself a divine hour of love and comfort with him when she could say this beyond doubt. It was all so easy to her. The simplest way in which to say, Now Foley we can be married. Her dream ended and began in marriage. Of course they would be married. They would go to Dublin together and come back and say, Now we're married. Well, what could be simpler?

Grania was absolutely confident in Foley's love for her. She did not for a moment doubt that she filled the thoughts of his days and nights with the same agonizing strength and sweetness that was in her thoughts of him. She was a wild-blooded but a single-hearted child. There was nothing light or easy about this loving of hers. The idea that there could be a successor to Foley in her life never trembled on the edge of her mind. He only was her love, and if they parted she would die. She was as sure of this as of anything, as sure indeed as she was of his love.

And now she was tired. She turned from the window and rubbed the chill of the river air in her cold fat arms and thought of her bed where she would sleep away this exquisite mindless exhaustion, and of the morning when she was to meet him early and ride out with him. . . . Already her plans were laid for it, her lies were told. And now, good-night. Good-night to these poor cold creatures outside the ring of her thoughts. Good-night to that spry and secret Sylvia, who had no secret like Grania's to keep to herself. Say good-night to the silly sweetie your mother, and how she would cry and go on, beg, persuade and forbid if she knew the truth, and then hurry away to confide the whole thing in Nan. Nan

again, Nan all the time. She was the beginning and the
end of Aragon.

Except to Sylvia, and Sylvia had always kept her own
secrets, and Nan as well as everyone else respected her for
it. Sylvia had put away her embroidery now, and she and
her mother were playing a game of Bezique, snapping the
little score boards up and down, dealing out the cards
with quick precision. Sylvia didn't much like playing
Bezique but she was as concentrated on this occupation
as any other.

" I'm going to bed," Grania said after her wordless
rehearsed good-nights, and came over from the window
to kiss her mother good-night.

" You're looking pale, darling. Are you tired ? Try to
remind me to write off for some more of that expensive
tonic. Now what was its name ? I can't remember
names—Bezique, I think, dear, that's another 100. Good-
night, Lammy. The child *is* looking pale. . . .

" Bezique," said Sylvia.

Grania went up to bed.

V

MUCH LATER Mrs. Fox sat in front of her dressing-table while Nan brushed her feathery grey hair. She put her hands up to her mouth yawning luxuriously. Then she slipped off her rings and settled down to a good gossip with Nan.

It was never admitted to be a gossip, of course. It was a sort of grave council on the affairs of Aragon, and only as though by accident shaded off into the provocative, " Well, I know I shouldn't say," prelude to luscious detail and unbrindled confidence.

Mrs. Fox loved the feeling of the brush in her hair with Nan's strength behind it, she could lie back relaxed, in no great hurry to speak, when she did speak her words came in a calm easy flow, without trouble, without trying.

" Do you think, Nan, Miss Grania should take that tonic again—what was its name ? '

" Syrup of Phosphates."

" *Of course*, does she look a little pale ? Of course it's the weather too. My primulas, they were limp to-night, quite limp. If I hadn't slipped out to water them before dinner, well, I ask myself—Now that reminds me, what's the good of telling Kane anything ? Only this afternoon I said to him he was to be *sure* to water my primulas."

" You know what ails him, or perhaps I shouldn't say it, *Nellie McVeagh*."

" That ugly little thing. Are you sure, Nan ? "

" And her mind's not on her work for one five minutes either. ' Nellie,' I said to her to-day, or was it yesterday, maybe it was Tuesday, ' Nellie,' I said, ' Your mind's not on your work, and where is it, Nellie ? ' I said. Well, she went the colour of a peony, so I said no more."

Mrs. Fox settled the faintly grubby little cape of lace and bows that she wore for these hair brushings, and pursed her mouth at her reflection.

"Keep your eye on her, Nan. I don't like to even *think* it, but those McVeaghs . . ."

Nan said, with resignation, but with a condemnation in her voice that was a little frightening :

"Ah, those McVeaghs—they were bred to be hot."

Mrs. Fox nodded regretful agreement. That condemnation of the joy of sex, that forgetting of their own past joys, and heats, fears and failures, left a curious blank streak of cruelty equally in her and Nan. Love and the mating of bodies, was really vile to their minds, they could not avoid this mental attitude. It was as much a part of them as their own noses.

Of course when everything was circumspect, restrained and satisfactory, love was quite another thing, spoken of in another language. Its relation to any natural heats and lusts transcended, forgotten in the glorious mists and romanticism of veils and tears and orange blossoms, and the happy solidity of marriage portions, and a nice sense of permanence. But that attitude of mind, though real enough, was not so straight from their souls and stomachs as the first revulsion from the obscenity of sex. In the second there was a loathed thing to forget. In the first there was nothing but the loathed thing to remember. But it was nice to play with the idea, in the proper spirit of disgust, of course.

"Do you think . . . ?"

Mrs. Fox said, now raising her eyebrows in a horrid query : "Well, last Thursday evening when I was passing down by the grove to post a letter, what did I see by the giant rhododendrons but two bicycles, and one, if you'll pardon the expression, was a man's bicycle. Yes, indeed."

It sounded most unutterably dirty. What was not said about the embraces enacted in the shelter of the giant rhododendrons was implied by nods and ghastly pauses. A stretching of a silence, a withdrawal, a faintly renewed implication.

"Oh, dear." Mrs. Fox sighed, a sigh of luscious dis-

approval. " And was to-day her afternoon ? My goodness, Nan, of course, it's Thursday again to-day."

" Aha, no wonder those primulas went dry."

They stared at each other for a moment in the glass.
Nan's lips grew tight. She picked up a ribbon, and put
it round Mrs. Fox's pretty feathers of grey hair. Knotted
the bow with cruel decision.

" I'll keep my eyes open," was all she said.

Mrs. Fox went back to the subject of Grania without
bothering where her thought led from.

" Pale. She does look pale. Nan, what did you say
the tonic was called ? "

" Syrup of Phosphates. I'll order it. But she's well,
ma'am. She was always that kind of colour. She's
healthy."

" Girls are difficult, Nan—one never knows."

" Ah, you and I would remark it, dear. . . ."

" She asked me to leave Mr. Craye out of the bridge
to-morrow."

" She'd never have asked that if it meant anything."

" Oh, dear, I suppose not indeed. He's such a nice
boy, Nan, and I was presented at the same court as his
mother."

" Perhaps it's not my place to say it . . . ? "

" No . . . What, Nan ? "

" I've been thinking lately that Miss Sylvia and
Captain Purvis . . ."

" Now, that would be nice, what makes you think so,
Nan ? "

" Well, now, it's very few Miss Sylvia'd ask advice from
on the subject of a horse, unless it's my Foley. Still, she
and Captain Purvis were about a half-hour up in her
show horses's box last Sunday. Why I know is I was up
to the garden for a couple of heads of lettuce Kane forgot
to leave in, and there they were and I going up. So I
stopped up to gather green gooseberries for the Fool, and
when I was coming down, yes, indeed, imagine, there
they were still in it."

" Well, Nan ! "

" Well, indeed. ' Well ' is right."

" We'll watch it, but tact of course."

" Oh, tact, ma'am, tact is the thing indeed."

" And how do you think, Miss Pigeon, has been the last few days, Nan ? "

" Tch, Tch, Tch, Oh, I've had some terrible times with her. You'll excuse me, pardon, ma'am, but would she sleep in her bed last night ? No. She said she'd get leprosy sleeping in a bed, and it was out on the stairs in her nightgown, with an eiderdown and a pillow, imagine ! Well (not that it would signify one bit), but I lost the best part of my night's sleep before I got her back to her room."

" Poor Nan, what a time she does give you."

" Oh, I wouldn't grudge the time, or the trouble, but the way she'd take against me over every little thing is cruel."

" And you are so sweet to her. Nan, I wonder if you could, tactfully, keep her away from the tennis paryt to-morrow. You know, sometimes she can be so embarrassing."

" Oh, I'll think up some excuse. I'll tell her there's a black man coming. She has a horror of those blacks. If you tell her you heard there was a black man seen about the woods she won't put a foot out of the house for a week."

" Well, tell her anything you like. But, of course, don't frighten her, Nan."

" Is it me to frighten her and she the only baby I have left ? Ready for bed now ? Don't forget to drink your milk, and there's a new kind of biscuit in your box. Try one. Don't let the crumbs in your sheets. Is your bottle nice and hot ? Well, good-night, now ma'am."

" Good-night Nan, bless you."

VI

NAN turned out the gas, and shut the door with comfortable assurance. Out in the dark passage above the well of the staircase she stood alone with her candle in her hand. She was less alone now than at any time. For here she was close as flesh can be to spirit with all the dead Fox's of Aragon; as close and comfortable with them as she was with the living Fox's, as unsurprised by her own strange consciousness of their crowding presences as she was unsurprised by her strong powers with the living. Nan was the only person who knew the ghosts at Aragon familiarly. It was like nothing to her to go into a room and know the movement, the fullness, the stirring of air that told of its occupation. Now, as she went down the shallow steps of the stairs, candlestick held carefully in one hand, she reached down her other hand to a certain height for she felt that one she called " the Child " was with her, and it was late and dark for the creature to be about. She did not pay much attention, for she was searching by the light of her candle for the cobwebs invisible by day. Three she counted, and pursed her lips thinking of what she could say to Nellie McVeagh in the morning. That such a slut should let cobwebs and dust gather on the pictures of dead Fox's was abhorrent to Nan. She went on down to the servants' hall, where she made herself a nice little bit of supper. The other servants had gone to bed so she got the end of the gooseberry tart and some thick cream. A nice little piece of lamb first and then a cup of tea, strong Indian tea with rich cream in it.

Upstairs Aunt Pidgie, waiting for Nan to come up, lay on her face in bed, a shawl was knotted tightly round her stomach, and a pillow doubled and put between her body and her mattress; she found this a good way to appease the hunger that so often overcame her at night, so that

she was sometimes sorely tempted to eat up the morsels
she had saved from supper for her Diblins. To-night she
thought longingly of the backbone of a herring and a
small quantity of cold boiled rice stored away in her
sporran for their breakfast in the morning. There had
been three blackbirds' eggs in her sporran this evening
too, but these she had eaten herself with the bathroom
door locked on such a shocking exhibition of greed.

VII

FOLEY O'NEILL's house was up near the mountains.
Near, but not very near. There was a little valley with a
stream at the bottom and a wild hill covered in bracken
and gorse and crowned wildly in dark fir trees between
his house and farm, and the real mountains. Once there
had been a rocky little laneway deep between loose stone
walls leading from the main road up to the O'Neills'
house. But Foley and Nan had civilised the approach.
There were solid bright white gates now, with a latch
that could be opened easily from a horse's back, and
inside the dark walls that sank to the depths of the lane
were white timber rails, rather like a racecourse, this
partly for the safety of a couple of brood mares and their
foals, and partly because Nan admired the smart look
they gave the place.

The house was on the left of the laneway. It had been
a steep grey farm-house of infinite squalor, standing
undivided from its wet steep yard where fowl scratched
morosely at the steaming manure heaps, and housed
calves bayed for food, and chopped furze was laid thickly
in the slush so that you walked dry-footed round the house
on dark winter days.

Things were different now. Two gay, villa like bow
windows were built on to the south face of the house. A
square of garden was divided off from the yard by a

whitewashed wall. Two neat grass plots, parted cleanly
by a gravelled path, squared each side of the hall door.
Two beds of begonias were there carefully minded because
they looked so well. But hydrangeas flowered untended
and bluer than any summer mountain because they have
a tiresome preference for such situations.

When you opened the hall door you looked straight
down a narrow passage to the kitchen. If both the inner
and outer kitchen doors happened to be open at the same
time you looked right across into the mountains. The
intervening land and the yard at the back were cut out
by the height on which the house stood. It was as if there
was a house and mountains in grand isolation. The two
things that counted. The mountains for wildness and
cold hours. The house for shelter.

Foxes' masks, ruffed by faded brushes, were hung on
the walls of the passage-way. A couple of hunting prints,
divorced from their series, took the place of the holy
pictures that might have been there. The parlour door
was on the right, the dining-room door on the left. The
parlour was papered in brownish cream with a gay dado of
cornflowers. There were panes of blue and red glass in
the sides of its bow window. Dampish chintz clung to the
intricate outlines of the elaborate suite of furniture spaced
accurately round the room. Paraffin oil lamps with globes
moulded and frosted in red and white glass stood high
among forests of photographs of Nan's aristocratic
patients and nurslings. Foxes of all ages were well represented, from Mrs. Fox in her court dress bouqueted and
feathered, to Grania, photographed in her vest by Speight.
But there were plenty of other treasures, including a
couple of coroneted ladies, with fondest Love to Dearest
Nan; scattered through the collection were pictures of
Foley's progressive moments of triumph in the horse-world.
From the time a smart little boy sat his show jumping
pony with stylish ease, to the time when a rigidly
nonchalant young man was taken on a Dublin show
champion—that most dreadful and triumphant of all

horse pictures—Nan had kept and framed them all. Her pride in Foley's horsemanship and all it meant was as strong in her as a well grounded hate is strong.

Across the other side of the passage was the dining-room. It was bow-windowed to corresponded exactly with the parlour. There, one picture of the Pope, and a few common family photographs, were allowed on the walls, wedding groups, the brides all wearing navy gabardine and roses in their hats and the grooms with collars swallowing their ears and one large possessive hand laid on the bride's shoulder as they stood to attention behind her chair. The walls were papered in red. Both lace and red velvet curtains shrouded the windows into the proper gloom for dining. The silver cups Foley's horses had won in shows decorated the sideboard. In a couple of the slenderest shape, bouquets of imitation carnations had been arranged.

VIII

DONATIA, Foley's cousin, was sixteen. She would have been at her convent school, but her prayers to the saints, her horrid influence on her fellow pupils, and her disregard of the Sisters' and Reverend Mother's holy influences or spiteful punishment, had set her free from the fifth of these sacred prisons, and here she was in April back with her mother and Foley at Mountain Brig. That was the name of this house now, although in its less smart days it had been called Clonamore. But Nan thought Mountain Brig sounded much more civilised, as indeed it did.

Donatia was a small strong black little gipsy. She was deeply religious, a terrible liar, and a tireless worker, a tireless worker for Foley because she loved him with the worship of childhood turning into the sad passion of the adolescent.

Sixteen and possessed of herself in a curiously simple way. You could see it in the air and swing with which she wore her clothes, in the confidence of her walk. She had been the spoilt child of older men, men who belonged to the world of horse-dealing, or to the racing world, whose business it was to know people and horses. Such men have a sophistication of outlook so complete that they can turn their own simplicity to account, and hardly know they do so. They have a confidence, and a right confidence, in the importance of their trade, which is not acquired from any association with a sophisticated aristocracy of customers, but grows from within. It is acquired through hardship and gambles that go wrong, and successes sometimes, and a life where perception is keyed to an abnormal pitch and quickness is all. That quickness of eye and ear and sharpness of mind had been alive in Donatia since the age of ten when Foley had first taken her about looking at horses, or to a summer race-meeting, or a point-to-point, perhaps, if he was not riding, or in later years if he was. She would ride out on her pony with him in the mornings when the early silence hung hollow as a bell over cold fields, and she knew enough at ten years old to keep her mouth shut, and to keep herself and her pony out of his way at these times. If she made a mistake she was cursed with cold emphasis, and she would a great deal sooner have been beaten.

When she was thirteen she was a well-known person to Foley's friends and customers. As sharp as a needle and as bright as paint, she never stuck herself into a conversation unless invited. She called all his older friends " Uncle," " Uncle Charley," " Uncle Jack." When she was little they would send her ponies to school before they were sold to the parents of rich little boys and girls. She did not really civilise them completely, but they could be sold as hunted by a child. Now she seldom rode a horse except one of Foley's. She was his stable slave and gloried in her usefulness to him. She was a marvel to catch the boys out if they idled. There was no horse he put her on

that she would not ride, in the pathetic confidence that
if Foley said she could ride the horse, to do so was well
within her powers.

But now, now at sixteen, the proudest age of all, a very
terrible and darkly secret thing was happening to Donatia.
It was eating the heart out of her, though so far no one
knew. She was growing frightened of horses. All the
strong bright unruly horses she had ridden were only like
ghosts to her. No strength came from the knowledge that
she had ruled their strength.

In Donatia's room there was a little plaster stoup of
holy water, a dusty sprig of palm stuck behind it since
last Palm Sunday, and on the little table below was a
very imposing statue of the Blessed Virgin. So blue, so
white her robes as clouds and summer skies ; so unreal
those folded plaster hands, they would have made a fable
of any story. And it was to her Donatia prayed unceas-
ingly for strength against her sinful cowardice. From her
praying she would turn to that picture of Foley (the same
one that his mother had in her bedroom, the picture of
Foley on Teltaletit. Superb in confidence and strength
and ease). It seemed to her as if she caught her heart in
her teeth as she told herself that he must never know. At
sixteen you do not own that you love your gods—you are
contented to worship them.

I X

SIX O'CLOCK on an April morning and the birds shouting
in ecstasy when Donatia woke in her hard familiar little
bed. She lay quietly, accepting a consciousness of fear,
new every morning after the night, measured out to her
in small realities ; the cold sound of stirrup-irons touching
in the half-dark morning air came from below ; horses
moving in their boxes and the muffled voices of the boys
still heavy and sullen with sleep, as they began another
day's work.

There was an ugly taste in Donatia's mouth as she got
out of her bed, she must get up now if she wanted to get
a cup of tea for Foley and herself before they rode out.
She shivered as she sat on the edge of her bed, her feet
feeling for the slippers underneath it. Donatia was as
small as a girl of twelve, but she was as tough and
muscular as any gipsy boy. Her strong black hair was
twisted into a little bun on the top of her head in an un-
affectedly female and untidy curve, small straight pieces
escaping pathetically to fall on the collar of her striped
pyjamas, a present from Foley when she had won a
jumping competition. They were too long by far for
the strong small body they covered. Cuffs were turned
back and trousers roped in folds round her waist. Her
face had the inscrutability of a head carved on a very
small walking stick ; precise features set carefully, a
sphinx-like straightness of line. If there had been some
abandon, some break, some wildness, some mistake, there
might have been some fascination too, but everything was
closed in and shut down in the terrible reserve of youth.

She took off her pyjamas and stood, a dark naked little
image in the cold early air, the holy medal she wore on
a chain round her neck gleamed in its pale circle above
her bare breasts, and swung out on the length of its chain
as she stooped for her clothes.

" Mother, have you our tea for us ? " She was dressed
and down in the kitchen where a lamp still burned in the
daylight, and Mrs. Bohane, a great overgrown gipsy, bent
across the table reading the advertisements on the back of
a week-old paper. Her black hair was still in curling pins,
and her white skin greasy from sleeping. She had put on
a tweed skirt and jumper over her nightdress, and there
were no stockings on her beautiful legs. She was a
gorgeously shameless slattern, an ageing beauty whose
riotous blood perforce subdued its excitement to shoppings
and gossipings and local births (the more difficult the
better), deaths (preferably by cancer) and love affairs
which she investigated with a bitter condemnatory
enthralment.

" Have I your tea, love ? Of course. There you are
now, take the blue cup up to Foley. Look, wasn't it the
luck of God I took a glance at this paper, I had it in the
fire itself when I caught a sight of this hat . . ." her voice
followed Donatia out of the kitchen door and paused
comfortably poised in narrative until her return. . . .

He was in his shirt sleeves and shaving—why shaving ?
—when she came in, pulling his face into terrible angles
and preoccupied with more than morning silence. She
put the cup down beside him. A blue shirt and his new
jodhpurs—why not his red jersey and old breeches ?
He gave her a smile, half a " thank you, child," and as
she was going out he said, " Would you like a surprise ? "

" I would, Foley."

" Well, you can ride out the Knight of Aragon horse
this morning."

Her hands shut into fists and her eyes for a second
closed too—Mother of God be near me.

" Would you be able for him ? " the voice went on
teasing and affectionate. He had no doubt as to her
ability, the hardy little thief.

" I'll tell them to change my saddle, they have it on
the pony."

She nearly whispered, her voice was so dry—the Knight of Aragon horse, oh, dear Mother of God, didn't he fire Mickey Brown in two small shots of bucks only yesterday? Why not the pony? Ah, why not the pony?

"Then tell Mickey to lead the pony on—there's a lady wants to ride him at school, we'll go down through Tin-a-curry bog."

A lady? At this hour of the morning? It was no hour of the morning for ladies—or for questions, Donatia knew. No doubt one of those dream-like creatures, pearls, tweeds, glamour and shooting sticks, who stood rounds of drink at race-meetings and leaned and whispered to Foley after they had "had a couple" (how well Donatia knew the signs of slight intoxication in the aristocracy), and drove away in rich pale-coloured motor cars, back into their own soft lives, had taken a crazy fancy for riding out when she could be in her bed—well she'd get her fill of it schooling over the Tin-a-curry fences—Oh, Jesu, had she forgotten? Even for a moment had she forgotten?

"And will you ride the Aragon into the Bog double for me."

It was her thought spoken for her but turned into such a sweet intention of flattery that she was warmed and powerless to speak of fear.

"I will, of course."

"You will? Great little girl. Run on now and hurry the boys."

He picked up his watch and frowned as he buckled the strap, his mind for a moment occupied with a thought of Donatia, his little Donatia. I wonder is she able for him? Ah, she is, I think, she is. Anyway I couldn't give Grania anything but the pony. He was knotting his tie, very tight and neat and pinning the end with a worn gold safety pin, smooth and sharp from all its years of use. He would sooner lose £3 than lose that pin, though he could scarcely remember now how he got it. He would wear his second good coat, it would look too remarkable if he wore his good coat as well as his new jodhpurs. He reached it down from its hanger in the cupboard, and put it on with that strained carefulness that the least vain men show when it comes to their coats, and Foley was vain enough in a simple way. He liked a good coat, but if it was *his* coat (or horse, or dog, or woman), it became good any way. He was very faithful and undoubting in possession and careful about things too, this morning he had said his prayers before he dressed so that he would not have to kneel down in his good jodhpurs. He drank his tea now and went downstairs, his mind on what was immediately to do, not so far on as meeting Grania again.

In the kitchen Aunt Gipsy was still reading the advertisements on the table, and her voice rose again from where it had ceased for the second time that morning when Donatia went out to the yard.

" And do you know, Foley, I always find it very hard to buy a hat. Why it is I don't know, but the styles now aren't what they were, and when you do chance to see a thing that would suit you, you should nip to it quickly, wouldn't you say that yourself ? "

" I would, Aunt Gipsy."

" Maybe I could get a drive into town then on Tuesday, maybe. There's a nice sale on at Aherns."

" You could, Aunt Gip, if any one was going."

That was the way to take Aunt Gipsy, easy, and leave yourself a way of escape, don't let her pin you down.

" I might bring Miss Grania back to breakfast with us. She's trying out the pony."

" Oh, Holy Hour ! I'll have to hurry myself, child."

She would too, he knew Aunt Gipsy. Everything would be nice and a credit to him when they came back. There would be fresh eggs, and fresh bread, and sweet salty butter, and good strong tea in the flowered china pot Aunt Gipsy had bought at an auction, taking a passionate leave of her senses and bidding against a Dublin dealer. Yes, everything in Foley's house was all right. He was pleased with it.

He crossed the yard slowly, not at that almost trotting
little walk that men whose lives have been spent with
horses mostly adopt. Everyone was very grave in the
morning before riding out, everyone in the grip of himself,
and horses unfriendly and set in their minds away from
any kindness between horses and men. They stood darkly
and crookedly in their boxes. No boy whistled yet or
spoke cheerfully—the reality of to-day was present and
unpitying.

Donatia was leaning where the sun struck a patch on
the wall of the Knight of Aragon horse's box (leaning on
her lion's cage). She was yawning, as she felt very very
sick, and the collar of her dark coat was turned up
against the green thin line of her jaw. Her mind and her
body seemed to stand apart coldly afraid for each other.

"Doatie, ride your pony down to the bog, and let
Micky get up on that laddo first."

Mickey said, " I have Miss Doatie's saddle on him, sir."

A wave of fury towards Micky swept through her,
Micky who didn't care what horse he rode or how often
he got fired, to crucify her like this. She was stretched in
pain while Foley paused, before he said, carelessly.

" Ah, swop your leathers."

He did not know why he had suddenly changed his
mind about Donatia's ability for the horse. It wasn't that
exactly. She was well able to ride him, but that hardy
little thief, Micky, might as well soften him for her first.
The child looked sick this morning, any way.

Reprieved, Donatia felt the full heat of the sun again,
felt life in her hands again, and the loosening of a cruel
knot within her. A tide of gratitude flowed through her.
She caught her breath to steady herself. If she had acted
with freedom then she would have reached out to touch
Foley's coat ; to kiss its stuff in love and gratefulness.
But she stood quietly against the wall, and he never
guessed she was so much afraid, and he knew nothing at
all of that flame of adoring gratitude that rose in her
beside him.

Because of her relief she mounted the pony with forgotten confidence, she did not remember how she had lain awake the night before thinking and seeing with taut hands how dangerous the pony could be.

Micky ran into the saddle room to look for his stick, and the big horse was led out and round the yard—to Donatia he looked infinite in strength and evil. Cold as a snake's eye his was. The early sun shuddered across his bright and beautiful body. Donatia knew he was filled as full of bad intentions as a horse could be. She had seen one of the boys cross himself in the dark of the stable before mounting him. This was not Micky, who came out swinging and fastening his coat, his own little stick in his hand, stepping lightly towards the horse and speaking easily, gathering up his reins, and holding up a leg to Foley.

" Right ? "

" Right, sir."

Up through the air with the greatest of ease, in the saddle away by yourself from the help of man, and to think it might have been herself up there on the cold bad horse's back ; but she was saved, saved for a time. They had four miles to go before they got to the bogs, and Micky would have the worst edge worn off him by then.

Foley was mounting now, like a gentleman from the ground, one foot in his stirrup, for this horse was going to England. Donatia turned her pony's head, and rode warily down the deep lane. She could hear Micky's voice growling a threat to his horse, and knew without looking behind how the horse's back was in an iron bow under the saddle, and his neck straining to drive his head away and down beyond control. Her pony stopped to shy at nothing inside the field, and Micky's voice came urgently from behind her.

" Keep going, Miss Doatie."

She caught hold of the pony and sent her on again.

Out on the wider road Foley rode up beside her.

" I thought Micky was gone when the pony stopped in

the lane—the horse was gathered up under him ready to pelt him."

"Imagine, was he ? " Donatia answered politely while her heart turned in sympathy for Micky. And Foley was laughing. He always laughed when people were in danger from horses. He was so seldom in danger himself. With strength and confidence and the little ways he had, he would fool horses into doing his will. He had lovely ways with horses. Even when they hated him they appeared kind and easy when he rode them.

"Oh, look, look ! Poor Micky. Stay there, Mick, you're all right boy ! "

A goat in the hedge raising her drab ivory face, struggling with spancled legs, was enough to set the big horse swerving and bucketing across the road.

"Ah, Micky, I thought he had you that time."

And Micky, smiling and patting the lion's arched neck, saying :

"The beggar's only watching his chance, sir."

The sun shone out more kindly as they rode along. The little unawakened houses looked like toy farms unpacked out of a box, as definite and unliving in the earliness. The blackthorn blossom was laid along the banks thick and quiet as wreaths on a grave. Willow trees flowered and dropped their yellow dust sadly on the low shine of water beneath them. A grass road as old as anything in Ireland took them past the arches and broken towers of a castle. It was flung up high against the sky, and the hills. Sky and hills were framed like light cold water-colours in its windows and doorways. Rooks flew across and through the airy roofless heights of walls and towers. Brave, bold and elegant the horses strode by under the castle walls.

Foley looked up at a certain window as he passed, but he saw no sign or message there for him to-day. In these troubled times he was so far involved with Ireland's Republican Army that he knew where to look for such signs.

Beyond food, shelter and silence for any flying column that might call for these things at his house, he held to a thorny neutrality in this war between the English, from whom he made his money, and the Irish who sought to drive the English out of Ireland. He betrayed neither one side nor the other, but maintained a tricky balance between the two. To-night, two tired boys on the run might have the food and the shelter of his house. To-morrow afternoon, two smart hardy young British officers would be schooling horses with him, and standing him a drink after the school was ridden. That was the situation. He might as well accommodate the boys pleasantly as be bullied and beaten up, perhaps shot for refusing them a refuge when they needed one. And most certainly he was not going to abandon his trade with the soldiers before he could help it.

Much of Nan's passion and skill for the intrigues and situations of life was in Foley too, he loved a good reason for diplomacy, it was like a game of cards to him. But just lately, from whispers he had heard, only whispers, he was getting a little watchful and nervy. He was glad to see no sign or signal at the castle for him to-day.

They went on by a track a little paler than the sallow fields. They rode through a line of gaps in walls built thinly of the castle stones. Foley and Donatia talked a little. He said :

" Aunt Gipsy's wild to buy a hat. She saw a very nice hat in the paper this morning."

" We have to take her in to get Confession some day soon. She could try the hat then."

" And we could go to the pictures."

" Will she ever get her hat, and the pictures, and Confession all on the one day ? "

" We'll go to the pictures while she'll be at the hat."

" Oh, she'd die if she didn't see this fellow that is on this week, what's this his name is ? "

" I wouldn't know."

" I wouldn't either, but she's stone mad about him."

" If that's the way it is we'll never get out of town. Will we give these horses a canter ? It's what they want."

A wide field sloped up and away from them. Here many a contest had been won or lost under cold grey skies with wind and rain driving, and on bright hot mornings with flowers in the drenching grass and the grey and gold of honeysuckle along the banks and groups of foxglove spires all furred in dew. And mornings like to-day where nothing was yet but promise and those black and white grave-wreaths of thorn to show that promises ended in death, and primroses in all the sheltered places growing on for ever in soft placid contradiction.

" Right, Micky ? "

" Right, Sir ! "

The big horse moved crookedly, his head to the east, his tail to the west, fighting his bit, waiting his chance, his eye cold and his neck black with sweat. A bird in the hedge gave him his chance. One—two—three—with the grace and quickness of a panther and the strength of a bull he fired the bucks out of his wicked body, and at the third Micky was gone, shot out of the saddle to land uncannily on his feet with the reins in his hand.

" Hold on to him now, Micky," Foley said quietly as he dismounted and gave his horse to Donatia, Donatia trembling and pricking with a sweat of sympathy—her own pony unruly in the fracas. And Micky, poor lion tamer of the circus, brave, stupid slave, standing again as he had stood in the yard, patting the untamed strength of that neck, ready to be thrown up again, even to death.

" Are you right, Mick ? "

" Right, Sir."

He was up again and the horse trembled in the light air as Foley led him on half-threatening, half-cajoling, round and round in a circle.

" I'll take him around the field now, sir. I'll soberize the beggar."

Micky edged away from the other two horses and set going up the long slope of the field.

" That's a great boy," Foley said to Donatia, watching them over the rise of the hill.

" He is." A great pang of envy rose in Donatia's heart to take the place of the awful pity she had felt for Micky.

Foley lit a cigarette, his eyes watching all the time to see Micky reappear, before he took his horse from her.

" Would you be very cross with me if I asked you something," he said.

" I would I suppose." She was so used to the unmeaning caress in his voice. She had known it since she was eight years old, as long as she had loved him.

" Ah, you'd be mad with me, I think."

" Go on. What is it ? "

" I think I'll leave Micky school that fellow to-day. I wouldn't mind him being green, but the beggar's too rough for you."

" Ah, Foley."

He mistook that cry of relief for disappointment.

" Well, we'll see," he said.

" Whatever you say yourself, of course."

" You wouldn't be real mad with me, Doatie ? "

" No. I wouldn't care."

" You can ride him to-morrow. We'll let Micky knock him round to-day."

" Who's the lady you have for the pony ? "

He hesitated.

" One of the Miss Fox's. I think it's Grania they said would try him."

" I wonder Aunt Dymphnia didn't mention it. She was over yesterday."

" They're getting big girls now—maybe they don't tell their Nanny everything."

" Ah, go on, Aunt Dymphnia wouldn't wait to be told."

Foley laughed, a faint acquiescence in his mother's ability to find out what she wanted to know. He picked up his reins and rode off across the field, riding away from Donatia and her questions. He wondered if he had laid up trouble for himself in this lie about Grania buying the pony. Doatie was so sharp and so close. You couldn't tell what was in her mind, and it was such an easy explanation of Grania's early morning appearance, he was a master of the easy word.

Out of the fields where Micky and a quieter horse waited at the gate, and down a steep lane through gorse and heather to a crossroads where the wind blew clean and naked across the sallow bog land.

Grania's hair was blown back like the grass behind her head. Hair and grass had the same strange shining life in their pallor as the wind caught and turned them in the light. She leant against a bank, her little black bitch sat on the bank and leant against her cheek. Grania looked so bold and uncaring leaning there, her coat was full of mends and holes, her boots and breeches very clean and expensive. She gazed on Foley and spoke to him only, after a faint good-morning to Donatia and Micky.

" Oh," she cried, " I thought you were never coming. Poor Grania ! Do you know she bicycled all the way here ? Yes, really, honestly. Do you think the bicycle will be safe if we pop it inside the gate ? Don't let me if it's going to be stolen ? "

" It wouldn't be a big loss," Foley was standing beside her, he had given his horse to Donatia to hold with not a glance. " That's a dangerous yoke." He was considering the bicycle. " Look ! not a brake on it, and the back wheel nearly off."

" It was all I could find and I thought I'd be late." She had dropped heavy eyelids and her mouth trembled as he stood near her.

" You'll be safer on my pony."

" Yes, Foley."

X

" You'll be safer on my pony." What was there in that absent insistent voice of Foley's that bred in Donatia such a gush of venom towards Grania—" My pony," why not, " Doatie's pony ? " It was always called Doatie's pony ? The ponies were all called that, always. Donatia was well used to his politely caressing ways with the ladies who came to buy horses, the ladies who fêted him on the race courses of Ireland, but these were strange ladies, often married ladies, with their bold, uncaring, gentry ways. This eagerness in his meeting with Grania was another thing. He had known Grania for years. Foley's mother was Grania's nurse. There was no need for her to live at Aragon and work for Fox money, but so she did. Donatia could always remember when she was Nannie in the nursery before she became friend and counsellor, and those afternoons when she was taken for a great treat to have tea with *Miss* Grania and *Miss* Sylvia. Her mother would bring her over, and both she and Aunt Dymphnia would watch her all the time to see that she did not disgrace herself or them by common word or rude vulgar act. Doatie was not very old before she knew that Aunt Dymphnia watched her mother in the same way dreading that she would betray herself in over-politeness to the other servants, that she would not keep a distance as befitted Nannie's sister-in-law, or that some slight grossness in feeding would be observed and retold in the servants' hall. But she was always nice to her sister-in-law, if a little eager to speak for her in society to which she was unaccustomed, and to hint in invitations to nursery tea at Aragon what clothes she and Donatia should wear for the treat.

Later than nursery days Donatia's skill and bravery with her ponies and her success in children's classes at shows had put her in a position to which the two Misses

Fox, inept but ambitious equestrians, looked with envy and respect. Donatia always saw the hunts they could not see, and caught the judge's eye on ponies infinitely inferior to their own. It was rather grand to be seen talking horse to Donatia in show grounds, and they were not ashamed to give her their ponies to civilise when they proved beyond their own powers. Then in school days they drifted away from any familiar contact with her, and now at seventeen Grania came out to meet Foley with such gay challenge as Donatia could not mistake.

Donatia could not name the jealousy that pierced her and shook her with an anger she had never known, an anger that purged her of fear and left her in a state of hot intention. She would show the fat, shameless thing the kind of girl you had to be to please Foley, the hardy useful kind that he approved. Soft blondes were but by the way, no matter how kindly he looked on them, or sweetly smiled.

It was while Foley mounted Grania on the pony with every care and watchful attention that Micky (and not sorry either) threw Donatia up on the big horse. She walked him off down the road, feeling her way with him, strong and confident in her new anger.

Foley was delighted when he saw what she had done. There was a kink in him which liked to see Donatia in danger, liked other people to see her surmount that danger, the skill and courage in her little body triumphant. Together with Donatia he resented Grania's spoilt softness, resented that she had never had to work for anything, remotely disliked the knowledge that his mother worked for hers. Though he did not know it Foley was on Donatia's side and against Grania this morning.

"You're a very bold girl," he said to her and she laughed, recognising the indulgence in his voice. She rode first through the gate that Micky held open, the gate that led into the waste bog-lands where death might be her portion.

Donatia did not care. She was freed from her fear she

had taken it wholly upon herself and now it was gone.
Her horse plunged under her as Grania's little black
bitch flew screaming across their path, her rabbit prey in
view. Donatia caught up that wicked strength between
her hands and her knees, and thrilled to know she ruled
him.

" You could leave her at home another day," Foley
had said, surly. " I hate dogs around young horses."

" Another day . . . another day . . ." was this not the
first and the only day ? Donatia's heart turned with the
gull that wheeled chalk white in the strong air : the wind
across the bog blew on her coldly, but the wind never
blows warm across a bog, and far off the mountains turned
a chill indigo. A wave of evil intention came from her
horse, so strong that it brought the edge of fear to life
in her again. He knew it. He knew it. He was looking
for his chance again. Anything might give it to him.
Grania jostling along carelessly on the pony, her dog
splashing its way after a bird through bright sparkling
pools in the rushes, a bird alone, or the shadow of a cloud
across the bare land. Why had she got up on him ? What
did anything matter except the far-off warmth of safety,
the comfort of being on your own feet ? Now she would
have given everything she had twice over to be safe again
and out of this cold purgatory of waiting for danger.

" All right, Doatie ? " Foley asked as he had called to
Micky earlier and :

" Right, Foley," she answered as they jogged down the
edge of a field and he reached for his bit and leaned
heavy in her hands. Down in the corner was the first
fence they jumped in this school. He remembered it and
the remembrance excited him, but she was strong enough
for him still ; hold him, present him, and pop him up
on the bank, and into the next field with style. Ah, she
was warmer then, she could feel her confidence subduing
the power set against her. Brave again for the next bank
and the next, but now between each fence he would make
a drive to be off. She knew she had only to weaken by a

very little and he, not she, would be in charge, but still she was not tired, she could ride him.

Foley and Grania rode together, talking quietly, the pony hopping on and off the banks like a dog, and who had taught her to jump so well, and so neatly ? Doatie, poor Doatie alone in her danger now, and no one in the world to care at what moment disaster would overtake her.

It was Grania's Soo that caused the trouble, Soo scream-ing in pursuit of a rabbit running under his tail as he fidgeted on the far side of a fence that Foley's horse refused behind him. The dog and the sound of Foley's stick together were too much. He gave one sickening plunge and flew down the field.

Now it had come, now danger was here, she had no fear, yet she could not stop him. She could not turn him. She must not tire herself yet, drop her hands, cod him, deceive him, talk to him. The field was wide, she could turn him round and back to the other horses, keep him going round the field, Ah, but she couldn't turn him. His neck was set like a neck of iron, and he gathered strength below her like a big ship, like an engine, and can you stop it ? But she was not tired yet. Time to steady him still, and only a little wall with bushes laid on the top of it between them and the next field. No, but she could not stop or steady him. They galloped into it, hit all the bushes, sent loose stones flying, and landed anyway in the farther field. A stirrup gone now, and the wind knocked out of her, she sobbed to him in panic anger. Could nothing give him a second's kindness ? She caught her stirrup again as they galloped through a rough gap. Better, she had got her breath back ; now he nearly slipped-up down the side of a little hill ; two quiet asses grazing and a stream at the bottom—picture of another world. Recovery unbalanced, and on out of control through another gap, up a laneway, whirling up it, swerving and driving on.

Tired, oh tired, and he forever strength, wicked, bloody strength beyond her, beyond all compassing. Sick and silly and full of a terrible loathing, riding him worse each minute, she was finished. She saw the lane ending, ending in a high black barrier of thorns, built strong and high for her destruction in the bright field, and the bright cruel morning beyond. She dropped her hands and caught up the reins again, pulling the bit through his mouth with a last sobbing effort before he galloped into the fence. Then violence beyond all violence struck her and there was nothing more.

XI

GRANIA came flying down the lane on Donatia's pony, tears poured down her face, and sobs blew back in gusts through the air behind her. It was her fault, all her fault. She had killed little Doatie with her stupidity bringing Soo and all. She screamed with rage at Soo who screamed back, thrilled and flying along like a little black whippet beside her. Lovely, Soo thought, it was the best morning for a long time. Birdies and bunnies and horses all flying before her. She had frightened the life out of everything she met to-day.

There was a great breach in the obstacle that fenced the lane's end. Bushes and stones and an iron bar all burst out into the field beyond, and Foley was stooping over a terrifying little huddled bundle on the short grass, and the Knight of Aragon horse was standing with a foot up like a dog, afar off; staring and raging with reins hanging straight down from his upflung head and his tail out behind him like a horse on a monument on a hill-top. Oh, it was a dreadful scene of confusion, and frighteningly quiet, with a horrid after battle subsidence in the air, a dip towards unreality.

"I don't like moving her," Foley said to Grania. "I think her collar bone's gone, and she's clean out. Go and get a door some place and a blanket."

He was taking off his coat to put over her, and Grania hurried off hers, delighted that he seemed to have forgotten the dreadful things he had said to her and Soo not five minutes before ; now he spoke quite naturally, his hands feeling over poor little Doatie like a doctor's.

A man came running heavily down the side of the hill to them, the splendid thrill of disaster bore him to them as surely as a land-coming wave. He was disappointed that disaster's victim was still alive, he had viewed the fall, and thought she had no business to be.

" She set spurs to him, and she whipped into it," he told Foley. " Look see, look see, he flew through the bars of iron like a pigeon through smoke, and he tumbled his body three times through the air before ever he hit the land—oh, it was noble."

Grania redeemed herself a little by catching the horse. But the redemption turned a little sour in her mouth when she saw how he hobbled beside her. Foley would have something more to say about that. But he said nothing. He was smoking a cigarette and looking down at Doatie's dead little face, flat on the ground in the sunny shelter of the bank. He stooped down often to wrap the coats more snugly round her, and often looked over the hill behind to see if there was any sign of the man's return with door or blanket. It is the isolation and slowness of competing with such disasters that unnerves the waiters. Doors are not lying about, waiting to carry the wounded to hospital, nor do blankets or doctors grow on the bushes, and there is always the inconvenient horse which cannot be left to its own device and wild purpose. You must wait and watch the still, suffering creature until help comes, pieced so slowly and clumsily together from sources foreign to the accident.

To-day the kind vulture man returned soon with a company of helpers, and Doatie was carried to a house where a priest had been summoned. There was every circumstance of tragedy until the doctor's arrival, and his disappointing opinion that she was not too bad, and had

better be got home and to bed as soon as possible. She
was put in the doctor's car with Foley holding her.

Grania and Micky took the three horses home, Micky
riding Foley's and leading the wounded lion, while Grania
(though very worried as to how she was to get her bicycle
back to Aragon) rode the pony.

They talked ceaselessly.

" Well, wasn't it a fright, Miss ? "

" Oh, it was too shattering."

" A holy fright to God."

" Ghastly, and all Soo's fault. Oh, Soo, you naughty,
wicked——"

" It's little troubles her, and mind you a bird in the
air would do the same with this beggar, if he choose, he
choose and Miss Doatie's not equal to the likes of him."

" And poor Soo, really she didn't do so much. Just a
little dash out after a rabbit, poor sweetie."

" Dogs is a black and bloody nuisance around horses."

" Do you hear that, Soo ? Now you know."

" And I suppose the little she done was why he soared
through the air with buck, lep and kick, and away with
him into the firmaments, I suppose ? "

" Oh, it was terrible. He was gone in a flash, and then
Foley couldn't get his horse over the fence and didn't
know what to do, and Soo was barking like a mad woman,
and then if you only heard the crack he hit the wall—
I don't know how Miss Doatie stayed on him."

" Ah, she's hardy. But she's not hardy enough for the
likes of he. God help her she shouldn't be so venture-
some."

They turned in at the gate of Foley's house and rode
down the deep lane. The dark walls were alive with little
ferns wedged in the shade as bright as lizards in the sun.
A group of five cherries held their flowers pretty as dancers'
skirts on the dark edge of a grove. Cherry is the only
white flower with gaiety and none of the ominous waxen
quality implicit in white flowers.

Foley was waiting in the yard. He took no heed of

Grania but gently led the lame horse into his stable and closed the door.

Grania was in a state. What to do next? Did Foley not take in her difficulties? Where was the bicycle? Where was the doctor, who would surely report where he had seen her? And no matter either if she had not lied about it. Fishing for minnows indeed, a queer story to tell Nan. Oh, what should she do? and what had come of this daring morning outing but disgrace with Foley. She felt furious with Soo, but could not resist her when she came mimbling along for love, she must come into your arms again, little sweetness. Grania sat on the wooden stump of mounting block, her short hair pouring over Soo as she bent her head, dividing at the back of her neck as cleanly as water parts.

She lost herself in thoughts of Soo. Soo was like so many things. Smooth as a blackbird, supple as a cat, fast as a tiny deer. When she laid herself down to gallop a thrill would pierce Grania to see that flashing speed, those jinks and turnings. Filled with hunting lusts her gait of going was different, the procedure tremendously thought out. Then she mimbled about carefully in sight with her ears laid back flat against her head, she would edge up to the mate chosen for the day's sports and give him sly and wicked looks ; saying, watch me, keep your eye on me, I'll give the signal. Waiting until, even for a breath, Grania's attention was distracted ; even a breath is long enough, and like a horse jumping into its bridle, she would be off at a wicked bullet-like speed, tucking herself into herself and firing herself along, a black bee with no wings. A passion that knows no conscience possessing her, savage and extreme in her desire, she must reach the coverts and the wild, and pursue the game, which she so seldom captured. If, one day out of a year of days, she did by some chance turn of speed, or by some immemorial dig get her teeth fastened in the choking stink of bunny fur and flesh, her mouth, alas, was too weak to hold her prize. A moment there may be with fulfilment in her grasp, paradise between the teeth, then a couple of bounding kicks from her prey and he is gone from her, lost to her. Only frustration owns the cruel moment.

Who can tell, there may be other times, when a nest of blind and naked baby rabbits falls to her share, and she can bloat herself on their succulent delicacy. But she never returned full-stomached and bloody from her hunting—or if she was bloody, blood cannot be seen against her blue-black coat. One thing is sure, she never came back other than spindle-bodied and hungry. Her belly touching her backbone. There are bracelets of platinum bound round her bird-thin forelegs where traps and snares, the wicked gins of men, have snapped into her flesh in dark rabbit runs, where for hours she has striven and suffered while Grania searched and called for her fruitlessly.

There was once such a night when the trapper went his rounds, and a tough tinker he was, but to Soo a man, and men are kind. As she saw him approach her agony held her silent in anticipation of mercy and release. Now it was dusk and her torment would soon cease. He was coming to her through the wet, blood-red bracken, through the cold, through the pain. He came nearer. He paused. Soo's black back was arched in her pain and terror.

He turned away and left her. A black cat, he thought. I'll bring my gun and shoot her in the morning. For black cats touch no chord of pity in any poacher's heart.

None can ever know or tell about the night that followed. A new height of suffering and terror must have reached its pain up towards the chill stars and screamed, mercy, to the night.

The next morning she was loosed, in such a cold extremity of exhaustion that she could hardly make her way home. Two hours it took her to cover a distance that she could have done in twenty minutes. And when she got back to her house, to Aragon, no, she could not even cry ; but crouched and licked her wound in the cold dewed grass near to the dark of the rhododendrons, there she was found and succoured with passionate and healing love.

So Grania dwelt and dreamed on the thought of Soo, and held her and forgave her foolishness, and murmured to her, What shall we do now, Soo? We're lost. What fools we were.

Then Foley was standing at her shoulder saying coldly, "I wonder would you go in and give Aunt Gipsy a hand with Doatie?" Saying then with an intention that left her breathless in its promise and forgiveness: "I'm going to drive you back to your bicycle after breakfast. Don't fret about the horse, he's all right."

He picked Soo up. "Weren't you a very naughty girl. Give us a kiss now and say you're sorry," his eyes at that trick of holding hers across what he was saying. "I must go back to my patient," as Micky came out of the kitchen door with a pail of hot water. "Run along now, and don't be keeping my mind from my work."

Freed and insolent, knowing she was restored to her place in his love again Grania walked across the yard, away from the smart line of boxes and towards the house.

The old yard sloped up towards the back of the house which, unadorned by bow-windows or porches of coloured glass, had the tall dismal dignity of a narrow old farm-house. Low white walls came up to each corner of the house and thick fuschia hedges, clipped year after year to impenetrable sturdiness, jutted roundly above the curved wall coping. The windows in the back of the house were small, small-paned and dark looking, set with purpose and carefulness in the walls, flat to the extreme outside of the thick walls. You thought the house to be higher than it was, the drop of the yard below gave it a faintly towerlike look. The outer walls were so sour and flat you supposed them to be thin, but they were built as solid as a castle. The back of Foley's house was so unlike the front of it that the contrast gave you as quick a shock as the sight of a skeleton sitting on a sofa might give, or the geniality of a friend suddenly turned to bitterness and accusation.

Grania opened the high latched door that led into the kitchen, and stood within, looking about her in the quiet gloom of a farm kitchen where for years food had been prepared for people and for animals, and where many people had lived in the poverty and dignity of daily life, before the idea of masters feeding apart from their men was known, or the dreadful style of parlours.

Aunt Gipsy's voice came calling down the stairs for someone to boil a kettle, and Grania called back, " I'll do it." She put the kettle on and stirred the fire, alone and responsible for this slight act. She was curiously excited, it was absurd for there could not be a smaller thing to do, but the air in the long dim kitchen seemed full of presage as the stars, the whitened walls leaned inwards and towards her. Light rode down a lean beam from a window deeply dug in the thick wall. Such light never came directly in, the windows were too high and deep sunk to the outer wall, but there was a softness and warmth of light that melted against the limed walls and poured back from them into the air. On the table there was a wide bowl, pale brown outside and white inside. Nine fresh eggs it held. They were so new that a sort of bloom lay on their shells. A smell of bread came strongly from the oven. She opened the door, and found a cloth hanging on a chair to turn the pan of bread. A sweet volume of warmth came from the open oven door.

She felt drunk with this contrast to her morning of danger and hardihood. The warmth enclosed within walls, the delight of a house, the sweetness of new bread, all these things touched the realm of the exotic now. Common joys were new to her, making bread or making love. She was awed and enchanted by them newly, and deeply ignorant of both. She was beyond and outside herself and reality, in a world of different wonders and unguessed at values.

Grania was far too young and inexperienced to take love

at all lightly. The idea of passing love, was not born in her. It had not dawned on her that Foley's love could mean only a little. She thought everything in him and of him was for her, as he was the breath of life and the only meaning of love to her, so she must be to him. She had no doubts of him whatever. She was only un-questioningly wildly glad that by a miracle he had found her to love. She pinched her fat arms now, hurting herself into the knowledge of reality. She was well lost indeed, a fat beautiful blonde.

Now the boiling kettle checked her pleasant dreaming and she lifted it clumsily off the fire, and called up the stairs :

" Mrs. Bohane ! Mrs. Bohane ! " and only the gabble of quick praying came down, in a hammer-like mutter, in answer to her calling. How she wished Nan and not Mrs. Bohane were in charge of poor Doatie. There would be more nursing than praying done by Nan in such a case.

The praying went on. You could not hear any words, only the rhythm that repeated prayers make on the empty air, despairingly mechanical.

She took the kettle and went up the steep stairs, a feeling of carefulness and responsibility alive in her. She opened the room through which the sound of praying came. Mrs. Bohane, smartly dressed in mauve for her breakfast party, was kneeling by Doatie's bed, and a young and dirty girl knelt a little apart, as was fit. Mrs. Bohane led the prayer and the girl responded. Doatie moved a little and waved her poor head from side to side on the pillow. She was no more than half-conscious.

" Oh, Miss Grania, my heavens, you'll have to excuse us, oh, really, you will," Mrs. Bohane sprang to her feet and began to drag the curlers out of her hair, her toilet not having progressed to its conclusion before catastrophe was sprung on her.

" The kettle boiled so I brought it up."

" My heavens, will you ever excuse us ? Mary, what are you thinking of ? Take the kettle from Miss Fox. Oh, we all need a cup of tea, don't we? Go down and make it, Mary."

" How is poor Doatie ? "

Mrs. Bohane shook her dark head despairingly.

" Oh, the doctor said he'd be back in a couple of hours. Indeed, my great heavens, look at her. She might be gone by then, wouldn't you say so yourself? It's the priest we might be calling, don't you think so ? "

" Oh, Mrs. Bohane, I thought the doctor said she wasn't as bad as we thought."

" Oh, doctors say this and doctors say that, but I can see the Blue Shadow on her face, and we all know what that means."

" Oh, no ! "

" Oh, yes, indeed, and a corpse in my tea cup on a Friday, don't tell me she'll ever leave that bed again but in her little coffin. A child's coffin would nearly do her, perhaps. Indeed I'll have to get into town to see about it."

All this conversation streamed in a galloping whisper from Mrs. Bohane, and Grania's answers had been murmured back, so when Foley came into the room and said in a low but natural voice :

" Breakfast's ready. How's poor Doatie ?." it really seemed as though he brought with him the possibility of life. He stepped over to her bed and stood there considering for a moment before he found her hand, with a half-yard of striped sleeve below it and felt her pulse. Then he felt under the bed clothes for her feet.

" What about a hot bottle ? " he said, " Two in fact. She's perished. Her little feet are like stones in a river."

" Oh, my God, I had the kettle boiling and I forgot what I had it for, imagine ! I sent it down for the tea."

" I suppose you were laying plans for the funeral party."

" Oh, Jesu, what a rap ! "

" Go on and get the two bottles now as quick as you can."

" There's but the one in the house, dear, I'll have to get into town and buy another."

Foley tucked the clothes gently round poor Doatie and went down to the kitchen.

"Mary," he said, "get me a hot bottle. Have you only the one?"

"I have an old jar some place."

"Quick now, good girl."

He had a great way of getting things done; small necessary things. Cosy fundamentals, and he used people without bullying them. Grania watched him, back in Donatia's room in five minutes after he had left it, wrap the jar and the rubber bottle in two vests of Doatie's and put them in her bed, felt a surprised respect for such handiness. Suddenly she saw his likeness to Nan. Just so did Nan deal with things. The same hard, quick strength and dexterity; more comforting when you were ill than all the warmth and kind chatter in the world. Seeing this likeness so plainly frightened her a little. For a flashing moment she saw that there were things that mattered to her which would be no more to him than to Nan. She might keep many things she loved a secret for always. The way she thought of the silent pleasure-ground at Aragon, of the still river air feeling its way with watery quiet into the drawing-room, poems of De La Mare, poems of Grania Fox, ah, but what had love to do with such cold things? How compare those joys belonging essentially to your loneliness to this glory, and this longing shared.

He held the door of Donatia's room open for her and walked after her down the stairs at a cool and courtly distance. She was so vulnerable to him that even this could hurt and surprise her. She walked through the kitchen with her fair head reared up, swallowing tears and spit. She wanted to say, I did boil the kettle. I turned the bread, I'm not useless.

In the dining-room Mrs. Bohane sat importantly behind her teapot facing the Pope.

Foley said, "I told Mary to stay with Doatie till you go back to her. She shouldn't be left alone."

" Oh, pardon and excuse me, Foley, Doctor said leave
her perfectly quiet, and if there was ever a bull in a
thunder shop that's Mary."

" Well I'm going into town after breakfast, and I'll
bring out a nurse."

" A nurse, indeed ! You'll excuse me, Miss Grania,
but whose daughter is Doatie ? And who should nurse
her but her mother ? Not one of those brats in a white
bib, I suppose, from the County home, imagine, making
work for nobody through the house, don't tell me."

" Well, she may be your daughter, Aunt Gip, but whose
horse was it nearly killed her, poor child ? and who
should get her a nurse ? "

" And whose dog nearly killed her ? " Grania suddenly
felt impelled to a share in Doatie's misfortune.

" Oh, don't think of it, Miss Grania. Look, what am
I doing ? You haven't a bit to eat, do you take sugar
in your tea ? Really I'm so nervous I'm getting quite
forgetful."

" You're not fit to nurse her after the shock, Aunt
Gip."

" Indeed it must have been a great shock for you, Mrs.
Bohane."

" Shock, dear ? When I saw the doctor's car from this
window, Oh, I said to myself, what will I do, if he's come
to break it to me she's gone ? Now, I wonder, I said to
myself, what will I do. I could see myself at the little
grave, Miss Grania—really now I could—all in black and
a black hat. Isn't it well, I said to myself, I never saw
that nice little flowered hat on the paper till this very
morning, or it would be up there now in its box, and I'd
never knock a turn out of it the summer long."

" Aunt Gip——"

" A broken collar bone, Mrs. Bohane, the doctor said.
Is that only all, I said. I knew it was only softening
the blow he was——"

" Aunt Gip——"

" Well, there's a touch of concussion too, he said, and

with that my head commenced to reel and it's reeling yet."

"Aunt Gip, you'll let me bring the nurse out now, won't you? It's for your sake as much as Doatie."

"Very well, dear. I'll come in with you and see have they the little hat yet at McBirney's, and get a few little things for poor Doatie."

"Milk and water's all poor Doatie'll want for the next few days, and I'll tell them to keep the hat for you, Aunt Gip."

"Ah, Foley, how would you know it from the picture? I'll have to see it my own self." Aunt Gip was getting desperate.

"Now, listen, when I bring the nurse out to Doatie I'll bring you in to Ahern's. Will that satisfy you?"

"Now, it's not for any pleasure attached to it, but I do find it very hard, imagine, to buy a hat that suits me, and it's only an economy to buy one hat that suits you, where you could be buying three you couldn't wear."

"That's a fact, Aunt Gip . . . Look"—he put in a smile instead of "Miss Grania"—"we must be off. I don't want to hurry you but I have a lot to do."

"Are you driving Miss Grania back to Aragon, Foley? Will you see your mother?"

"No," he said shortly, "I won't."

"Oh," said Aunt Gip, and she sat in a surprising silence and stillness staring at the Pope for at least a minute before she wove her complicated good-byes and excuses and compliments round Grania. But there were no messages for Nan.

Foley noticed this. He said to himself, "The old bitch is on the line, God blast her. . . . I'll not do a thing about the hat or she'll get more suspicious if I'm too nice with her."

XII

" Miss Pigeon, up, now, it's time to get up and dress yourself, and your bath morning too."

Aunt Pidgie curled herself down in her bed. She longed to be a sitting hen that no one could disturb for twenty-one days, no one could throw her off her eggs. Ah, but they did come and throw the hens from their nests, the poor birdies, but I would steal my nest some place where no one could find me, Aunt Pidgie decided. In the old ice-house perhaps or maybe a nice empty manger, a sturdy deep manger of worm-eaten wood. She saw herself blinking in the blue seedy light of an empty stable ; the quiet stuffiness ; the light coming through slatted windows in dusty bars. She would purr to herself, spreading her feathers, and tap gently on a hot egg with her bill, pushing it back beneath her heavy flattened body. Her body would cling to those hot eggs and she would be steeped in quiet and queen of quietness and warmth.

" Miss Pigeon, are you never going to get out of bed ? And such a glorious day it's a shame for you to be wasting it. Come on now, your bath's none too hot, and it's not getting hotter."

Nan spoke in a voice in which cajoling and threats were equally balanced. A nurse's voice, a voice that knows the body well and cares nothing for the extravagances of the mind.

Aunt Pidgie bundled herself desperately to the edge of her bed and stretched down those tiny blue veined feet for her slippers.

" My slippers, Nan, my slippers."

" They're there," Nan was collecting towels and soap.

" They're not."

They were, of course. Nan came over and clapped them on her feet as if they were irons. Clapped in irons.

That's what the pirates did to you, and there was something else, a shadow on her mind about irons. Who did they put in irons?

" Who do they put in irons, Nan? "

" Who's been talking to you about irons, Miss Pigeon? Wait till I meet them. No, you'll never come to that, dear, indeed no, not while you have Nan to look after you."

It was a terrifying little speech delivered with goulish becks and nods and veiled understanding of possible horrors not to be explained. It was by such innuendos that Nan kept Miss Pigeon in order and alive in her a recognition of Nan's protective power. Miss Pidgie knew there were things Nan could tell that would get her locked away for ever in the asylum, that terrible prison on the hill where you never saw a fire or felt the soft yielding heat of a hot-water bottle (such as Nan sometimes very kindly gave her on particularly cold nights, not every night of course), where terrible people called Brutal Warders knocked you about, and you got stewed mice every second Thursday for your dinner, and there were lice in the beds and bars on the windows. . . . Oh, hurry, hurry to your bath and no moaning and shivering about it if it ran cold, for if you were not good you might find yourself taken away from Aragon, and out of Nan's care, so you had to be very careful not to annoy Nan, and never, never to complain about her or about anything she might say or do.

Nan washed Miss Pigeon with firm carefulness and left her floating in the warm water, her body nearly as transparent as a frog's, while she went down to get the breakfast tray.

" But only a minute now, Miss Pigeon, and you're to be dry when I get back. There's your hot towel, and there's your vest."

Alone in hot water, and it was hot to-day, Aunt Pidgie lay back and luxuriated at her ease. Oh, delicious warmth, soaking into her bones, why was one always cold? The torture of coldness, now she wondered if she

couldn't be a little hotter, how comfortable to have the
water one degree hotter and one inch deeper. Nan would
not know. Miss Pigeon pulled herself up and carefully
with both hands turned on the hot tap. An exquisite
dribble enlivened the temperature of the water. Aunt
Pidgie sat near the tap, sponging the hotter water
over her shoulders, holding hot spongefuls on the back
of her thin neck, smiling with ease and pleasure, forgetting
all the worries and responsibilities of her life.

Suddenly she heard Nan's returning step, quick and
loud and busy, and at the sound her hands flew to the
tap to turn it off. Even if she was not dried and in her
vest she could not be found committing this iniquity in
her bath. And now the tap would not turn off. She
twisted at it with weak fury but it would not budge.
Regardless of her effort the water ran on, deepening her
crime, comfortably cruelly running into the bath, already
far deeper and hotter than Nan permitted. Aunt Pidgie
was in a terrible state. She splashed and clattered about
in the water trying to deaden the sound of the running
tap until she found some means to stop it flowing. It was
too late when she saw that she had been twisting at COLD
not HOT, for Nan was back again, a ferocious mixture of
wrath and injured trustfulness.

"And so this is what happens when I leave you and
trust you ! Giving yourself a good boil the way you'll
catch every chill of the day when you go out." Nan came
whirling in. "Have you no conscience, have you no
thought for others, living here at your ease in the
Mansion of Aragon ? "

"Oh, Nan, Nan, I'm sorry, I'm sorry. I didn't mean
it, you know I didn't."

"I know you're boiled as red as a prawn this living
minute." Nan picked up a brass jug and began filling
it under the cold tap. The pupils of her eyes were like
black pin heads.

"Stand up there, now," she spoke jeeringly, "till we
cool you off."

"Nan, no, Nan, no. Not cold water. It hurts me, it does things to me . . .."

"Stop your screeching, now. Stop it, do you hear me."

Nan stood magnificently above the cowering white body crouching up the shallow end of the bath, her beautiful grey hair had not a curl out of place, her apron was as crisp as virgin snow, her perfect teeth showed in a curious smile. She trickled an icy dribble of water out of the spout of her can in front of Miss Pigeon, and Miss Pigeon gripped the grandly shaped arm that held the can and whimpered in a frenzy of fear.

Nan emptied the can out into the bath and burst out laughing.

"Aren't you very easily frightened, Miss Pigeon? Don't you know I was only teasing you? All the same it was a very bold and dangerous act to go turning on the hot tap. I once heard a true story of a lady who got boiled in her bath for doing that very thing indeed. Couldn't turn the tap off, fell back in a faint, how are you, and hit the back of her head, imagine, stunned herself, think of it, and boiled herself to death, fancy!"

She helped Aunt Pidgie out as she talked and wrapped her in a towel and dried her as carefully and gently as if she was a baby, even a Fox baby.

Poor Aunt Pidgie. She was trembling still and at the same time whimpering with relief. Nan was so kind, so strong, so good, one shouldn't be so silly as to mind her little jokes with cans of cold water. She would show she was sorry by hurrying into her clothes. Aunt Pidgie wore quantities of underclothes. She had combinations and knickers and white split drawers on top of the knickers, that drew in at the knees with embroidery, and three different spencers with long, medium and short sleeves. Her legs, about as thick as a heron's and white and hairless as a chalk stone, were eaten up in thick black stockings. The legs of the combinations were folded down below the knife-sharp promontories of her knees, and held up by tapes that went across her shoulders and down the back, cross-pieced by tape in front and behind. It was a very good device and she had worn it since her last pair of corsets gave out about two years ago. Some day Mrs. Fox was going to buy her a very special new kind of corset, but she had so much to think about it was hard for her to remember everything. That was all the clothes you put on in the bathroom, the rest went on when you go back to your own room.

XIII

AUNT PIDGIE'S room had once been the nursery and it still kept that curiously forlorn look which nurseries have when their children are gone. The linoleum clings to the floor. The high iron fireguard with its brass rail has never been divorced from the fires it once guarded. The paper on the wall may be different, but who is going to take the bars off the windows, or patch up the mouse hole in the wainscot that so many oddments were put down for the mice, or put back the two missing handles on the white-painted chest of drawers, much less repaint it? People who don't matter to anybody are put to sleep in old nurseries. This is odd when one thinks of the time when the nursery was the most considered room in the house. Now there is about it the sad unnecessary air of a deserted beehive. The rocking-horse in the window ramps eternally idle on his rockers, no nor always idle, for sometimes when Miss Pigeon knew herself to be alone for hours she would mount him very slowly and carefully and rock herself gently while she gazed out of the window, from which she could see the river water and hear the river water flow, sliding past her and beyond her, as now everything went by her, people and happenings all unrelated to her life, all but Nan.

Now she was back in her room and the rest of her clothes were lying there ready to put on. First her sporran had to be adjusted, which was always a business as Nan objected to the lump it made under her skirt when it was full of precious things, so she would tie its top by the very ends round her waist and sling the paunch down between her legs. Then came her black and white checked petticoat, and to-day was the day for her purple skirt. She liked her purple skirt though she always wished she had a blouse to match it as then the violet colour might reflect in her eyes. But a navy blue blouse was the best she could do, with a cream lace guimpe upstanding, a little boned palisade, round her neck. She wore a couple of cardigans, the inner one a marled black and white weave, the outer a very long navy blue model with a tasselled belt blousing it slightly at the waist.

She sat in a chair while Nan put a towel round her shoulders and did up her hair. Her hair, once so yellow, and now the indeterminate colour of water in which many teacups have been washed. She still wore the yellow combs in it that had matched it so well. They felt just the same in her hair now as they had done in that person's hair who had been herself, herself before she got ill. She did not think of herself as particularly old, only as ill and cold and always rather tired.

Nan put her boots on too and she sighed as she did every morning about that sharp lump inside the left boot, or was it the right boot? which ran into her foot like a dagger before the end of the day. But in the morning she could never remember distinctly which foot it was, as she did not feel the lump until she had walked a bit, and Nan would bamboozle and mislead her, saying, " Are you sure it's not the right foot you mean, Miss Pigeon? Make certain now, and I'll take them back to the man in the boot department. But I'd want to know which for certain," all the time lacing up the boots like wildfire so that Miss Pigeon got confused and would not say for certain which foot it was.

Grania would often call in to see her at breakfast time, Grania in a ragged blue kimono with a stork on the back, on her way to her bath. Grania had a fancy for the nursery bathroom and often came there for her bath and if she was not in too great a hurry she would look in on Aunt Pidgie.

Somehow these visits gave Aunt Pidgie exactly the same feeling of being apart and alone as the sight and sound of the passing river water under her window gave her. Grania's fat little behind would waggle cosily inside the tightly clasped kimono, and her fat white elbows would come through the long split sleeves, her hair would be screwed up in curlers and she would sit down or lean across the rocking-horse in the window, and make conversation to Aunt Pidgie for a few minutes.

" Lovely morning, Aunt Pidgie."

" Yes, dear, I think it's an east wind though."

" Oh, Aunt Pidgie, how can you tell ? You haven't been out."

" Feel it all over me."

" What are you having for breakfast ? "

" Just a cup of tea and a little bread and butter."

" You ought to eat more, Aunt Pidgie."

" Oh, I couldn't touch another thing, not possibly. People eat far too much, that's what I always say. Just a slice of bread and butter for me, and a little piece over for my Diblins, that's all I want. What are you having for breakfast downstairs, I wonder ? "

" Kedgeree perhaps. It was salmon last night for dinner."

" Oh, a lovely pink heap of kedgeree with chopped eggs in it and some parsley on top, I expect."

" Shall I save some for your Diblins ? "

" Oh, nasty indigestible stuff. You'll give every Diblin on the place the height of indigestion," Nan might put in.

" Nasty indigestible stuff," Miss Pidgie repeated sadly after her.

Grania laughed. " Oh, well, perhaps it's not kedgeree at all."

" Perhaps it's bacon and eggs ? "

" Perhaps."

" What are you doing to-day, Grania ? " And whatever Grania was doing, riding or playing tennis or going
down to see the salmon net drawn it was so apart from
Miss Pigeon that when it was told it seemed to drop
Miss Pigeon further and deeper into the cold shaft of
loneliness where her life was lived. . . . Still she liked to
see Grania in the mornings. Grania was still a little like
the baby and the child Grania that Aunt Pidgie had
spoilt and patronised and fascinated with stories of her
Diblins. She was not like that stuck-up little Sylvia who
had never really believed in Diblins, Aunt Pidgie knew,
nor in T. Runk, the God of travelling either. Sylvia had
always been cool and calm and collected, and it was
always her dog, that nasty neat, smooth fox terrier that
Aunt Pidgie found nosing round the secret places where
the Diblins' food was left for them. Aunt Pidgie hated
Titsy. She would never look when Titsy was going
through her repertoire of tricks, she could do them all so
well and neatly and with such dispatch and obedience,
but Aunt Pidgie preferred Grania's Soo and would get
her to beg-up, jump-up, and die for Ireland in endless
opposition to Titsy's accomplishments. And if Soo was
not there when Titsy was showing off Aunt Pidgie would
shut her eyes and groan loudly at the applause. Another
faintly annoying thing about Titsy was that she never,
never got in the family way. Not even when Sylvia
intended that she should. She was indefeatably spin-
sterish. She bit her lovers and sat down firmly and snarled
at all advances ; while Soo, poor passionate little gipsy,
could hardly be restrained from the most indiscreet affairs,
she had been desperately in love with a mastiff, and many
other gentlemen had fancied her too.

That was one of the games Aunt Pidgie and Grania
played with most enjoyment, talking about Soo's life and
asking Soo questions about it. They would think up
questions to ask Soo in front of Sylvia, about what Soo
thought of Titsy, and make up Soo's answers, but Sylvia

was so abominably quick-witted that she often thought
up on the spur of the moment the most devastating cracks
back for Titsy, and Grania and Aunt Pidgie, who were
neither of them very quick—though they were painstaking
—would be reduced to broadsides, such as : " What a
pity Titsy's such a fool." " What a pity Titsy lost her
figure."

It was only through such childish games as these that
Aunt Pidgie climbed out of her loneliness and felt gloriousy
equal to the glorious young. To-day after her fright in the
bath she felt more thrust into herself than ever, and she
was still rather shaky when she sat down to her tea and
bread and butter.

" Where's Miss Grania to-day, I wonder," she ventured
presently.

" Fishing for minnows." Nan always prided herself on
knowing the exact whereabouts and occupation of all the
Fox's at all hours of the day or night. You could not
catch her out.

" She'll catch cold, out so early."

" People don't catch cold as easy as you think."

" No."

" No, they don't, and I think it's high time we took
away one of your winter blankets."

" Oh, Nan, I'm so cold at night. I want them all."

" Well, want must be your master (that was a favourite
saying of Nan's), I can't have you getting yourself into a
perspiration at night just for a fancy. No, Miss Pigeon,
that wouldn't do at all. Who's responsible for your
health ? Who has the job of nursing you when you're
sick ? Who ? Tell me that now, who ? "

" You, Nan."

" And you don't want to give me any more trouble
than you can help, do you ? "

" Oh, no, Nan." Miss Pigeon gazed at the loaf of
bread longing for another slice but much too frightened
of giving extra trouble to ask for it. Nan was very busy
dusting now, she hooshed and flapped with her duster

making a great to-do among the photographs and ornaments on the mantelpiece, her duster flew out like a kite,
and folded up as absorbent as a sponge, and went into
all corners after the most invisible specks of dust or
untidiness. She rattled an empty match box and Miss
Pigeon screamed out :

"Oh, my eggs ! my eggs ! "

"How should I know your eggs were in there. Are
they for your Diblins."

"Yes, Nan, yes."

Nan opened the box, " But these are blown."

"Yes, I blew them last night."

Nan looked at her curiously, and Miss Pidgie began to
think of excuses for having blown her eggs, but after a
pause Nan said, " Well, why shouldn't you ? " and shut
the box laughing. Miss Pigeon was very relieved that no
further questions had been asked. But that danger past,
as always happens, another difficulty blew up in her mind
to do away with the joy from relief that she had briefly
known. Now she was in quite a fidget to get out because
if she did not get out soon it would be too late. . . . Aunt
Pidgie's life was just a vortex and a tangle of plans and
adventures that nobody knew about.

XIV

FRAZER, the butler, knew his place all right, and he knew
a lot of other interesting things too, but knowing his place
came first. He was not English, though he sounded very
English, he came from the North of Ireland, and had a
sour, abiding dislike of these Southerners, and no one
could have been more unpopular with the natives of
Aragon than he was. He always managed to know who
stole what, and who idled most. Oddly enough he and
Nan disliked each other intensely. There was not room
for two such powers at Aragon, and Nan's way of dispens-
ing her power was far more imaginative and grand than
Frazer's. She was royal in the disposition of favour or
rebuke. He was meticulous and petty and could overlook
nothing that he saw wrong in the house, or the garden,
the river or even the stables, for he would poke his nose
into every department of the estate, and appraise its
conduct to a nicety.

He was very partial to the soldiery who visited Aragon.
They seemed right and civilised to his mind, with their
clipped moustaches, clean flannels, well-made shoes and
good manners. They represented the things he respected
most, and he hoped he would see Miss Sylvia married to
one of them. He had a real liking for her. Yes, she was
a lady. Her little cold ways and clever fingers, her skill
with horses or her skill on the river were very nice to him.
He admired her tidiness and punctuality. There was
something low to his mind in Miss Grania's dirty childish
ways and in Mrs. Fox's airy flexible irresponsibility, and
her indulgence towards delinquencies on the place, and
her familiarity with Nan. He had often timed those long
cosy talks at bedtime or the day-time murmurs in the
morning-room. Their length filled him with disproportionate jealousy, although he would never have permitted
the freedom to himself. He knew his mistress's place

better. A " Yes, Madam," or " No, Madam," from him could always put her in it. There was an inverted pleasure in keeping the family in its place. Then he knew better than Nan did their comings and goings and exactly which of the young officers was paying most marked attention to the young ladies. He read all postcards religiously, and could remember every telegram that came to Aragon in the course of a year.

Although it was far from his place to do so he often prepared platefuls of chicken and cress sandwiches with which he would waylay Miss Pigeon in some out of the way spot saying with tremendous ceremony, " For the Diblins, Miss, and if you would kindly leave the plate beneath this laurel bush I will collect it in due course." Then he would bow and leave her among the gloomy leaves of the rhododendrons. He would not have dreamed of watching her as she darted in among the dry twisty branches, rooted and layered to the ground.

Frazer hated Nan, that was the truth. And Nan loved to torment him. To seek him out in his own pantry and torment him, show her power and boast to him till she had him in a frenzy of annoyance. On some morning when he was feeling particularly sour and conscious of his ills she might come crisply in, and the conversation go something like this :

" Good-morning, Mr. Frazer."

A pause while he swept three crumbs ceremoniously off a table. Then " Good-morning, Mrs. O'Neill."

"Would you kindly leave out a bottle of light port wine for Miss Pigeon's lunch biscuit, Mr. Frazer."

" I thought you had a bottle of that last week, Mrs. O'Neill."

" *And* how many glasses go to a bottle, will you tell me ? Am I dreaming or is it seven ? "

" I'd say Miss Pigeon did most of the dreaming where that port was concerned, Mrs. O'Neill."

That was how it would go on between them, or it might be :

" May I glance at the *Irish Times*, Mr. Frazer ? I'd like to see the results of the Clonmel Horse Show."

Again the scene would be in his pantry, just after the post came in.

" I have it folded for the drawing-room, Mrs. O'Neill."

" I'll fold it again. I just want to see if my son's horse won a prize ? " She knew very well he had. So did Frazer. And he was not going to wait to be boasted to either. He would not give her that much satisfaction. Certainly not. He made for the door, a tray of letters in his hand. But he found he could not get out, not get out of his own pantry. Mrs. O'Neill was between him and the door and deaf to all, " Excuse me's," " Kindly allow me to pass."

" Am I stopping you, Mr. Frazer. Excuse me ! Oh, look——" flapping wide the paper and folding down a page of photographs——" ' Mr. F. O'Neill on ' Mountain Brig,' winner of the class for hunters up to 14 stone.' Well, isn't that nice. Foley will be pleased. And such a gorgeous picture of him, isn't it ? Don't you think so, Mr. Frazer ? "

" I scarcely noticed it, Mrs. O'Neill."

" A lot of horses in his class and a Baronet and an Honourable and a Lord showing in it too, fancy ! "

" Pardon me, Mrs. O'Neill, but I have my·morning's work to do, if all you want is to read the papers. Kindly let me out of my own pantry."

" Oh, Mr. Frazer, excuse me every time. What was I thinking of ? Only such a triumph would make any mother thoughtless, wouldn't it ? "

Long and long ago Frazer had looked on Nan with admiring eyes. Nan had known it and with every light malicious twist in her had shown how she despised him then. That was very long ago, but the seeds of hatred it had sown between them had thriven well. Frazer knew many things about Nan to her detriment, but not enough, never quite enough for her undoing, but he had waited years and he could wait longer for that hour. It might not be so long now either for he sensed something that was afoot between Miss Grania and Foley O'Neill. It might be nothing. It was too soon to say. But there were signs about, things that needed watching. For instance ; the day Miss Grania was so late for dinner, a ferret of Foley's breed had joined the horrid hutchful in the stables. Everyone knew these ferrets with the spot. Of course it might have come through Nan. He was preparing a test for her to find this out. And where had Miss Grania gone this morning ? He had seen her, through the pantry window, bicycling down the mist-ridden avenue going at high speed past the fogged sleepy groups of black cattle and pale towers of the lime trees. It was early hours for one who liked her bed so well as Miss Grania did. He put on one of his tests at breakfast time.

"Shall I leave the lamp under the coffee for Miss Grania, Madam ? " he asked Mrs. Fox as she was distractedly sorting her letters from bills and catalogues before she flew down, rather late, to see the cook.

"Always late. Yes, I suppose so, yes Frazer, please."

"I thought perhaps she would be out for breakfast, ma'am."

"Out ? She's not up yet."

"Ah, I must have been mistaken, madam."

"Oh, ' mistaken,' Frazer ? "

"I imagined I saw Miss Grania cycling down the avenue at 7 o'clock this morning, madam."

"Oh, no, Frazer, you must have been mistaken."

"Obviously my mistake, Madam."

So, she was off on the quiet was she, and why ? For what ? There was something more in this to nose into. And she wouldn't be back to breakfast this morning, not likely. Whatever business had Miss Grania out of bed at six would be important enough to occupy her well into the morning. Perhaps he had been foolish to say anything to Mrs. Fox, but at least he now knew there was something queer about this morning's business. His mind went back to the glimpse of her pedalling madly down the avenue. What was it that had struck him as peculiar

about it ? Why, of course, she was in riding clothes. . . .
Frazer pulled the little spirit lamps out from under coffee
and silver dishes and extinguished them each with a sour
smile. No, Miss Grania certainly would not be back to
breakfast.

As he cleared the table he saw Miss Pidgie scurrying
along the path between the house and the terraces. He
saw her against the shining water. The sun glistened and
the wind blew in some black cock's feathers in her hat,
turning them to ice green. Everyone seemed on business
bent this morning. He opened the window to intercept
her, in his hand a plate of scrambled eggs, fried toast and
bacon. " Excuse me, Miss," he leant out towards the
black feathered hat with tremendous ceremony, " for the
Diblins, Miss, and if you would kindly leave the plate
beneath that laurel bush I will collect it in due course."

" Oh, thank you, Frazer, thank you. It's a hungry
morning for them, isn't it ? "

He saw her change her course and disappear down a
dark little side walk towards the river. " Now I wonder
what *she* had for her breakfast," he pondered, " If I could
fix that on the old bitch I'd be content. Starved that's
what she is, starved to death, and no one gives a damn.
These cursed Irish they're all the same, rich and bloody
poor, they're all alike," for in his own extreme self Frazer
had a loose way of talking that would have shocked
deeply the self he had made.

X V

THE WREN'S NEST. Foley did not mean to stop at Roche's public house that morning, but he saw the sign the boys used when they were there at the door. The wooden crosspiece of a plough leaning against the wall. The boys knew his car well enough and someone would be on the lookout to report they had seen him go by when the sign was out. It was the sign of the Irish Republican army and he dared not pass by.

He stopped his car in the sunny road. A black-faced mountainy sheep skipped back across the low stone wall to the heather and gorse stretching high and wide and away up to the sharp blue cloud shadows that travelled the mountain distances. The gorse and low spring heather were dry as cages, he knew because he had lain on the mountain this morning with Grania in the sun and light wind, teasing her and making love in the morning sun until she was wild for love.

She had all the unshamed and natural dignity of her wild blood. For so young a creature she was superb and at her ease. Afterwards she lay in the dark heather laughing at her lover and talking in a deep low voice. Presently she said, picking at a tight curl of bracken that pressed itself like a blue question mark out of the ground.

" We're all right, aren't we, Foley ? Not that I'd mind whatever happened, would you ? "

" Mind what ? " He was wondering how soon he could leave her and go on to get the nurse for Doatie.

" Mind if we started a baby."

" Good God—you don't think ? "

His voice disturbed Grania. There was nothing in it of what she had supposed would be there for her if she told him this. There was no tenderness, only rough alarm.

" You're not trying to tell me anything, are you ? "

Grania laughed and moved away from him. A dizzy

little panic that would not be quite forbidden came over her. I won't say any more. Not till I know. Not till I'm certain. I won't speak of it. Not to this stranger.

He was a stranger, they were not together. This was the first time it had occurred to Grania that they could be apart without a rush of understanding and sympathy. Always she had followed his mind in doglike devotion, in apt anticipation. It was not such a business really. His mind was not so complicated. But that hers should go with it was one of the miracles of this loving. Now, in a moment, from a tone in his voice, she guessed and would not guess how different things might be between them, how short a way his love and mind might go with hers.

" You're very silent," he said.

She was looking away from him and he turned her chin back towards him with one finger.

" Sulks ? " he said. His eyes laughed at her, caressing and reassuring. He adored any resistance. Fostered it by teasing. " You look like sister Sylvia now," he said. " Why don't you talk to me about the price of oats ? "

" Oh, how dare you ? " Grania never could resist a giggle at Sylvia. She let her head fall back in the arm crooked ready for it. First and last he knew how to make you comfortable. Cosy was the word for it. Her seeing moment retreated. She only knew she would not tell. Not yet. Soon. Not to-day.

" Do you think she talks about oats much ? " Only for something to say. It was nice talking in a dreaming voice with the sky above you and an arm under your head and the sun on the bank behind.

" I wouldn't know. I wouldn't want to know."

" Does she have kisses, do you think ? "

" Not much I shouldn't think."

" That's why she's such a sour puss, do you think ? "

" Who would she have them with ? "

" Michael Purvis."

" He's nice. He's easily the best of the fellows in the barracks."

" I don't think he would be very good for kisses."

" You haven't tried. He might be lots better than me.
I think he'll buy the horse that flattened little Doatie this
morning."

" Do you ? Would he be able for him ? "

" Yes, he would. He's got sense about things. I like
him. Is he really courting Sylvia ? "

" Oh, they're so cool. Love is like a frost with them.
She keeps away. He keeps away. I don't know why I
say it's an affair, but I'm sure it is."

" That's right. That's what you'd expect."

His tone of approval startled Grania.

" Do you think everyone should keep away or only the
Sylvias and Michaels ? "

"Only the Sylvias and Michaels," he laughed and pulled
her close. " Don't you begin it."

" I'm rather late to, aren't I ? " Grania said. She did
not know that her lip trembled.

" Well don't. Promise. Promise ? "

She nodded. Her hair flew about in a breeze and shone
in the sun. He gave her a cigarette and lit it and his own.
Grania did not really like smoking. But, of course, one
must not be childish. She was not old enough for that.

" And poor Doatie," he said after a minute. " You
should be ashamed of yourself keeping me here when I
should have the nurse back to her by this."

" I'm not keeping you."

" Yes, you are. I can't help myself, see ? I have to
stay with you."

He pulled her to her feet and they parted as he intended
they should part, with Grania looking for love, waiting
for her next hour of love.

Foley wanted nothing of her beyond this. She was no
real mate for him. He did not understand her careless
chatter born of the idleness and centuries of rich living
behind her. Her absurdities and importances were like
those of a child to him. He did not once in his mind cross
her mind. Her very freedom in love seemed shameless to

the peasant in him and his own wickedness in taking her love frightened the Catholic that was behind his character. It was a terrible thing he was doing. It was against all his beliefs and all his conscience. Nothing was engaged in it but his body, but that could not give her up, he could not let go. Every time they were together he had to make a plan for the next time. Between their secret meetings he was full of fear and disgust at himself, and a kind of coarse pity for Grania. For she was doing everything he most despised in women, there was nothing he could at all respect about her. When they met publicly they had no common ground. She was ignorant about horses and talked a great deal of nonsense to him about them. She had no racing technique. She was not like Doatie, whom you could entrust any time to get £25 on a horse at the best price and with lightning speed. No, Grania could never back a horse. She couldn't put two shillings on without telling everyone she knew that it was a certainty and why and who had told her and who had told them. She was a silly in everything that mattered to him except one thing, and he could not give that up.

This morning when he left her near Aragon and turned his car round to drive to the town for Doatie's nurse his mind was far more with Doatie in her injured and useless state than it was with Grania. He blamed himself disgustedly for all that dallying and love-making in the heather and now at the Wren's Nest on the crosses, he was held up again for the Boys' Sign was out.

The Wren's Nest was a yellow-washed house built long and low and thatched deeply against the mountain weather. It stood at the meeting of five roads and was the only public house for miles around. A cripple man and his mother kept it, and between the Boys on the Run who sheltered with them at night and the British soldiers who searched the place for them by day, their lives were kept on a perpetual rack.

Foley greeted Popsy the Weasel, this was the cripple's name, who was sitting behind the high counter bar where

the light darkly met the dark bottles, all set within the
reach of his long arms. His arms stretched and reached
like a spider's dark limbs as he served the drinks and
washed glasses without moving from his stool because his
legs were withered, no bigger than those of a child of five.
His little feet were twisted round the legs of his stool while
his big body and pale face leaned about in the darkness,
and he talked with nervous affability to everyone, and
pinched the quantity of drink he served whenever he
thought he could.

" Good-morning, Popsy."

" Oh, what a beautiful morning, isn't it, Mr. O'Neill?
What will you drink, Mr. O'Neill? Or is it too early
for you, Mr. O'Neill? "

"A Guinness, Popsy." Foley chucked his head towards
the door that led from the public house to a little dark
private room. " I'll bring it in there, boy." They would
be waiting for him in there, he knew, though what they
wanted from him to-day he did not know. Transport for
someone in his car, he supposed . . . it was always that,
when it wasn't money or a bed for the night. Indeed they
might not want him at all, but the sign was out for
someone.

He walked into the room with the friendly kind of
swagger he affected towards the boys because he knew
they mistrusted him. Not that they had any cause to do
so, his trade in horses was reason real enough for his
association with the English soldiery and their like in the
country. He had to live. He had never refused bed, food
or shelter to a lad on the run, though God knew how he
hated the whole business. All he wanted was to be left
in peace to make a bit of money out of his horses. But
on all sides he was beset, lying to one, lying to the other,
held fast by old oaths to Ireland and the boys; by
inclination, association and livelihood easy with their
enemies.

Three tired grave young men were sitting in the little
dark hole of a room behind the public bar. They sat

round, two of them on the stiff little couch and one on a straight-backed chair rather as if they were at a tea party, they hardly looked as though they had been out in the mountains all night, but their eyes were tired and sly and fierce as ill-used dogs. They were all three wearing their belted mackintosh coats, because they were hunted men, at any moment ready to run, always on the watch for their lives. Three or four or five of them up here in the mountains and a regiment of soldiers in the garrison town below, yet they have no cunning to put against these three or four or five.

"Hallo, Tim. Hallo, Matty. Hallo, ——" he stopped at the third name. Bold, dark, and tough, he was slouching across the end of the table and looking up towards Foley though his head was bent.

"Captain Cussens—Mr. O'Neill." One of the other boys effected an introduction with the formality of a rectory garden party.

Foley shook hands with Denny the Killer, so this was him, the brains and the daring behind many an ambush. When Denny was around there was trouble, dirty trouble for all. He was not sent from headquarters for nothing. Where he was things moved along. He could frighten the guts out of the lonely country people, and at the same time light anew in them the burning flame for Ireland. He used men and women and sent them to their deaths, and slept all night and the night after it too. His own bravery and cunning and ruthlessness were so great that he required and got a higher measure of the three from others.

"Take a drink, boys?" Foley invited them all politely, and they all shook their heads. Foley sat down with a great show of ease. His mind was cursing and fumbling, wondering what the gunman was doing down here. What he and the boys wanted of him, for they were not surprised to see him come in. They had known he was around all right. It was for him the sign had been out. Still they did not speak to him. Foley got angry.

" Anything I can do for you ? I was on my way to get a nurse. Someone met with an accident at my place this morning."

" We'll not keep you long," Killer Denny spoke. " All we want from you, now see, is a little information. You're the man that can tell us what we want to know, now see, you're the only bloody man."

Foley sat dark and silent on his chair. He seemed strangely of the other side, too much and too little a gentleman in his smart clothes, the breath and the smell of Grania close about him still, in this dark old cold little room with these three quiet toughs.

" What do you want to know ? "

" Oh, you mightn't have the information to-day, or to-morrow even, or the next day, but we'll depend on you getting it, now see, before the end of next week shall we say ? "

" What's this you want to know ? Maybe it's not the right Bureau of Information you're at, at all."

" Well, if I had any doubts, Boy, they were settled after the kissing and fondling I seen this morning on the mountain side."

Foley stood up.

" Mind your own bloody business," he said. He stood over the other.

" Easy, now, easy." They were all smiling. " We've all got guns now see, and what have you but your nice gentlemanly feelings ? And you wouldn't expect chaps the like of us to understand them, would you, eh, would you, Boy ? Now take it easy. Sit down. Sit down."

Foley sat down. What else could he do. Guns or no guns they were three to one. They could beat him up here and now and lead him off to a lonely little execution in the mountains any time they liked. He knew enough and too much about all three of them and their where-abouts and secret hiding places for them to chance letting him go free as their enemy. Only as their comrade and agent would he go free of them. He sat down, their hostile faces closed in on him in the stuffy room, dangerous, hunted young faces. Killer Denny's was insolent and darkly vain. His hat slouched jauntily over his eyes, his jaw was shaved navy blue, even in the mountains he managed a shave. His neck was strong as a young bull above his collar. The other two were weaker, commoner types. Matty had bright intelligent eyes, a long ugly nose, thin ascetic mouth and a sharp chin. Tim was pale and delicate looking, he had a restless cough and a poisoned finger, and a martyr's obstinate fatality looked out of his eyes. He had left a good job in the Post Office for this hell for Ireland game, the agony and discomforts of it came cruelly hard on him, and he would have been the first of the lot of them to put a shot into Foley, for he was a nervous, tortured, rabid little patriot.

" Well, let's get the thing straight now," Killer Denny spoke at the heavy end of a pause. His pause, of his making, and his voice was changed to that of an officer giving his orders. " We need information as to the comings and goings of certain British officers who visit regularly at Aragon house, and from your familiarity with the Fox family, O'Neill, you should be able to tell us all we want to know about their movements."

So that was it. He was to do the spy for their work. This was to be his cursed punishment for all he had done with Grania. He had always known that such wickedness (and with a Protestant, too) would only bring its own punishment. Here he was now, trapped and tied and circled by his own ill-doing. " Your familiarity with the Fox family," the threat and sneer had been patent in this politer phrase. They must know he could get what they wanted. Foley's heart knocked disgustedly against his ribs, sick for his powerlessness.

The little room that saw no sun was sticky with their breath and the smell of tired unwashed bodies. The fight for Ireland was planned and won in many such sordid sad corners of the country. Tired men afraid of one another laid plans against overwhelming odds ; dirty ambushes

and cowardly assasinations they were called by the
British officers who persistently refused to conduct
themselves as though they were at war and in an enemy's
country. They must have their game of tennis, their
day's shooting, their hunting too, though at every turn
of the road death might be waiting. It made cruelly
hard situations for those natives of the countryside who
were in any position to give information of their comings
and goings between barracks and country houses. In
those extraordinary days there was every chance of
bloodshed after tea and tennis with strawberries and cream.
Gramophone dances started at four o'clock in the afternoon and lasted, grim tests of endurance, until the next
day, for to travel the roads at night, where bridges might
be blown to bits and stars look upwards from the black
water below, or barricaded roads gave masked ad-
venturers their opportunity, seemed (even to a young and
hot-blooded British soldier) a slightly foolish undertaking.

Foley knew all this, knew to a nicety his probable use
to Killer Denny. He could not dramatise whatever
murder was to be done here and to the doing of which
he was to be instrumental, into an act of war for Ireland.
It was no more than a job, a mean dirty job, and the
Killer would see it got done too. He came to a place for
one reason and one reason only, for a killing.

" I see all right. I understand what you want." Foley
spoke with heavy indecision. Keep them guessing was his
idea, keep their faith in him somehow and he might
scramble through yet. " I can't promise I'll be all that
use to you though I might be able."

" Oh, you're able right enough, the only manjack of
us that is able." Again the jocose sneer from the Killer
and sour smiles of disapproval from the other two sick
ascetic boys. Yes, they had all seen too much. He had
no defence on that side.

" Who do you want news of particularly ? "

A dark look ran between the three. He saw from it
that they trusted him so little that they would not give

him the names of the wanted. It was not to be in his power to give any warning. The meanest class of spy work, that was all he was good for and his own side could not even trust him the full length in that. God curse him they were right, rat and louse and ill-living fool that he was. A wave of revulsion towards himself was followed by a fury of sudden anger against the three of them. A voice that delighted and set free some hot and glorious thing in Foley was speaking for him. He did not know, cute and tough and calculating as he was, where it found the guts to betray him.

" God blast you and your dirty work," it was saying. " Take me out in the heather now and shoot me as you're well able. I'll not play the bloody spy for you. I've given help and shelter and put myself in danger time and again for you boys when you came to me quenched with fear and cold, and I'll do it again any night. But I'll be no go-between to bring chaps to their bloody deaths, chaps that come to my house and buy my horses, decent poor fools of boys whichever side they fight on. Get on with it yourselves for blast the word you'll get from me."

" Shut that." The Killer had his gun on him. Foley put his hands on the table, leaning forward, white-faced, helpless in their hands, three men with guns who sat and sneered at him. It was then that they heard the cripple Popsy the Weasel's shrill voice rising high in the other room.

" No, sir, Mr. O'Neill's not here, sir. Yes, it's his car all right, indeed, but he's gone up the mountain now not ten minutes ago, up to the little farm above to see a poor man's sick ram."

And the voice that answered was the clipped educated voice of one of the soldiers Foley knew—Captain Purvis.

" Oh, well, he'll be back soon I suppose. We'll wait. What about a bottle of beer, Tony ? "

" Bit early for one, old chap. Got such a thing as a drop of milk for this little dog ? Little devil, she's been underground for two days. We had her up here badger digging on Sunday morning . . ."

Patsy went softly to the door, opened it a narrow slit and peered through. He turned round from it with blazing eyes.

" He's there," he whispered.

" Bit of luck O'Neill should be about," the voice outside went on, " We'll get the doctor to look at that bite, Judy-girl. Here's her milk. Thank you. Doesn't want it. Never were one for milk, were you."

They were squatting on the ground like two little boys trying to persuade the tired terrier to lap milk when Denny and his boys walked in on them. They had their backs to the boys as they coaxed their dog in a patch of sunlight that came through the open door from the hot sweet May morning outside.

Foley heard the scuffle of their capture. The two boys had sprung on them from behind while Denny covered them with his revolver from the doorway. Someone had kicked or trodden on the terrier, a piercing yelp of pain and then a moment's silence before the cripple's high agonised voice screamed out, " Don't do it here, boys ! Don't do it here ! God blast it, I'll never get the place clean. For God's sake spare the cripple and take them outside ! "

In the dreadful little anti-chamber to death Foley sat staring through the open door. He could not see the group, the bar was the other end of the room, the door on to the road beside it. Fools, he was thinking, poor bloody fools, up in these mountains, unarmed probably, to look for a dog they lost badger digging. Yet looking for the dog was the only part of it he could understand, if it was a good dog. Ah, she must have been good to stay down with a badger two days. He had heard Michael Purvis had a good terrier, how had he heard it. He knew now, his accurate unwavering memory set a finger on the knowledge, Grania had told him when she told him about Purvis and Sylvia. That was why they had chosen him to spy on the comings and goings to Aragon. It was Purvis they wanted, and now they had got him without any help from Foley. They had got him, and some other poor chap would have to die with him. It was too dangerous to let a live man go. It was their lives or his life. That was fair. That was only fair. Oh, God help them, Foley was thinking, but he knew they were past helping now.

Denny the Killer came back into the room and closed the door.

" O'Neill," he said, " we've got the chap we want and without any help from you. Now see, you'll drive us up to Mooncoin caves. We want to get a bit of information from them and that's a quiet place."

" I'd as soon they didn't recognise me," Foley said. He was thinking how he had planned to sell the Knight of Aragon horse to Michael Purvis, and of the roan cob he had bought from him and of that afternoon he had come over to try him at Mountain Brig. He knew well enough there lay no danger for him in their escape. There was no escape for them. Denny understood this. He had grown very quiet since his easily won capture. The tough bullying side was subdued. He seemed only gentle and intent.

" Right, boy. They're blindfold." he said. " Take us up to the caves and that's all we want from you for the present, now see." All the time he was talking so quietly, he had Foley covered with his gun. He signed him to come out through the door and Foley obeyed. He could do nothing for the two soldiers ? What part of a chance had they, and what part of a chance had he if he informed. It might not be to-morrow, it might not be next week or next month, but the boys would come for him and get him all right.

The two young prisoners were standing up against the dark fireplace. Their eyes were bandaged and they held their hands behind them. This attitude gave them a curious nonchalant look as if they were just waiting about for their drinks. Their pale tweed coats and flannel trousers, their soft well-cut shirt collars, the scent of their hair oil, all these things were so widely at variance from their immediate killing, it was not possible to grasp that they would in such a little space of time be dead.

"Outside, boys," Denny spoke and the other two guided the prisoners towards the door which they had shut and locked. As they went down the room the little terrier jumped up on Purvis. He turned his head in the direction of nobody, because he could not see, and said, as he supposed, to the cripple :

"Would you be a good fellow, look after the little dog for me, and if you let Miss Fox of Aragon know that you found her straying up here, she'll give you a reward." He turned his head again, "If that would be all right by you," he spoke politely to his captors.

Before Denny could answer the cripple was shrilling from his chair :

"Let yous take the bitch. Take her with yous and stone her and give her the lough. You'll have the damn' soldiers on me, God help me, with your fashionable bred dogs."

A look of awful despair broke across Purvis's bandaged face. "I see," he said, quite patiently. "Well, perhaps she could come with us ? I'd be very grateful if one of you chaps could shoot her for me. I hate drowning dogs, don't you ? "

"Oh, I wouldn't drown a dog," said one.

"I couldn't shoot a dog," said another.

"I wouldn't harm a little dog for any money," said Denny the Killer.

"Take her away, take her out of this ! " screamed the cripple.

It was quite a situation. Foley forgot they were not to hear his voice.

"I'll take her," he said. "I'll see she's all right. I will really. She's a lovely little thing."

"She's as brave as a lion," the other boy said. He was

trembling. " Could we have a drink ? " he said, " How many of us are there ? I'll stand a round." He put a pound note on the counter. " Keep the change," he said to the cripple, " that's all right."

The cripple took the note and stuffed it away. He served six exact double Irish whiskys. One of the boys put the glasses into the prisoners' hands. Not one of them touched the drinks on the counter. Popsy the Weasel eyed them, greedily planning to bottle them again—four double whiskys—as soon as the party here left for the execution.

" Well, outside, boys." Denny said again. Matty unlocked the door and the sun flooded in hot and yellow, smelling of gorse. The prisoners held out their empty glasses, and the cripple reached out his long arms for them eagerly, afraid that they might be dropped and broken, and he hated to lose a glass.

Denny looked up the road and down. It was empty and full of sunshine. He signed the rest to come out. Denny said loudly to the cripple, " When Mr. O'Neill comes back tell him he'll have to walk it home."

Foley felt grateful for this misleading piece of nonsense as he started the car. Tim sat beside him with his gun across his knee. The other two guarded the prisoners who were squeezed up like children on the floor in the back, the little terrier between them.

" Drive on," the Killer said.

XVI

SYLVIA was ready for her tennis party. She was beautifully dressed in a white pleated crêpe de chine skirt, and long white alpaca wool jersey with a tasselled belt at the waist and a neat V neck, out of which her round throat rose as pretty as a bird's and circled by her row of river pearls. Her fair hair was neatly waved and tucked into a small gleaming bun at the back, not one hair ever got out of place in the most strenuous games, unlike Grania's yellow feathers that flew more wildly at every ball she missed. She wore white silk stockings and white buckskin shoes, whiter and softer and sounder looking than new tennis balls even. Her well-made little body swelled and retreated at precisely the right places inside her clothes. Strong, and poised and determined she looked and as rooted and suited to the life she led as young flag leaves are to a river bank. She looked truly set and exactly meant for marriage with the most eligible young soldier possible (just such a one as Michael Purvis), one who in due course would fall heir to a nice estate, most probably in Norfolk, and even his mother would be able to find no fault in Sylvia Fox of Aragon.

Aragon was at the supreme height of its beauty this late April afternoon. The house was like an elegant woman sitting quietly in front of her mirror, restful and still in her perfection, for Aragon was a very female house both within and without and wore the more exquisite moments of the year with a wonderful grandeur and quietness. About her cherry trees there was nothing girlish or fluffy. Their groups were frozen out against the dark of other trees, on the hill behind the house, and down the fall to the river below. Flowers and shrubs and flowering trees were all a litttle apart from the house. They did not flounce and jostle against the austere walls. Shallow gracious heights and wide sunny spaces of grass were empty between the sheltered groups of azaleas and camellias, magnolias, rhododendrons, and thickets of slight bamboo enclosing a light blue fog in their narrow straight pillars. Camellias, white and red, flowered freely, their foreign expensive faces looked as if they had been cut out of leather and painted and put smartly together and placed in position in the healthy gleam of their leaves. But the magnolias narrowing purple and white cups held all the secret dignity and resolve of flowers that come to perfection on hard twisted wood. Never in all their history had magnolia flowers been placed in a posy with lace paper and ribbon round. They are too wildly uncomplacent. Funeral wreaths have not seen magnolia either, for its death is too quick for deaths delayings. Great lilac bushes were softer than cats and the cut sallow leaves of golden oaks sharper than paper crowns. Red rhododendrons reared their ways, striving like horses up the hill. Azaleas, low as sheep in comparison, went in honey-blond flocks downwards to the back of the house. In the strong sunlight the garden gave nothing of what it was. It only waited, falsely gay, protecting itself, holding back its strength till the evening time, its flowing hours.

It was three o'clock, the brightest most nothing-like hour of afternoon. Sylvia was in the hall taking new tennis balls out of their box, and their separate dressings of tissue paper. The bright purple writing looked very smart on their whiteness. They smelt of rubber and clean unplayed games. The hall was so gloomy cool that the great jars of lilac smelt only of lilac in the rain, all richness frozen and quelled from its scent. The leaves of the lilac drooped a little exhausted, although the branches had only just been gathered and put in water, because in these days people were not so knowing and sophisticated about their flower decorations as they are now. They liked lots of nice greenery and thought gypsophila and asparagus fern went very prettily with sweet peas, and maidenhair fern with carnations and everything looked its best in a silver vase or, failing that, a tall thin green glass which, like a long green throat, swallowed the length of stems and posed the flower heads neatly where they should be.

Sylvia was happily of her age and time. Competent, not wild. Pretty in the right and accepted way. Nothing embarrassingly clever about her. Everything she had was buttoned up and put away in little boxes. She was strong. Two of her girl friends arrived. They came on bicycles and leant their bicycles against the pillars of the portico and came into the cool hall with their rackets in their hands.

" Hallo, Sylvia."

" Hallo, Cecily, Hallo, Violet."

" Hallo, Sylvia."

" Lovely new balls."

" Who's coming ? "

" Tony, Michael, Major Radley, John Wade, I think."

" How nice."

" What fun."

" I like your new blouse, Violet."

" I did all that faggot stitch myself."

" I hope there's coffee cake for tea."

" Yes, there is, greedy pig."

" Are they going to stay late ? "

" Shall we dance ? "

" We might. There's lots of cold food for supper."

" I want to play ' Whispering.' "

" The gramophone's outside."

" 'Whispering while you cuddle near me', oh, it's so lovely."

" 'Whispering so no one near can hear me.' " They sang, wandering out of the house in their white shoes and stockings, carrying rackets and tennis balls to the smooth sunny grass where white painted seats were set in the wide fern-like shade of a cedar tree. There they waited for their men to arrive, pulling at their clothes and preening their hair like hen birds picking down the lengths of a breast-feather, answering each other absently, their minds put forward to the gay challenge of the hours to come.

Presently Grania came out and joined them. She was not fond of Sylvia's two girl friends. They played tennis too well and spoke to her almost kindly, but now she felt so grand and whole compared to them, half-living on kisses and glances and little no's that she was able to compete with them.

"How late your men are," she said, beginning with a wholesome broadside. She threw herself down on a rug, feeling the short grass with her hands.

"Just as well, dear," Sylvia said. "It will give you time to tuck your shirt inside your skirt, and even put on a pair of stockings without a hole in them. If you hurry."

"Oh, I can't really go to all that bother for a few men." Grania lay closer to the ground. "Though I admire you girls a lot for the trouble you take about yourselves."

"How are your other backhand shots getting on?" one of the friends asked.

"Oh, not bad at all."

"Don't underrate yourself, dear, you broke the drawing-room window so cleverly yesterday—one of your best strokes."

Grania giggled. Sylvia couldn't upset her. Generally she felt hot and ashamed when they tormented her about her tennis. Really she felt quite earnest and embarrassed at her shocking inaptitude for the game but to-day she didn't mind how many smart young soldiers treated her with silent contempt and indulgence as she panted and flew about the courts, trying and failing, a bundle of nervous stupidity, so different from the serious capable serenity of Sylvia and her friends upon the courts. Laziness was behind Grania's failure to play tennis. The same laziness that left her clothes in holes and her hair unbrushed and her mind in a wild chaos with only the most immediate question uppermost. She could never

sort herself out. She would never know herself to a turn.
She would grow older confusedly and accomplishing little.
But all through her life there would be spread flat places
of unbelievable calm where her idle mind could laze
unreproached by any better self and her body could
indulge itself without cruel recrimination from a soured
and defeated sense of the supposed right. She had the
exact reverse of her sister's nature in working or playing.
There was no nicety about her or skill, only eagerness and
strange aptitudes which she hardly or never followed
through to any conclusion. And for that very reason her
aptitudes would keep their charm and novelty for her.
They would never be worn smooth by too much attain-
ment. Always, as now, she would feel elated if she
answered back to Sylvia, because she would never own
so quick a wit that its speed or flexibility could fail to
surprise herself.

Now they might say what they liked to her, Sylvia and
the girls. Her shot was spent, but it had got home, she
could ignore them contented. She parted Soo's black hair
for fleas, but found not one. The hairs closed over again
into a dog's coat with the sunlight on it like a polished
shell. Soo was lying in her mouse shape, humped behind
and head low between her forelegs.

The girls played the gramophone. It was totally wrong
out there with its silly little drift of music. But they
fastened their girlish emotions to the tune. Ten minutes
more passed by. Twenty minutes.

Grania raised her head from her arms to say :
" Why don't you have a girlish rally, dears. Your
boys seem to have forgotten you, don't they." She had
given herself time to prepare this one.

The girls laughed nervously. The idea of being the
forgotten ones is so lessening. So cruelly depriving of
confidence. They could not even answer back to Baby
Grania. Sylvia said, " Well, perhaps you're right. We'll
each give you a lesson. That ought to take our minds off
anything else, oughtn't it."

Grania said, " No, I'm far too tired to be scolded and made run about."

" Tired ? What have you been doing. What do you ever do ? "

" Well, I rode a school this morning, that's more than any of you can say."

" How very interesting. What horse did you ride. And whose ? And where ? "

Grania knew she had been a fool to say so much. It was pure boasting. An effort to put these tennis players in their places. But if she had been foolish she was not going to be silly enough to lie about it now.

" A young horse of Foley O'Neill's," she said grandly. It always sounded better to say " a young horse " or " a four-year-old " at the oldest.

" Really. Since when have you been getting out of your cosy bed to ride Foley's horses."

" Since to-day, actually."

" Fancy, and is he a jolly companion in the early morning ? ' Steady yourself, Miss Grania.' ' Hit her a good one now ' "

Sylvia's imitation of Foley's voice was mercilessly right. It placed him accurately where, till so short a time ago, he had belonged in Grania's estimation too. But now it filled her with a flame of pure defensive rage that swept all sense of proportion out of reach in her loving angry heart. She sat up, her cheeks crimson, tears almost in her eyes.

" Oh, yes, it's all very well for you to laugh at any one in that beastly way. The laugh's the other way when he rides rings round any of your soldier-boys. He makes them look a pretty silly lot of row-the-boats coming up the straight, doesn't he ? Well, doesn't he ? "

Sylvia looked at her with live curiosity. What was this ? There was something here to look into.

" Yes, he's a very beautiful jockey," she said, " and a wonderful man to show a horse. Better than any one I know."

Grania's eyes subdued themselves. The crimson in her cheeks died. But she still trembled a little. This admission from Sylvia showed her that she had let Sylvia guess too much. Sylvia was such a one for keeping things quiet. She would have to cover Grania before the girls. But afterwards. . . .

" Well, what about it ? Shall we have a ladies' four ? "

Till tea-time they played their uninterrupted ladies' four. Their white legs flying about the bright court. The new balls thudding high and with lovely precision in the sunshine. Lonely girls' voices called the scores and commended each other's play. " Too good." " O, Sylvia ! " " Can you ? " " O, good *shot*." " Played, partner." They gave as religious attention to their game as though their men were present to admire them. Even Grania, excited and upset and hitting only one ball in five that came her way, could not turn their holy practice of lawn tennis into an irreligious game.

XVII

TEA-TIME. Dozens of little iced coffee cakes and cucumber
sandwiches with gentlemen's relish. Hot cakes and a
confection rich with fruit and wine and age, china tea
and many many blue cups that had been set out early
for the lost party. This tea was served in the green spaces
of the drawing-room. The tide in the river was full, and
a boat with sails came up on it. This boat provided a nice
subject for comment and speculation. They had to keep
talking, each to show the other that she cared nothing
for the society of men. Only Mrs. Fox wondered, alone
and shamelessly, why her party had been forgotten.

" It's very odd, isn't it, Sylvia ? Tony and Michael are
so keen on a game of tennis."

" And Major Radley adores playing bridge with you,
Mum."

" I wonder what's happened ? "

" Oh, we'd have heard if anything had happened,
really."

" Yes, of course we would."

" Bound to." One of the girls bit an iced cake in half.
The other asked for more tea. Everyone was bent on
showing everyone else that things were just as they should
be.

The tide flooded smoothly up the river, milk green as
honeysuckle leaves. But the young leaves in the afternoon
spring light turned the old water to grey. It was a grey
light reflected back and up into the windows of the
drawing-room and made the girls' faces look paler than
water-weeds, alas for all their jolly disregard of sad
possibility.

Frazer came in. He was only faintly disordered and
moved when he said :

" Captain Michael Purvis and Mr. Tony Craye are
reported missing since this morning, madam. The

soldiers are out in parties searching in the mountains for them."

Sylvia was very white. She said :

" What did you hear exactly, Frazer ? "

" I heard they went up after a dog they lost badger digging on Sunday, Miss, and the Fenians got them up there, poor young gentlemen."

" Oh, the poor children," Mrs. Fox cried out softly. She would soon be in tears, consoling herself. Sylvia and Frazer's eyes met and her voice came to him in a wintry whisper :

" Anything else, Frazer ? "

" I heard no more at the Post Office, Miss, but I was thinking of cycling into town to find out if there was any news."

" Yes, please go, Frazer, please go."

He was back in an hour's time. There was a look of such triumph about him that their hearts leaped in anticipation of his news.

" They haven't got the poor young gentlemen," he said, " but they have arrested Mister Foley O'Neill."

XVIII

NAN was sitting sewing in her kingdom, the nursery, that bright afternoon. She had sent her poor baby, Miss Pidgie, out for a walk. The sun poured in on the grey behind of the rocking-horse. From this big window there was no watery intimacy with the river, as there was from the drawing-room windows. The nursery windows were not formed to curve voluptuously towards the swelling or retreating tides, they did not drink in the river light and breath, but flatly sprucely curtained they looked demurely out upon the river below, and some hedged fields, and hills, and airy blue of mountains beyond.

Nan had a pile of linen to mend beside her, fine soft linen that was a pride and delight to her mind and to her hands ; Fox linen, Aragon linen, linen that had been in the house, some of it, for generations, cool and gentle with age and darned and patched with an exquisite patience and skill worthy of its luxurious frailty. Nan revelled in the smooth coldness of the sheets, their less than knife-thick hems, the pillow-cases as fine as handkerchiefs, and the old face towels woven soft and with little fringes to finish their ends. The new house linen, of which she had Mrs. Fox buy a supply every year, was always of the finest to be got and Nan would mark and number it in tiny clear sampler lettering sewn in special red thread that would never run in the washing or fade from its colour. She was very careful of this thread and had a supply of the spools put by, for, like so many other things, she maintained you could not get it now. A friend used to send it to her from Paris and the friend was dead or the shop was shut, or something had happened to add immeasurably to the value of the red thread which marked the linen at Aragon.

Nan felt very calm and powerful as her needle went in and out making a tiny ticking sound in the darn as small as sixpence which she was putting into a towel. On her finger was a large gold thimble which Sylvia and Grania had given her once, it looked older and paler than it was from constant use. Nothing had such an easy look as a well-used thimble on a clever hand. Nan's beautiful grey hair curled crisp and healthy on her strong brown neck bent over the sewing. Her white collar went round it as crisp as a petal and narrow white cuffs were sewn to the wrists of her grey dress. Her apron was so white your eyes blinked once before they found rest in the contrasts of its curvings and shadows.

The top sash of one high window was open and Miss Pigeon's tea was laid neatly at one end of the square centre table. The air that was more of summer than the present spring flowed gently into the room and Nan's thoughts were running and rippling pleasantly about her as she worked. . . .

These towels have worn well ; yes, glancing at the date she had worked in the corner, of course, that was the year she had been in Dublin at Horseshow time, the year Foley had won the Championship of the Show. How elated and easy she had felt. Nothing but the best was good enough to buy for Aragon, the better than best. The hours she had spent, thumb to the corners of choice samples of linen, and at last the shopman, appreciative of and indulgent to a connoisseur, had agreed with her on a special weaving. Yes, this linen marked the sort of ecstasy of success she had reached that year, with Foley winning the Championship and Sylvia's first grown-up Horse Show too. And such a success the child had. Nan had not expected it. Miss Sylvia looked a Fox and a lady. That was the best she had ever thought of the child, but something had been added to the Fox and the lady. The little body carried clothes with a distinction that you could not miss. The girlish white dance frock took on a *chic* false simplicity as if worn by a successful beauty of thirty. And why ? Nan smiled secretly, knowing why. The small whys. The neat posy unpicked from its meaningless perch on the shoulder of the white taffeta gown and pinned decisively between the breasts. Nan had a great appreciation for such small gestures to the male. " Bold and cold and pity help the boys." Nan with a white apron over her navy blue skirt and elaborate blouse thought with satisfaction of Sylvia as she bustled about the hotel bedroom tidying up such few things as Sylvia had left out of their proper places when she went out to dine and dance. The blue habit to be brushed and pressed for the next day, and the child would look a little queen when she rode Foley's horse in the ladies' class. Nan gloried to think of it. She held the small firmness of a pair of rolled stockings tight in her hand and paused to think of it ; of herself leaning on the rail by the ringside, silent, missing no detail, drinking every detail of the scene with strong effortless perception of the moment. So certain of her cast-iron memory that she used not consciously to memorise anything. Afterwards she would know without a thought which of the ladies had a hair astray. A tie badly tied, a spur unpolished, She wasted not a thought on the horses. They were not her province. Not even Foley's horse, except that Foley owned him and Sylvia rode him. But the riders would not escape her tongue unscathed. Hers was the present mind that sees and acts and grasps the moment, ever conscious, unknowing the power and the glory of its strength. . . .

The cunning way a stranger from the Heythrop country did her hair. " A couple of clips in front of the ears, Miss Sylvia and the bun a roll, not a plaster." Poor old Lady Alice Montgomery had a new patch on the seat of her breeches this year. A coloured tie looks very common no matter who wears it, but a veil with a small spot is always nice. Oh, but such a look as she gave the judge, oh, the *look* if ever I saw it, watch for trouble there. She's a light little piece and her family were all the same. And she would watch Sylvia passionately as the horses galloped round her, leaning forward to be more with her, revelling in the set of the small straight shoulders, the skill that

went with so little strength. Nan's own eyes were to her
as the eyes of many, and as she watched she fed on the
praise that must be given, given to Sylvia and to Foley
and to Aragon—all to the glory of Aragon.

Now she was sewing quietly and intently and her mind
had gone back to that evening in a Dublin hotel when she
had folded away Sylvia's clothes and thought about the
to-morrow which was long since past but as clear to her
as her own plans for this evening and the next day. All
her life was as clear to her as if she opened an atlas and
looked at a map. It would be a map of Aragon with the
blood of her life and the strength of her mind and her
body marked on it in strong visible ways.

The bright rich surfaces of the furniture. How many
slave girls had she driven to the polishing ? The exquisite
store of linen, the children's straight backs, Miss Pigeon's
subjection, the nut walk, the late peaches, the breed of
fighting Bantam cocks, the wide and easy curve of turf
steps up the pleasure ground—the slightest glance
towards the time past showed these few of the many
marks that Nan had left on Aragon. But none, only
Nan, would ever know the secrets that Aragon had left
with her. The marks and wounds of grief and rapture
and of bitter failure. The calm of patience that can build
over again.

The dark storm of her youth ; now she could look back
to it as a whole thing, a separate piece of her life, not
the only stuff of life itself. Because of the grief and
rapture of her failing her power over Aragon and her
love for it had grown. Power must grow with secrecy.
Power is force controlled, and there is no control like
silence. To have kept silence half a life-time is to be
strong.

XIX

SINCE Nan was a child Aragon had been the dream in her life. The house was spoken of by Nan's mother hushedly, secretly. Tales of Aragon were never told before Nan's father, but when the child and her mother were alone they would pour between them. Nan's mother had been in service at Aragon before she married and it was hard to tell whether it was as hell or as heaven that she looked towards the house. Her life had been somewhere between hell and heaven, a glorious and dramatic purgatory, before she had married one of the keepers and settled in the lonely house where Nan was born, where the river got small, and the woodlands scarce, and the mountain heather began.

Nan's mother was a stupid loquacious slattern with blackberry coloured eyes and honey-coloured hair. There she would sit and talk by the hour, her stories always changing a bit more towards the remarkable. Looking out of the door towards the mountains, tears would start in her purple eyes as a new torture inflicted on her in the past by Ann Daly, the head housemaid, was composed and related. With the torture went the splendour of such a life. Compliments and presents from lovely ladies of title. Accounts of their ravishing ball gowns, their tiny feet, their propped white breasts, where diamond pendants hung in mists of tulle and roses.

" Ah, I was a whack hand to lay them out on the beds. Ah, not every young girl would have the taste for such a thing. The way I'd lay the dress on the white counterpane, a pinch in at the waist, and spread wide the skirt, you'd say a ghost lady was being dressed, for I had a knack of enticement with them, indeed, under a red silk canopy, perhaps, and all the branch wax candles burning on the dressing-table, and a coal fire up the chimney, and curtains drawn full against the river fog."

The full-drawn curtains, the crimson carpets and canopies, the many, many oil lamps and wax candles (it was one servant's entire work to tend them, one of the untold number that served the great house). Nan's mother would tell about them all, and their work for the upper servants, everyone of whom seemed to have a couple of satellites, and Nan's mother had been slave to the upper housemaid.

"Because I was so neat, see now, and pretty and fit to be about the ladies. ' Where's Goldilocks ? ' Mrs. Fox would say, imagine. Old Ann Daly would take the strap to me if I pulled a curl out under my cap, ah, she knew right enough. I'm telling you, Dymphnia, hide your looks, child, hide your beauty from the gentry. It's a snap-trap on your own leg, now look, pet, for it's more than the mistress will see it."

There were noddings and whisperings and tales of childbeds in far corners of the big house, and pale heavy-breasted girls dragging themselves again about their work. Ah, Ann Daly was a whack-hand at any business like that, and the river is handy for any little things that you wouldn't want to be keeping. " Dead, dear, she'd say, and aren't you lucky ? Another cat for the river, she'd say, and she'd laugh, she'd glory in it, 'twas like a medicine to her. . . . The young gentlemen were very great with Ann. She had a bedpost filled with pieces of gold they gave her, and one way and another she served them well. She was a great one for boiling roots and seeds at the right turn of the moon and a terrible effect they took if a girl went to her in time with her trouble. . . .

" Master Hubert was her pet, Master Hubert was a bold unruly boy. God help me, he was . . . Oh, child, mind yourself now on a November evening when the lamps be scarce on the long passages. No delay, Dymphnia, but to get about your work and down to the company in the servants' hall, and a good plate of beef and the men roaring songs and the cook cursing and the tallow candles and the lamps burning. Light, child, light's the thing.

You wouldn't know where you'd be in the dark indeed. You wouldn't rightly know what you'd be doing, God forgive you. . . . 'Child' Master Hubert called me always for he never could remember my name. . . .

"Ah, Dymphnia, what a man he was, so proud and so kind, Ah, child, never do what I did. Never get yourself caught like that. You'll never know peace after. Your father is a kind man and a good man, but I knew too much before I married him, twice too much to be happy after. You're the only child I have, Dymphnia, and I'm proud you are, and proud you should be of your breeding, and ever good to your poor mother for you cost her a lot. Ah, well, my sports was finished when I came to live up here on the heather with the lonely grouse. Ah, but Master Hubert did it all for the best when he made the match for me with your Dada. He thought too much of me to give me over to Ann Daly, a sight too much indeed."

Such thinly-veiled tales of her aristocratic parenthood were the bedtime stories of Nan's girlhood, for her mother was an unquenchable gossip and neither the grouse on the mountain nor Nan's stepfather were specially good audiences for the passions and tumults of her.past in the grand house. She had not seen it for years, because John Briscoe the keeper, although not too proud to put shoes once on a gentleman's pleasure (and indeed it had been made worth his while), was strict to a degree with that whining weak-minded beauty to whose daughter he had given his name. In the fourteen years of her married life she had never been down to the village four miles distant. When she died of a belated stillborn child he knew for a certainty that it was his own.

Strange enough he loved Nan, and the gentry side of her made her take to him for he had the lonely free aristocracy of outlook that comes from living hard on mountains and rivers, with dogs for company and fish and birds to care. He loved his wife too, for she was a beautiful creature and in spite of all she might say to Nan of the

poverty of married life after the splendours of her short
love life, she was an amorous creature as well as beautiful
and was more than contented with him.

It was her stepfather who insisted that Nan was to train
as a nurse, he had the lowest opinion of domestic service
with the gentry, and when her mother died, he sent the
girl away as soon as might be to a hospital.

She worked hard and did excellently, discussed her
ambitions with no one at all and at the age of thirty gave
up a good position in a Dublin hospital, and went to
Aragon as nurse to Sylvia Fox.

XX

In 1900 Nan had got to Aragon. Even now she could
remember her first day breathing its air, the feel of door
handles as she opened Aragon doors, the consciousness of
dead Fox's stirring in her blood. She was not yet aware
how Aragon would drown itself in her power and love.
She was for the first year like a person on the edge of a
great and only love affair. She made strong her links
with the beloved, she set her feet firmly on the path she
wished to follow. Nan was going to stay at Aragon. She
invented little difficulties and delicacies for Sylvia, a wiry
and hardy child really, discussed them with Mrs. Fox
who was wildly anxious about her first baby, tried little
regimens and diets and brought the child on in a remarkable way, while maintaining the theory that her con-
stitution was far from robust.

Nan's control of Mrs. Fox had its roots in that first
year too. Nothing was too much for Nan to do to help
her, she nursed her carefully towards dependence. She
magnified the importance of little rests and glasses of
milk, she petted and flattered and never, never obtruded
herself. She sewed for the child with skill and pains. All
the time she stitched at the little dresses, stiff with em-

broidery, and awful white pelisses, her mind was gone
ahead to the day when her hands would be among the
Aragon linen, mending and marking and sorting and
putting aside.

Mrs. Fox had a miscarriage that year which put her
more completely into Nan's hands. Nan had brilliant
technique in encouraging people to love being ill.
Delicious trays of invalid food, fresh carnations daily,
temperature takings and head shakings, ever so little of
a serious look and then a professionally cheerful voice,
washings and powderings and scentings in bed, a bow to
tie the hair, blinds drawn and rests at the same moment
daily, Sylvia with her hair brushed round Nan's finger
brought in for long enough to amuse, not long enough
to tire.

Nan was so good looking then. She had a fineness with
her strength that came through her breeding. She was
tall and wide in the shoulders, with narrow hips and long
strong legs. Her gold brown hair showed in crisp waves
under her cap. It was good coarse hair and the com-
monest thing about her. Everything else showed her
father's quality and mother's beauty ; the long eyes and
rather thin mouth ; the line of the jaw cutting in against
the long neck ; all the look of slightness and small bones
in so big a woman came from Aragon. Nan knew this and
gloried in it.

When Sylvia was asleep on a summer night she would
sometimes leave the nursery maid in charge, saying
briskly that she would take a " breath of air " or a " little
trot." Then on with her long blue coat with its short
shoulder cape and the bonnet and veil that nurses wore
then. Going from the nursery she would pass the top of
the wide double staircase and standing there desire would
be in her feet to run down its shallow steps past all the
pictures of her ancestors and out through the hall where
the scent of lilies in their pots came strained through cold
space and muted light. But no, the respect for Aragon
was beyond such trifling. The nurses of Aragon did not

use these stairs ; they were for the family. So she would go through the swing door of red baize and down the narrow wooden stairs, where so many old prints in maple frames were hung, and a black plaster nigger in a blue starred petticoat that everyone thought so hideous, stood on the landing half-way down. She would go out through a side door, where a dark sticky escalonia filled the air with its delicious gummy scent, and a shadowy white jasmine breathed of sex and swoons against such cleanly briskness. She might stand at the corner of the house and look down its length of windows and urns and balustrading. She might breathe sharply, knowing her share in a serene magnificence that was as precious as flesh to her. Because this share was not owned nor admitted, and could not be, it was stronger in her than any good thing in her life. It was danger, romance, the very stuff and part of dreams. For how could her love for Aragon ever be admitted, or her share in the Fox family ever be allowed— the vanity and reverence for her own blood were the first to deny its admission. The long arms in their blue sleeves would move outwards in a small flowing gesture. Presently her feet would move quickly away from the house. Through the park she might go, where black cattle breathed heavily, moving about in heavy groups through the lime avenue where the scent came down like a great bell upon you, a light, pale, wide bell of sensation, and back then to the house, the summer air warm as milk about it, the night darker, the river sounds nearly audible.

XXI

THE YEAR Grania was born Nan put Mrs. Fox to bed for about six months. She was not going to have a mistake about this baby. It was to be a son for Aragon. Nan knew it, told it in signs and portents, things she said and did not say, mysterious calculations and assumptions all arriving at that, the only conclusion.

Hugh Fox was anxious enough for a son to be born too. He had had a pitiful time of it in the last couple of years with his wife's delicacy and miscarrying, and further delicacy and temperaments and tears, all consequent, they told him, on her loss of the babies. He was sorry for her, but sorry with the intolerance of the strong for the sick. There is nothing to undo love like the disaster of bad health. That is perhaps what lends to some women the strength for its defeat. But Mrs. Fox enjoyed her bad health. In and out of pregnancies she had Nan to stand between her and trouble. Nan to keep strong in her a faith in her own importance, Nan's will and power and care forcing her to keep this baby.

This was the winter of Nan's great trial, the trial between Aragon, her secret life and pride, and this other glorious calamity that was upon her.

She fell in love with Hugh Fox, her master and her half-cousin, and he with her. When the river mists were thick against the window panes in November, and the curtains drawn full and nice as her mother had told, she would lock herself into the nursery with the child Sylvia, enduring such contest of flesh and spirit as leave marks past hiding—the gay rocking-horse, the scattered toys, the sleeping child, her sewing, the white gaslight, what were these to the unbearable calling between them? Sitting there, the simple shape of nursery shadows round her, everything around her clean and simple and good, she was waiting, only living, for the moment when she would go in to Mrs. Fox's room to give her her medicine and settle her for the night. He would be there perhaps or maybe not. Oh, the doubt, the torture, and the knowing that because of her strength she would always say no to him.

He was the consummation and the end of all that Aragon stood for to Nan. Pale, fine, long-handed, narrow-eyed, like all their common ancestry. A soft thick mouth, and soft thick hair, weak and demanding and enchanting, the very counterpart for her strength and generosity.

Then Nan knew how all Mrs. Fox's gentle whimpering no's put him beside himself. She ached with pain past belief to comfort and give love.

Self-respect, vanity, obstinacy—whatever it is called, there is a quality in some people that they cannot be parted from but to their great loss. Nan had this. If she had yielded to her love she would have lost her very self, and for the rest of her life have had no reason for being.

Nan would go quickly down the passages from the nursery to the room where Mrs. Fox lay in a little piece of the big double bed. It was before the time when beds got low, and this bed was like a great pale country for sickness bounded top and bottom by dark mahogany. Pink duvets lay light as clouds. Yards of rose-wreathed chintz were gathered round in a valance to hide the legs of the bed. Drifts of white pillows were heaped behind the weak little back. A fair and faintly sticky plait of hair hung down over one shoulder, half-hidden in a smother of lace and ribbons, the prettiest bed-jacket of all. Everywhere in slender vases of silver and glass, pink carnations were sprayed about the room, their colour melted into the roses in the chintz. The wallpaper was white with silver stripes. The carpet *vieux rose*, and satin cushions to pick up its colour. A wood fire burnt lavishly. Scents of fresh and old lavender water and eau de cologne drifted here and there. A pekinese snuffled and slumbered in the embrace of its basket. Mrs. Fox was petulant. She had not been able to get a word out of her husband for the last half-hour. He sat in his armchair under the green-shaded table-lamp reading the same paper that he had taken up after dinner. Even the same page of the same paper. Sulking, defensive, secret, very much on his dignity if she spoke to him. His face pale and those full eyelids and black lashes low, his mouth set and not amiable. Very still, very dark in his black evening clothes, full of nervous restraint, answering, "Yes, my dear," "No, my dear," if she spoke, as though his mouth would never form her name, or not willingly. She was delighted to see Nan when she came in. It woke the room up, made a break, charged the air with life in some way. He got up and came over to the bed when Nan was shaking the pillows.

"Good-night, I suppose," he said. There was life in his voice. He bent over her and kissed the top of her head.

"Won't you come back."

"I've got some letters to write. You'd better go to sleep. Hadn't she, Nan?"

"Just as she likes," Nan said, she would not help him to keep away. "You had a sleep this afternoon, didn't you, madam?"

He straightened himself and held her little bed-warmed hand and smiled across at Nan.

"All right, come and tell me when you're finished with her. I'll be in the study." He was laughing at her. He knew she would not go to him in the study. There was something very natural and funny about the way he could sometimes for a moment laugh at all the weights of love that held him and tease her with her strictness. A light stick to sting her with. Everything about this love was light and impatient. Except Nan's reply to it, which had so much sorrow and dignity and value.

Nan put Mrs. Fox to bed, curling the feathery hair, folding away the ribboned coat, carefully, unhasty, forgetful of nothing, attentive to the disconnected chatter about this and about that. Sylvia. The flowers. The new housemaid. What the doctor said. What she felt about the baby, and how her feeling differed from what she had felt before the last disaster. It was all so little. It was still all there was of first importance, and Nan gave it the attention which was its due. She was fond of Mrs. Fox and saw nothing to despise in her because her husband's love had wandered. Under the circumstances it was not so very surprising. Nan knew it took a super-woman to hold a Fox true to her, that was Nan's outlook really. There were Fox's in the world and other people. There was Aragon in the world and other places.

Now she listened attentive and interested to the chatter of a Fox mother, though all her being was thrust away from her towards the room where Hugh Fox was sitting alone.

" Oh, Nan, look, do you think I've knitted enough to cast off yet ? "

" Ah, it's going to be a bigger boy than that."

" It is going to be a boy, I'm certain. Nan, there's how long now ? One, two, three, four months. To the twenty-third, I should say."

" It will be the twenty-seventh."

" I feel so much better than I did with the others. Isn't that a good sign ? "

" Not too good, you must keep yourself quiet."

" I wish they would send the blue ribbon from Dublin. They are so slow. I want to see what sized holes to make for it."

" The size you have done will be all right."

" I think that vase of carnations might go."

" Yes, indeed. I saw some red ones in the greenhouse to-day, but they aren't so nice for a bedroom, are they ? "

" No, I like pale pink in a bedroom or violets are nice. Mr. Fox likes violets. He said he shot a jack-snipe to-day. Tell the cook to send it up for my lunch to-morrow."

" It's no more than a mouthful, madam. No bigger than a moth you might say."

" I've got everything now, I think. My glass of water, my biscuit. I'll take my medicine, Nan, shall I ? "

" And your hot milk."

" You know I think that glass of milk gives me indigestion."

" Well, we'll leave it off to-morrow night."

" You've said that for the last three months."

" No, it's good for him ; it builds the bones."

" Well, all right. . . . Nan, go down to the study and tell Mr. Fox I want to see him."

" Couldn't you go to sleep, Madam ? "

" I've been asleep half the day. Go down yourself, Nan, don't send any one, and say I really want to see him. I really do."

" Don't fuss yourself, now, Madam. I'll see to it."

" Go yourself, Nan. Promise."

Poor little silly, she could recognise Nan's power, but not the implications of such power. There is felicity in such silliness.

Nan put the last un-needed touches to the complete order of the room before she went downstairs. She went down the wide staircase, her hand touching lightly along the smooth bannister. She took this way to lend herself a kind of strength, to borrow resistance from all the pale Fox's. The intensive vanity, the highest end of snobbery made possible the connection between Nan and these pallid brown portraits, hung and settled on the walls of the house. They did indeed influence her to a denial that was then close to martyrdom.

" Well, so you did come down to me ? " He was standing in front of the fire, smoking a cigarette. The restraint, the teasing of his upstairs-manner were gone.

Nan held the door open at her back.

" Mrs. Fox would particularly like to see you, Sir."

" Nan, come here to me. Please."

" I must go back to the nursery."

" Don't I matter at all ? " He crossed the room in a moment and closed the door behind her. " Don't you mind

about me, Nan?" His arms were round her. "Nan."
For a moment all the power that was in her was changed
into a strength of love, beyond thought, beyond resistance.
There was a force in this terrible loving that would never
be lost by giving.

She put him from her. Her eyes were dark with pain.
She would murder love. Her hands were strong and cold
with despair, and when she spoke her voice was strong.
She said :

"I don't want to trouble Mrs. Fox as things are, but
I should let you know, Sir, that I must leave when the
child is born. I am going to be married to Owen
O'Neill."

He stood apart from her. "I'm so sorry, Nan," he said.

It was then that she longed most to comfort him. What
was she that she denied him anything? Her love, her
little boy, her dearest and only cause and reason for living.

He had gone back to the fire before she opened the door
to go, and just before she went he said, softly and gently :

"Good-night, Cousin Nan."

It was a wonderful acceptance of her refusal. It gave
back into her keeping entire the world of Aragon, for
which she had just given her all, and to give your all is so
dangerous even for the strong. The object for which so
much is sacrificed must at the time be exaggerated far
out of the true, and when such lovely illusion goes, only
the sour emptiness of loss is left to the giver.

Now, in two words, her dream and her secret had been
made a reality. Hugh Fox paid her for a lifetime of
service with those two words, "Cousin Nan," spoken so
sweetly and gravely at that moment. He was of his time
in that faintly dramatic respect of a woman who could
withstand him, and of his time too in knowing the
strength and depth of value to Nan this brief recognition
of their cousinship would be. But he was real and gentle
in that he took the gravest means in his power to console
her for what he knew now she would always put away
from her. He knew she loved him far more deeply than

he looked for. He was afraid and grateful for her strength
in denying a force that might be beyond them both. He
was to have no easy joy of her.

Nan went down the passage slowly from the study door
to the hall. What he had said brought her no comfort
yet. She felt weak and suffocated by a kind of nausea
for which there was no relief. It was very cold in the
passage and the high hall where the gaslight was turned
down to a pale worm of light. Nan's arms were folded
across her white apron, her hands grasping either arm
above the elbow. Her tall body was bent to a hollow
weariness. She was empty of all resolve. If he had been
there now that she knew what her refusal meant. . . .
But he did not follow her. She was alone with despair.
Despair takes so long about its business. It has a sort of
mild finality, even in its first moments. It is an empty,
dirty house with old foggy windows.

Nan's only reason for going into the drawing-room that
night was her wish to hide for a little while. She could
not face the bright nursery and the curious eyes of the
nursery-maid left there in charge of Sylvia.

She opened the high thin mahogany door quietly, and
shutting it she went slowly, still stooping, across the room
to one of the windows that looked over the river. The
sharp stars were squared again and again in the small
panes of the windows. She was kneeling on the floor.
Her dress flowed free from her narrow waist, it was a
delicate, dark, sweeping line to the floor. She was not
crying. She was alone in her house, alone in body and
spirit. Her despair and her desire were too close and high
about her for any comfort to come near. It was not then
but long afterwards that the dead Fox's came near her.
That night she was comfortless, and that night her pity
for pain in others died. She would live to hurt somebody
for this terrible wrong she had done herself. She would
twist a revenge out of life yet.

She knelt a long time in the cold room above the cold
river, and when at last she got up from her knees she felt

as cold as death. It was a help to have any sensation that she could assuage, any feeling that said to the supremely sensible woman in her, "Have sense. Help yourself." She went out of the drawing-room and through the hall and up the back stairs to the nursery, where she dismissed the maid, and brewed herself a cup of tea.

That cup of tea in moments of crisis, whether disastrous or happy, is to the peasant Irish what his opium is to the Chinaman. Habit and her mother's blood were strong enough in Nan to make it her tonic and her opiate. Its strong comfort was ready for her to-night and gave her back some reliance on herself. She shuddered as she drank the first mouthful, but then, catching herself together half-angrily, she drank for her good concentrating in the pleasure it gave her. Then she wrote a letter to Gipsy O'Neill saying she would come to tea with her on her next free afternoon. The letter contained an arch reference to her brother, Owen O'Neill. When Nan stuck up the envelope there was a look about her mouth, a wry, hard look, that Aunt Pidgie was to see often in later years.

XXII

NAN left Aragon before Grania was born. She could not trust herself to stay near Hugh Fox any longer. She arranged her marriage with Owen O'Neill and went to live at Clonamore. When her son was born she was very happy. He was a lovely child, although there was much more of the O'Neill than the Fox about him. His father died of pneumonia when he was three years' old and when he was six, Nan left him in charge of her sister-in-law and went back to Aragon. Hugh Fox had hurt his back so terribly in a hunting accident that the doctors said he could not live six months. Nan kept him alive for twelve, and then she was glad to see him die. After that she could never leave Aragon.

It was when he was dying that she first knew the ghosts in the house. The ghosts at Aragon were only seen and heard by the Fox's, and the Fox's were usually afraid of them and denied their presence. When one of the family was near death they would keep all together and lights burning and drinking, and fires roaring up the chimneys, and no lonely venturing round the house after nightfall.

But for Nan it was another thing, and a glorious thing. She went towards the hauntings, the shadows, the fullness in empty rooms, with a great embracement of spirit.

To her this proof of her Fox blood was a wonder and a satisfaction beyond price. She accepted and gloried in their presence. If a door opened a little, Nan would get up from her chair, leave down her sewing, and open it wide, wide to her dead. She would set off like a happy ship down the dark passages to fetch trays from the kitchen at night, trays which the servants were frightened to bring though they saw nothing, heard nothing, but their vulgar minds were full of the house's old stories.

It was on one of these excursions that Nan first knew the height of the one she called " the Child " trotting beside her, and knew when she stretched down her hand where its hand would meet hers. There was happiness in the air when it was there. But there were other ghosts at Aragon not quite so happy. Were the girls such as Ann Daly had dealt with (and many a one before her) coming back with their wrongs, a crazed haunting of the beautiful house where they had been coaxed or forced to wickedness and where babies' bones were little and green scattered skeletons on the river bottom? Nan passed off her knowing of these with a shrug—such things were. Take it or leave it, such things have been. She could turn over and go to sleep when she had been woken by the clash of duelling swords on the path below her window. The path that ran between the house and the shallow terrace and the drop to the river.

Aragon's living and dying and dead all turned to Nan in that wonderful year of her return, so filled with sadness and satisfaction. Afterwards she would turn the events of that year over in her mind, its happenings were like objects, she could put them away in a bag and take them out one by one, almost in her hands and turn over and dwell upon them.

Nan had a wonderful enjoyment in using words. No matter how often she might discuss or dissect an incident with Mrs. Fox she always had new words in which to state its outline and embroider its detail. Away from the glorious details of illness and death, funeral wreaths or a difficult birth, what might she picture? Grouse—a brace of grouse, and how shall we eat them?

"They are young birds, Madam. No spurs, see, imagine, and their feet as soft as a baby's. Would you have them roast? Not too much done, see, on a piece of soft toast, a good thick slice that will hold their goodness, and a rich brown sauce, and a spoonful of crumbs, and a nice bread sauce, and we'll start in on the late line of peas, and a few mushrooms, and a sharp salad, and a half-bottle of the old Burgundy—the birds deserve it. And a grill of the legs for breakfast with scrambled eggs and sliced tomato and chippy bacon. How would that be, Madam? How would you eat that? Wouldn't it be good?"

Food is wonderful and consoling when it is spoken of by a clean enthusiastic woman, especially when it is not her business or province. But life was Nan's province, every aspect of life on which she could lay a finger, some octupus like quality in her seemed able to reach out its sensitive strength and grasp the essential of what she heard or saw, and hold it tenaciously within herself until the moment for its use should come.

Little by little Nan had achieved the ruling of Aragon. There was no coarseness or violence shown in the methods by which her opponents were weeded out. Slowly, and one by one they went, and with their going, her power over the rest tightened its grip. Everyone on the place was afraid of Nan and Nan's influence on Mrs. Fox, who was the perfect doll to be manipulated by Nan.

Perhaps, for all her power Nan's only enemy was Frazer, and Frazer knew her too well to come out into the open in his defiance. Besides what had he to hold against her except his hatred, and his shadowy knowledge that Miss Pidgie often went hungry for Nan's pleasure.

Frazer hated pleasure, and life, and himself, and other people, and Ireland. He was bitter and efficient and savagely honest. He hated Catholics. His chilblains gave him a lot of trouble in winter-time, and his digestion all the year round. He used to write his grudges and his discoveries about other people's wrong-doings down on dirty little pieces of ruled paper torn from his notebook, and lock them away in a drawer in the pantry, against the time they might come in useful. He was a horrid little man, but an excellent and honourable butler. Even Nan's and her own dislike of him had not been enough to make Mrs. Fox dismiss him, and for years, as long as Nan's, he had remained at Aragon. Sylvia he liked, and Miss Pidgie he pitied, the more hotly because his pity was linked with his hatred of Nan and her easy powerful ways in every

province of the house . . . and for her son, for that thing
abhorrent to all bitter old servants, one who is not so
far above themselves but who, because of an ability and
knowledge they will never attain, is accepted and
questioned and respected by the gentry they serve in their
different measures. For her son, Gentleman Bloody Foley,
as he called him from between the teeth of his mind,
Frazer had a dislike equal to and beyond that which he
felt for the mother. He hated horses and never for a
moment dissociated a racecourse from evil and dishonest
practice of every description, and Foley was the prophet
of all these matters. The young soldiers who came to
Aragon would rather talk to him than to each other if he
chanced to be there. He had sometimes come to a meal,
and Frazer regretted that he hardly ever drank, because
it deprived him of the satisfaction of stinting the drink he
poured into his glass. Never were there such fairy slices
of game placed on any plate as on Foley's. Almost, if the
butler's marrow in his bones had not prevented him, he
snatched the vegetables from him as he handed the silver
dish. He could not possibly recognise the natural tough
simplicity of Foley's character which made him take the
elaborate service of meals in the big house as easily as he
would take the boiling of eggs for his own tea, and service
from the stately Frazer as indifferently as service from
Doatie or Aunt Gipsy.

XXIII

WHAT a moment of supreme and blissful triumph for Frazer, what an exquisite hour of fulfilment was here on that spring evening as he closed the drawing-room door on the ring of pale faces, faces paled and shocked by his story, faces consternated in the still air of the room, when he left them to go, before any could forestall him, and carry the tale to Nan's kingdom, the nursery. He did not hurry, he paused and rolled the taste of each moment on his tongue as he went steadily up the staircase to the nursery. It was a strange way to him, for, though Nan might sail into the pantry with dreadful unabashed freedom when the notion took her, Frazer never, never went near the nursery. So to-day when he knocked at the door it was like knocking at the door of a strange house—his enemy's house.

" Come in," Nan called. If she was startled when she looked up from her stitching and saw him there instead of a maid with the tea, she did not show it, but bit the end of her thread and snapped a new piece from the spool before she said :

" It's a pleasure to see you up here, fancy, Mr. Frazer."

" It's not for my pleasure but for my duty I come into this room, Mrs. O'Neill."

" Duty, really, fancy again, Mr. Frazer ! And when did your duty go beyond cleaning silver with your thumb ? "

" Ah, Nan O'Neill, my thumb and my duty alike are my business, and I know my place. I know my place and I keep my place, and I never seek to puff myself up with power, like some I know, not so far away."

" Oh, it's great sport to hear you give out a sermon, all the same, Mr. Frazer."

" Like some I know."

" Not so far away, didn't you say, Mr. Frazer ? "

"Like some I know that will get the cap of conceit torn off them in a way they *don't* expect."

"You and I have lived here a good few years now, and the only cap I have left off is my nurse's cap, at Mrs. Fox's special request." Nan passed her fingers through her strong grey curls with an expression on her face of overbearing and maddening self-content. She was Queen of Aragon, and maybe this was her last contest with one who had been for so long a spy and a dark opponent. Her eyes danced for the battle, and her quick brain went flashing down the possible methods of his attack and her own counter thrusts and out-manoeuvring to come. She was a little discountenanced when he sat down without invitation and laughed—a rude and certain laugh.

Nan got up and folded away her sewing, an angry colour in her cheeks now.

"If it's all the same to you, Mr. Frazer, would you remember that Miss Pigeon will be in to her tea at any moment, and that happens to be her chair you are settled in."

"Poor Miss Pigeon, indeed. A chair is about all she does get for a meal, tea or any other meal, a chair and little more than a crust, don't I know it? Don't I know where my good grouse goes, or my nice ham, or my bit of sole and melted butter I send up on a hot plate, so tasty from the dining-room? Don't I know who starves and bullies Miss Pigeon for their own wickedness?"

"Would Mrs. Fox and myself and the doctor be the best judges of Miss Pigeon's diet, or would we get you in to advise us, now tell me?" Nan's face was livid. "What medicine do you think she should take, now tell me? What time should she go to bed, since you know so much?"

"It's little medicine she'd want if she got a square meal once in a way, God help her."

"The same as He'll twist you for interference."

"It's the twist of hunger in a harmless old creature you'll have to answer for, see, and good food in plenty all around her. Oh, I've kept the life in her, she'd be dead long ago, like a light old bird in winter, only for me. I know when she's hungry, though she never asked me for a bite yet. I know when I see that old disgrace of a hat you keep on her go nodding along past the dining-room window or the pantry window maybe, and the cold wind whistling out through the cock's feathers in it. I know she's hungry though she's too proud to look in the window, just by way of—only by chance, she'll go by. Ah, Nan, for all your cruel tricks, many a good plate of cold game or mushrooms and bacon on toast I've kept there for her from the breakfast, sizzling on the hot plate, 'Just a morsel for your Diblins, Miss,' I say, to save her pride."

" You'll kindly repeat every word of that before Mrs. Fox. Yes, and Miss Pigeon shall be there, and see then will she uphold one word of it."

" And, long ago, I'd have said it to Mrs. Fox, Nan, only I knew who would get the dirty end of that stick, and that's the old lady."

" And what ails you now to drag your lies and your dirty grudges into the daylight ? "

" Ah, things are changed now, Nan. Things are changed." He almost sang the words at her. He was trembling to deal her his blow. But there were other matters to be dealt with first, and bitter satisfactions that could not be foregone.

" For thirty years I've watched you in this place."

" And have you known me do a thing that wasn't for this place and the good of the family ? "

" Ah, the bastard's pride in you ! "

" John Frazer, you low, tinker bred scum ! Out now. Out, or I'll put you out ? You little rat——"

" Easy, Nan, easy a minute. It's the pride that held you out against the poor Master, I wouldn't blame it——"

" Don't speak to me, don't dare."

" I can, girl, I saw it. Ah, I watched you then with the eyes of love, but you changed my love to hate, and every year with more reason I hate what you are. You got all you wanted from life, didn't you, Nan? Full power over the house of your blood and the Fox's within it? But you charged yourself with the bitter loss of love in all your life of content, that torment is threaded in you, in and out, in and out."

"Hold your tongue. Hold your tongue. Have you gone mad?"

"The one good act you did, you did it for a bad reason, and the bad grudge it left in you is vented on the only Fox you are able to torment. The want of goodness through you and through you wouldn't let time pacify your lust, but had to twist it out of you in cruel goings on to one more helpless than a baby in your wicked hands."

"And what have I done? Speak up and say can you lay a finger on one of your wicked accusations?"

Frazer took a dirty little notebook out of his pocket, and opened its pages silently. Nan would have given much to snatch it from his hands and watch it fall far fluttering downwards to the river below, the river that had hidden so much in time past.

"April 3rd, 1917," Frazer read out, "Miss P. very lame. Have you a sore foot, Miss P.? I have a blistered heel, Frazer, she replied, there is a nail in my boot. Give me the boot, Miss P., I replied, and took it from her. There was a brad up into the side of her foot and a welt out in the leather in the heel. I adjusted the boot with a hammer. Is it long like that, Miss P., I inquired. Oh, a long time, Frazer, she replied, but Nan says the soldiers in France have more to put up with,' And that's only one little thing." He put an elastic band twice round the little book and put it away in his pocket. "Only one little thing in the ten years you're minding Miss Pigeon, and I'm watching you minding Miss Pigeon."

"And do you think any one is more likely to believe your lies, because you write them down, you fool?"

"They look better so. 1917 is a long way back. But I have day and date and time for many a thing."

" And what brings you up here to-day with your insults and your nonsense ? "

" What brings me up here to-day, is it ? Oh, didn't I nearly forget. Fancy, Nan, that I could forget such an important young chap—so gentlemanly, such a friend of all the officers ! Well, Nan, tch, tch, where's my head ? Indeed it's time I gave up my job."

" What are you talking about now ? Get out of here. I'll see you again with Mrs. Fox."

" Well, now, I'm going, I'm just going. But before I go I'd like to be the first to tell you that your son, *Mr.* Bloody Foley, is arrested and in the barracks for aiding and abetting in the murder of Captain Purvis and Mr. Craye in the mountains this morning ! Ah, ha, the Fox blood, the Aragon touch ran a bit thin in the laddo, eh ? "

Nan was white. She looked white all the way through to her bones and past them. Through and through her the blood of her strength had failed.

" I don't believe you."

" You do believe me," he said.

" Tell me more."

" You'll hear time enough." He shook his head and got up to go. He was a hard old man, righteous and hard as flint. " Run with the hare and hunt with the hounds," he said, " But it won't last for ever, will it, Nan ? " He was sniggering with pleasure as he went softly out of the nursery.

XXIV

NAN stood facing the window. The linen she had been marking lay in a pile on the floor, it looked like a great ruin of snow melting in wreaths and circles back to water and dark earth. An hour ago this linen had been rich and crisply dignified, an emblem of Nan's sound position at Aragon, exquisite and dearly bought. Nan looked out across the full river. What had Foley done ? What foolish mistake had he made that could put such words into her enemy's mouth, that could empower him to taunt and torment and insult her ? Frazer was the sort who would not hit until he knew undoubtedly his foe was down. He would have waited his lifetime, he would have died before he struck a meaningless blow.

Nan had never thought of admitting to herself that her treatment of Miss Pidgeon amounted to cruelty. Of course not. The moments of tense satisfaction when she knew Miss Pigeon's fear of her was a fluttering living thing, the moments when satisfied power made her indulgent, as one might be with a tiresome petted dog, not because the dog is less tiresome, but because some gland of generosity, suddenly freed, for the moment requires an outlet ; these moments she neither noticed nor understood, but thought of herself as a tower of patience towards Miss Pigeon's cracked childish ways, and as a healthy deterrent and guard against many nasty and rather dirty ways. She kept her clean. She fed her. She kept her away from visitors. She frightened her into good behaviour. She gave her pills when she was constipated, and saw to it that she did not cost Mrs. Fox a penny more than could be helped in clothes. She had done her duty by Miss Pigeon, of course she had, more than her duty. Yet a dark wind of fear was blowing through Nan. She could not possibly understand the reasons for some of the feelings she had towards Miss Pigeon, for some of the things she had done to her, she could not even remember them. What was written down in that little book ? What had Miss Pigeon told him ? How much and how often had they talked ? Some of Frazer's words came back to Nan :

" The bitter loss of love in all your life. . . . A bad grudge left in you and vented on the only Fox you can torment . . ."

Nan could reject his wild charges, of course she could reject them all, but with such charges went a loss of her dignity, of her great connection with Aragon. She might be watched. She might be questioned—the Queenship halted or lost, and what indeed was this about Foley ? She must go over to Mountain Brig after Miss Pidgie's tea. (Life, death or imprisonment cannot interfere with a good nannie's idea of a tea-hour.) Mrs. Fox would send her in the car. The anxiety for Foley was implemented in the anxiety for herself and for Aragon. She was far more proud than fond of him. She was not a fond person. She only had her passions—the one passion —Aragon. So far in life Foley, the handsome little boy, the prodigy of childish horsemanship—Foley, the clever big boy who passed all examinations so easily—Foley, the successful owner of horses, had been a credit and a pride and a bolster to her importance. The kind of son she felt it right that she should have. The kind of son other women did not achieve, other women without a trickle of Fox blood in their veins. Now, what had he done, what sort of trouble was he in, how would it effect and disgrace her? Could she carry him over it? Whom should she approach in his favour ? What next, what next ?

How late Miss Pigeon was for her tea. She was usually in early and sat waiting for her bread and butter and her slice of cake in a state of great expectancy. The maid tapped at the door and came in with the tray. Nan looked out of the window furiously and saw a little figure, far below, foreshortened as flat as a beetle, hurrying and bundling along the flagged path beneath the windows.

Miss Pigeon was panting when she came in, the speed of her coming still stirred the feathers in her hat.

" I'm a little late, Nan," she said anxiously. " My watch stopped at 4.15, and when I looked again it was still 4.15."

" And what does it say now ? "

" Oh, I set it by the clock in the hall as I came through."

" Well, Miss Pigeon, you must have been very quick to get round by the hall, and it not three minutes since I saw you come in by the side door."

" Oh, I was very quick, Nan. I ran, Nan."

" You're sure you didn't fly, Miss Pigeon ? " Nan's temper was mounting as it always did in these contests with Miss Pigeon. It made the excuse greater for punishment. To-night it had reached the " No cake " level in a flash when something halted her, made her look at the creature she had cared for so long. It was fear, fear unalloyed that stayed her mind for that second's looking. What a small creature she saw, small, unattractive and frightened. Miss Pigeon's face was pale under the big feathered hat. The blue ribbon bow on her breast jumped and quivered as if there was a wire spring behind it.

" Take off your hat, now, and sit down to your tea." Nan took the ginger cake out of its box and cut a large slice from it, the largest Miss Pigeon had seen for a long time. " And no more fibs to Nan mind, or it's early bed and no supper." She poured out Miss Pigeon's tea and went into the bedroom to dress in her blue coat and skirt, for she must get to Mountain Brig as soon as possible. Nan had a most trustworthy belief in her own power to compete with any situation better than anybody else if she could be on the spot where it was taking place, if she could gather its threads into her grasp. She could snap them and roll them up and tidy the tangle.

She was putting on her hat when she heard a voice, an

excited strong stormy voice speaking to Miss Pigeon in the nursery. It was Aunt Gipsy, Aunt Gipsy to whom Aragon was an Elysium of forbidden ground and unencountered aristocracy. Nan swung open the door before Aunt Gipsy could embark on the reasons for her visit to the tiny piece of faded gentlewoman who was begging her to sit down and offering her a solitary slice of ginger cake.

"Gipsy!" Nan said from the door, her voice an icy frame for reproof, "you've had your tea, I suppose."

"Tea, dear? No, indeed, nor dinner, scarcely what you'd see. Oh, Nan, what a day! Oh, Nan, wait now till I tell you all I know. Be brave now, Nan, to take a knock, but God is good and he will see you over it, and if we have a nice cup of tea wouldn't it hearten us? Well, don't trouble for me, of course, but it's a terrible business to take it out of you to buy a new hat. Do you like me in it? Well, when I was in Dungarvan I thought I'd be the right fool to pass it by, though it's not the one I intended buying."

"I think it's a show," Nan said sourly. She came forward into the room and put up a hand that was to put the room in two halves and divide the spate of words from Miss Pigeon.

"Would you care to go out, Miss," she said, "and take your cake, too. Perhaps another slice for those Diblins."

Miss Pigeon put on her hat again and hurried out. She was used to being shooed away when Nan had visitors.

Gipsy followed Nan into the bedroom. While she talked she kept diving between the two looking glasses. A close view in the dressing-table glass, a distant impression in the long one on the wardrobe door. Her pre-occupation with her hat made curiously light of all she had to say.

"How did you get here?" Nan asked.

"Oh, my dear, the car that brought out Nurse Dwyer for Doatie took me back."

"Nurse Dwyer for Doatie?"

"Oh, Nan, did you not see Miss Grania all day?"

" No." Nan paused. " She was out all day." What
was in store, what lay in that blank ? Gipsy must not
recognise her ignorance of any point. Gipsy, that vulgar
lesser creature, Foley's servant, her servant—and what an
indifferent one. What then ? What now ?

" You didn't hear herself and Foley nearly came home
with my poor child corpsed this morning to breakfast ? "

" I haven't seen Miss Grania. She had been away all
day."

" Well, I never will forget it. What a morning I put
over me. I hardly had my cup of tea in the kitchen when
I lit on this little hat in the paper. No, but it wasn't this
one, only the girl in Beirney's persuaded me this one was
the one for me, and only the three shillings between them,
so I said, I'll chance it. Well, my mind, dear, was very
taken with my little hat after they went off. Though,
indeed, I went out to the yard several times to see would
Foley's black hen lay a brown egg for his breakfast, and
made a cake of white bread on the pan with my own two
hands, mind, and slapped up a bit of fresh butter and
took the money out of the good teapot, and had all set
out as nice as you like ready for them to come back with
Miss Grania."

" How did you know Miss Grania was coming back
with them ? " The blank must be filled though she hated
to question Gipsy.

" Ah, dear, Foley doesn't keep back much from Aunt
Gipsy." Gipsy knew in a flash that Nan was ignorant
of any familiarity between Foley and Grania. She
wondered whether to build or to lessen that side of the
day's picture. Build, perhaps, since Nan knew so little.
" She's coming out with us to ride a school, Auntie, he
said, so get a nice breakfast, mind, and I think it was
then he said I ought to buy a new hat for myself. Ah,
child, I said, it's little indeed my hats troubles me, if I
can keep any old thing on me a bit decent for the chapel
is all I need. Well, Aunt Gipsy, he said, you must go to
Beirneys in Dungarvan and . . . "

" Gipsy, will you kindly forget your hat for a moment and tell me what has happened to-day."

" Hats, Nan, hats, I never give them a thought, only to keep a little bit of respectability going between Mountain Brig and the chapel."

" Well, what happened Doatie ? "

" Do you think one of them would trouble to tell me what that lion of a horse did to her ? Only to bring her home and lay her cold at my feet is what he did. Aunt Gipsy, he said, it's a black hat you nearly had a right to buy yourself this day. Oh, I could see myself—all in black and a black hat, standing by that little grave."

" And how is the corpse now ? " Nan shot out the question before the picture grew so gloomy that Gipsy must refuse to admit any possibility of recovery to her child. You could only guess at the truth behind Gipsy's accounts and the guesses even had to be daggered out by thrusting words.

" Oh, she's conscious all right, now. ' Where am I mother darling ? ' Those were the first words she spoke, and, oh, Mrs. Bohane, nurse said to me, what a mother's love can do ! "

" Are you sure it was nurse said it, Gipsy ? I thought you left her in charge and went off to Dungarvan to buy a hat."

" Well if it wasn't nurse, it was little Josie."

" Well, so Doatie's in bed with a hospital nurse in charge. You're driving round the country buying hats. And where, do you know, is Foley and when did you see him last ? "

" The last I say of Foley was driving Miss Grania back to her bicycle this morning after her breakfast, and when I came back from Dungarvan with my hat who met me in the yard with a white face on him and the eyes jumping from his head but Micky Brown. Micky, I said, is Miss Doatie . . . ? and I couldn't say the word. But it passed through my mind would they change the hat for a black hat. Keep the car Missus, Micky said, you might want it

yet. There was a party of Military here and you out.
What, Micky," I said, " did I miss the military? Did
they get a cup of tea? It wasn't tea, they took, he said,
but searched the place out till they found a little dog
Mr. Foley brought home with him to-day, and with that
they put Mr. Foley in the lorry and took him off. Oh,
Nan, the disgrace! For all to see him driving through
the country, a common prisoner to the bare light of day."

" A common prisoner to the bare light of day," that
was the phrase that struck Nan to the heart. What he
had done, what he might not have done, whatever bad
case of danger he was in, this was what stood out from it
for her first. Her son, proud Nan O'Neill's son, a common
prisoner to the bare light of day.

Nan looked round her wildly. She was shaking. She
moistened her lips. She put her hands up, pressing the
backs of them against her eyes for a second, pulling them
out against her temples, she leaned towards Gipsy, she
had to be at one with this fool for the moment, to find out
what she could from her.

" There was no word left why he was taken? "

" Not a word."

" What do you know, Gipsy? Do you know any more?
What did Micky say? That's a sensible boy."

" Micky said, ' Excuse me remarking it, Mrs. Bohane,
but that's a lovely hat.' "

" Gipsy, could you tell me straight, did he give you any
reason why the soldiers came to Mountain Brig to-day.
Was it to see your new hat? "

Gipsy whirled on her shrill and furious.

" Ah, your airs and grandeurs will take a toss now.
Yes, Nan, it's little a hat is to you or any little thing like
that that keeps life in the woman of a lonely place like
myself. How many years am I there, Nan, working for
your boy, and I love the boy, he's not his mother's boy
but my poor brother's, ah, the maker's name is on the
blade, indeed. But for all the gentry ways you may strive
to give him he's in a British jail, now, God help him, for

aiding his own against the enemy I wouldn't wonder, and
you laughing on the Q.T. at my new hat, the way you
always made yourself out a high cry above the O'Neills.
What finished me was how you came to marry my poor
brother. God make good to him the four years' anguish
he had with you."

"Gipsy, are you gone mad? You that I kept at
Mountain Brig . . ."

"At Clonamore as it should be called. . . ."

"And your little daughter all these years. . . ."

"Doatie worked for Foley since she was eight years of
age. How many children's ponies did that child make
and sell for him?"

"How much did I pay the good Nuns for the schooling
she and you were too savage and ignorant to appreciate,
tell me."

"And I minding Foley for you through every child's
sickness and you engrossed in your high life and your
gentry ways."

"Take care I'd leave you in it a day longer to mind
him."

"Ah, that's good, indeed, and the jailers tending him
now with a tin plate, who knows."

"Did you come out here in a hired car to rain down
abuse on me or what did you come for?"

"I came to tell you anything I knew about Foley, and
all I get from you is rude remarks passed on my new hat,
and who are you in any case to pass remarks? You never
could buy a hat that it didn't look a holy show on you and
your mind never rose above navy blue. And anything
you ever did put on your head has the forbidding look
of one who drove a pram before her for many years."

"Are we all gone mad, I wonder?" Nan's strength
came down to earth in a supreme gesture of sanity.
"Would a cup of tea ease our minds?"

"Well, I wonder now, would it?"

Quite suddenly they both fell from the heights of real
antipathy which they felt for each other to the state of

placid giving and taking which for so long their lives had required of them.

"Gipsy, take your hat off. And I will say it's not a bad little hat at all."

Gipsy took it off and twirled it slowly round.

"Well, it looks nice on the hand," she said, "but it had a big buck of a hairpin driven into my head till I could faint from the pain."

"God help you girl."

"And did I tell you that Micky said, 'twas a little dog they found shut in the loft fixed poor Foley for them?"

"A dog, Gipsy?"

"Micky said 'was belonging one of the officers who was captured."

"Oh, my God on High." Nan accepted the implication very quietly.

They went into the nursery where Nan's slave had left a fresh pot of tea and sat down, the neutrality of years settling again between them.

Two women drinking tea and the shadow of death between them.

XXV

DEATH and new hats, tea and fear and pain—Aunt Gipsy's remembrance of Doatie's pain. Grave clothes and lilies and mourning, grandeur and power, old grudges and mistrusts, the tremblings and small gaieties of Aunt Pidgie's life, all these things were so thick they were almost within the touch of hands on the old nursery air that evening. What was there then in the air of houses that is not now? Was it more stirred by the emotions of the past than now when the life of the present is gay and firm in the ether with the radio ministering to the loneliest. Radio has stirred away the hauntings and stillnesses in old rooms. There is not the same heaviness and langour in the air of afternoon, air that can at any moment be broken by the good, the vulgar, the wholesome, the beautiful, the terrifying, the useful things of the present. The waves of the past cannot lap and lap quietly encroaching on the solid sands of now. Houses and memories have less power to injure, less power to assuage. But this afternoon was April, 1920, an afternoon in the time of long memories and quietness and dull ageless stretches of time. A time when a bitter little war went untidily on, and news of its progresses went from mouth to mouth in whispers. Many old and beautiful houses that year had their last hours of life. They were stilled for death that summer. They waited in beauty and quiet for fire and the end. Did they have a foreknowing of their deaths? Was that air of desolate distance, of exquisite sadness, that lesser fainter appearance which Irish houses have in comparison to the stability of their kind in England, was it foretold in their stars, grown sadly in their very stones? An awareness and an acceptance of violence and desertion, desertion far more tragic than any sudden ending.

This tea-time pause in Nan's terrible day had the quality of waiting ; it was right and calm and polite.

Bad news and cruel words had been flowing about the
room, anxious thoughts and furious plans. Now stillness.
It was as if nothing had happened before tea and nothing
would happen after it. Small ships would sail up and
down the river between the grey willow trees on the
banks and senna coloured stumps, bare at low water, but
covered when the ships passed by, riding on bosomy tides
of olive water under olive skies. Her life at Aragon would
flow on. Its good and its bad ghosts massing quietly
along the generations, some ghosts so old that they were
quieting gradually in their graves and seldom stirred.
Some happy spirits like the child who must come back,
it had been so happy here, and sometimes a strong and
violent influence from bad lives and hard deaths of the
past would plunge into the present of the house and use
its air for cruelty and unnamed sports.

XXVI

SYLVIA said good-bye to her friends. She was so coolly,
perfectly modulated all through that even now she could
control any weakness towards hysteria, any relief that
might come to her from an admission of her love that
asked for pity. And within the tidy shell that held it
banded fast, her heart was in such constriction of pain as
she had never thought could be.

She said good-bye among the cool shadows and lilac
scents in the hall. She stood under the great porch to see
the girls mount their bicycles and ride off. On either side
of the porch at Aragon there is a surprise. On either side
there is an alcove for a statue and in each alcove is a life-
size nymph, an exquisite lime-white plaster girl, and the
alcoves are painted cold grey which looks like light blue
against the warm sallow walls of the house. Sylvia standing between them with the door into the hall open behind

her made the third. She looked as set and as unknowable as the two white girls in their blue alcoves.

She was thinking with a persistence more intense than any pain she had known, of his dead body. She saw his body clothed and dead and everything in her hard trim little body and soul was in agony. A pain that had no outlet in any remembrance of real love, its failure or its satisfaction, is an all pervading pain, holding the creature who suffers it in a torture beyond any consoling. Sylvia might have said, " My heart aches. I am cold," and these little words would have spoken their cruel truth taken from the trivial circumstances in which they are used and spoken. " My heart aches, my heart aches, and I am cold." She was quite stiff with cold. She trembled in the chill of the hall and sickened at the scent of the branches of lilac. She could do nothing. She would ask nothing. She was quite powerless for anything but waiting. She thought she would wait here in the hall, then she would hear the first of any news that was brought. Even at such a time Sylvia's orderly nature exerted itself to console her. If she waited in the hall she must have her needlework. She went into the drawing-room to collect it. Frazer was there clearing away the tea.

" Miss Sylvia," he said, " if you'll excuse me saying so they might get the young gentlemen safe yet."

" Frazer ? "

" Yes, Miss. And I'll take a further liberty in suggesting you might ask Miss Grania what she could tell you of Mr. Foley O'Neill's movements this morning. As little as she might know it could dot an ' i ' or cross a ' t ' for those who are looking for the two officers now."

" Frazer, what could Miss Grania know ? "

" Miss Sylvia, there's things going on and I am sorry for them but maybe Miss Grania could explain to yourself what she would be doing with a ferret of O'Neill's and why she set out on one of the boys' cycles in her riding clothes at crack of day this morning, yes, and in her best new jodhpurs too, and left a lie with the Mistress to say she was going fishing. Oh, there's wheels going nicely within wheels, Miss Sylvia, could have the axle of truth through them, mind you, though I don't forget my place in saying this."

Frazer hunched his shoulders like a sick crow, and stooped again to dirty tea-cups and crummy plates.

Sylvia said, "Thank you, Frazer." She stood a moment frozen in quietness and then shot out of the room like a poisoned arrow.

XXVII

POOR GRANIA, poor little lump of passion and grief, tears and despair and exhaustion. What to do? How to save? Who to tell? She was so far removed from Sylvia's dignified frozen acceptance of sorrow. There was no affinity between Grania and those plaster girls. She lay on her bed now sobbing with despair and excitement. What did they think he had done, her love, her dear? What might happen to him before the truth could be proven that he was innocent. Grania was caught between two beliefs. Her belief in Foley and her belief in everything that the British Army stood for. Half of Foley's glamour for her lay in his superficial likeness to the young soldiers who were his friends. He was a super imitation in all but voice, and in the fact that he did, fundamentally from the very roots of himself, and excelled in doing, the things that they more or less accomplished as a skilled pastime. Horses were his living and their life. Then beneath the surface he was tough, reasonable and tough. Not one of the young men Grania and Sylvia knew would have thought of being their lovers. Foley not only thought of this but put his thoughts into practice, and did this in spite of a Catholic upbringing. So he was really tough.

Although she could not know it, it was all this hard rough stuff that appealed to Grania. She was utterly ravished and facinated by her first experience of love, and had the most exaggerated view in the world of her lover's perfections. It is only when girls grow older that they can tolerate the idea of their lovers being imperfect, or in fact admit the idea at all. Grania, sobbing on her bed, great easy tears pouring through her fingers into her pillow, sobbed in a sort of hushed torment of heart that allowed every fear possible to assail her. Her fat arms even were wet with great salty drops. Her hair stuck like wet feathers to her temples. She squeezed her mouth against her pillow because even in her desperation she knew what an awful noise she made when she cried. It was not so long really since the days when she had roared for what she wanted, for this poor fat creature who sobbed with so much abandon was no more than eighteen on this shocking evening.

Grania's bedroom was a dreadful example of girlish taste of the date. There were blue birds swinging in pink rings on the wallpaper. The cretonne curtains were a mass of rich pink roses and frilled white muslin hanging inside them. A great many of the larger, richer blossoms on the curtains had been carefully snipped out and stitched on to the net and lace bedspread, which was laid across a piece of pink sateen on the bed, very pretty indeed. The china on the marble-topped washstand was equally be-rosed and be-ribboned, and the carpet had wreaths of darker roses on its paler ground shade. Here the girlish note might be said to have been struck for what it was worth, and the motif le sport added in emphatic super-structure. One fox mask hung down in ghostly realism, tongue out, lolling low between bright teeth. The relic was hung on a piece of leather, not stuck outwards from a shield of wood, and its place was the centre of the mantelshelf. Underneath the mask was a photograph of Grania (though Grania would have told anybody that it was a photograph of Grania's horse). Grania had been photographed at a meet and just a thought drunk on a glass of sloe gin. She was sitting beautifully and at her

ease with her horse standing just right. Rather long coat,
rather long leathers, rather large hat. All very 1920, and
most enviable and right. She often gazed in wonder at
that picture, and asked herself, " Can this be I ? " She
loved people to look at it, and then she would tell them
about the horse and how he was bred, and where he was
bought, and how good he was. This was not the only
picture on the mantelpiece. It was covered with framed
photographs, with other little unframed snapshots stuck
into their frames. There was no pictures of Foley except
in groups, but Grania had a sheaf of his photographs
locked away in her writing case, which she smoothed and
yearned over a great deal. All this gallery was composed
of sporting groups taken either at race meetings, point-to-
points, or ready to pursue the chase of the fox. And there
were quite a few pictures of Soo looking like a monkey
or a cat or a black satin shoe, but not in the least like a
dog. Not the same person that Grania parceled down in
her rug inside her basket at night. Down she would settle
like a bird in her nest and never stir till morning. No
toe-nailish wanderings through the night with imaginary
desires for a drink of water or an outing. No, Soo kept
her basket until Grania was called in the morning and
then came out of her cosiness like a little black snail out
of a brown shell. No photograph resembled her. She
was too rare. She could not be caught and hung on the
walls like those girl friends framed in black *passe-partout*
round vast white mounts. None of them were friends
that Grania cared much about but at that time photographs were such a habit that she even had one of Sylvia
(Sylvia translated winningly by Lenare) standing on her
chest of drawers. You had photographs. You did not
necessarily look at them. Then there was a small gramophone, from which the record " Whispering " had hardly
been removed this summer. Heavily and bluntly embossed
silver lay about on the dressing-table. Actually, as it was
kept shiningly clean it looked rather rich and nice on the
white spot muslin over pink calico shrouded dressing-table.

All this girlish tricking out of the rather bleak height and tall spare windows of the room gave it the look of a sad twenty-five year old girl who has never had a moment's success but is forever compelled to attend parties in debutantish tulle and taffeta, and Grania sobbing on the bed had joined now the sadness of the room behind all the flutter of muslin and bustle of chintz.,

She had quietened a little when Sylvia came in, and the nasty surprise of her coming made her gasp back her sobs, and take her rather dirty shoes off the net and roses of her bedspread.

Sylvia locked the door and put the key in the pocket of her jersey before she sat down in a little basket work arm-chair. She sat neatly and prettily because that was the way she would have sat even if she was being electrocuted. It was not in her to sit in any other way. A bird cannot look anything but tidy on its nest, no matter what deathly fears are shattering its heart.

" Grania," she said, " you were out riding with Foley O'Neill this morning, weren't you ? "

" Mind your own business."

" Exactly what I'm doing."

" Actually I haven't seen him for days."

" Oh, why bother to tell lies. You told us you were riding a school with him."

" Shut up, and get out."

" I'll do both as soon as you tell me anything you know about Foley's movements this morning."

" Why should I ? Why should I be cross-questioned by you ? What has it got to do with you what I do ? "

" My dear child it's got everything to do with me. Grania, I'm a fool to say it, but do you know what Michael means to me. And even if he meant nothing, don't you realise he'll be killed, he'll be murdered, if he's not dead now. Grania, you've got to say anything you know. The littlest thing might be the very link they need, don't you see that ? "

Grania flung herself on her pillow again.

"You always want to torment me. You're only trying to make me frightened. How dare you think Foley had anything to do with it? How dare you? You don't know a thing about him, and if you dare to think such a thing about him, you shouldn't say such a thing about him, so there! Do you think I'll tell you a thing?"

"Oh, don't be so gabbling and hysterical. Obviously you know more than you'll say. Don't you?"

"I'm a spy and a rebel, I suppose."

"Is Foley? That's the question, is Foley?"

"I know you'd like to think so, wouldn't you? You'd like to get me to say so, wouldn't you?"

"Is he?"

"Wouldn't you?"

"What are you hiding? What are you lying about?"

"I haven't got a thing to hide."

"Then why did you tell mother you were going fishing this morning when you were going out schooling with Foley?"

"I didn't intend to go till the last minute."

"Oh, nonsense. Don't be silly. You must have known there'd be a horse for you to ride."

"We're not all as bright as you are."

"Oh, Grania, don't be such an obstinate baby."

"Leave me alone, get out of my room, who asked you in here?"

"You can't answer a question, not the simplest question, can you?"

"I'll kill you."

"Why did you tell lies about schooling with Foley, and now that I know you were with him why won't you say where you went?"

"Because I won't."

"I'm arguing with you as if you were a child while Michael and Tony are nearer death every minute, if they aren't dead now. Don't you realise what you're doing? Can't you take it in, or what is it? Grania, does Foley mean anything to you more than one of our own friends?

" They are your friends, not my friends."

" They're surely more your friends than Foley O'Neill.
My dear Grania, you can't call him a friend of yours,
can you ? Nice as he is and all that, but he doesn't quite
come up to that standard does he ? "

" He's my friend, and if you're such a cad as to talk
like that about him, shut up about him, Do you hear me?
Shut up about him."

" Now you're going on like a poor class housemaid.
He's your boy, I suppose. Do you meet him on your
Sunday afternoon's off ? It must be a terrible strain
getting in by eight o'clock with such a fascinator. What
do you talk about when horses are finished ? The Irish
Republic, I suppose, and who's going to get shot from
behind a ditch next. And which of the brave boys will
do the job. Don't you see what you're stepping into,
mixing yourself up with people like Foley ? "

Grania had grown rather white while Sylvia was
talking. Her eyes looked strained and the tears were
lying in faint white rivers on her cheeks. Little pieces of
her hair were crisp with salt like seaweed dried in the sun.
She sat up on the edge of the bed. Soo sat up beside her
looking horrified and worried. Her tiny black sphinx face
regarding chaos with emotion for once. Sadly enough
there was a sort of desperate calm setting itself through
Grania. A maturity was coming quickly through her
tearful obstinacy and childish pigheadedness. A child was
drowning in strange waters—a child was passing. Poor
Grania ! She was not missish and well-grounded in the
fine joys of girlishness. She was dirty and passionate and
generous. She was greedy and had only begun to live.
She had not grown steady, learnt to fear danger, or
settled to any soberness in life. She wanted danger from
horses, and hardship any way she could get it. There was
something between her and river water, and the blood
of rabbits she shot, and the feel of wind in her bleached
untidy hair, and the feel of running, and the new-found
sight of something wild—an otter blowing out its cheeks

on a little shaley river beach, dark beneath alders—there was something between her and these things which made her strong. She knew she could never have enough of the salty earth. Her strong fat body could stand up to its pains and hardships, to cold hours of waiting, and hours of working, and long speechless times of idle silence. She had gathered her strength in these ways, and Sylvia's decorous probing and gibing did no more than pick the surface of her determination.

Now she said :

" I haven't got anything to tell and I'm not going to tell it."

" It will be very pleasant if they send up here from the Barracks to question you."

" They can't connect me with something I'm not connected with."

" They can and will if they know you were out with Foley this morning."

" All right. I don't mind."

" Are you going to say what you know ? "

" I don't know anything."

Sylvia got up and went out.

Grania went to her window and looked out of it. Up to the flowing slope of the pleasure grounds. It was seven o'clock and the light was still strong and full on the new yellow ribbon-green of leaves, the cherry blossoms glared like snow in Switzerland, the birds sang like awful choirs of children. There was no proper melancholy in the evening. To-night Grania forgot that peace had ever belonged to a spring evening. She was torn and torn again with anxious uncertain previsions, and outside the world was brightly and harshly divided from all her fears.

XXVIII

MRS. FOX came fluttering into her room. A tap, so soft it was like the brush of a frightened bird's wing on a glass pane, and she came in on top of it in her gentle headlong way, before there was a possibility of denial.

The vague serene face was crumpled and quartered in anxiety and disturbance. The grey little feathers of hair were raised and disturbed like those of a shocked hen. She affected deliberation to give herself a moment's pause, shutting the door softly and securely, her hand dwelling on the china knob as if to assure herself that they were alone.

" Grania, my child, my darling child, what do I hear ? "

" Some lying twaddle of Sylvia's, I suppose."

" Oh, my little girl, I am so glad you can assure your mother it's all a mistake. It is, darling, I know it is, just a ghastly mistake. Oh, poor Sylvia, poor pet, she's in such a state ! One understands. One has to forgive her, poor sweet, hasn't one, doesn't one ? "

" What did she tell you, mother ? "

" Oh, darling, I didn't believe her until I asked you, but she told me you were going about with Foley, Nan's son, Foley. She said you'd rather Michael and Tony were shot than say where Foley was this morning. Now, can that be possible, Sylvia, I said. Be careful what you say about the poor child, the poor lamb, my poor baby. It's not true, is it darling ? Of course not."

" It is true, mother. I did ride with Foley, why not ? Why shouldn't I ? I wanted to try the pony."

" Oh, darling, is that all ? From what Sylvia said mother didn't know what to think. But if that's all, it's all right. You've only got to say where you were, dear, it's too simple, and every one will understand. You just went to try the pony. Nothing could be simpler. Though, another time, Grania, let mother know before you do a thing like that. You are a big girl now, you know, and people start talking so dreadfully quickly if a girl gets too—too—well, you know. However, darling, I don't mind this time, as it's rather lucky really, you can come down to the Barracks with me and tell the Colonel just where Foley was when you saw him last—anything that might give him a hint that would be helpful. Sometimes just a word, you know, will prove something, and I'll tell Colonel James it's quite confidential."

The gulf between love and death and danger, and this patter of drawing-room values, left Grania somewhere in mid-air, stranded in a coldness of reality which frightened her. Her mother's free gabble of relief when her suspicion of Grania's intimacy with Foley lulled itself, was much greater than her anxiety over the other part of the situation. And her assumption that Grania would be too ready to betray anything she might know about his movements was hinged to the relief in her mind that his fate would have no importance to Grania. Vaguely, Grania realised that soon she would find herself in much more cruel difficulties. She sat on the edge of her bed, staring out of the window, chin up and swallowing tears desperately.

" I'm not going to say anything to any one about Foley. Why should I ? "

" But, Grania, my poor child, even if he's innocent you are associating yourself with him by this silence. Think what you are doing—a Fox siding with a rebel ! You've got to say something. It looks better."

" Mother ! "

" Well, it's the truth," Mrs. Fox said a little sulkily ; she had not quite meant that phrase, " it looks better," to get beyond her mind's keeping. But it had slipped from her unawares now, and even Mrs. Fox could see what a buttressed platform it would give to Grania's obstinacy. What childish mind could fail to grasp such an opportunity for heroism. Such phrases are spoken by their elders only to seal past all undoing the lips of their

young. "It looks better." Could any words be framed
that might put the matter on a lower footing? They are
dreadful little words taken in the slightest context, but
here with life and death to weigh against them they were
fatal—they put something like a flaming sword into
Grania's hand—an awkward weapon, and dangerous at
an age when one thinks only in extremes.

"You want me to make a statement about Foley's
movements as far as I know them this morning? So that
if possible he is accused of Michael and Tony's deaths.
Mother, do you know what you mean? I'm to do this
so that no one thinks Foley and I are in—are anything
to each other. That's what you mean. Isn't it, mother?"

"I should not dream of going so far as to suggest, or
let anybody dare to think that you could have any
interest in poor Foley, my dear." Oh, the dry, cold
retirement in the voice of an embarrassed elder. The
power to harm, the dangerous power to estrange for the
rest of human time together, and done so entirely for the
best of motives. Power used unkindly only to save, to
keep a child from disaster. Power used without brain,
blindly, clumsily, from motives of terrible excellence.
There is no pity in heaven and none in earth for the
tragic holders of such power. They are condemned to
lose so soon what they love and chasten, and chasten only
from their too much loving.

"Wouldn't you dream of it? Why not? Wouldn't
you dream of it? I'm going to tell you I love Foley. I
love him, and I'll never love any one else, so now. So
there. So now, it's true, it's true." She fell on her pillow
sobbing again. Tearing childish howls that seemed to
come from her extreme centre of emotion, deep ugly
crying.

Mrs. Fox was frightened, there was nothing in her to
meet such a situation, such an outburst, from reality.
Suddenly in an hour her happy fluttering sighing way of
life had been disrupted. Importances beyond the success
of her flowers and her games of bridge and gossips with

Nan at bed-time and new kinds of biscuits were suddenly thrust on her and she had no way to meet them. No familiar procedure to trust in and follow. She knew no course to take. She was lost indeed.

" My child, my poor little Grania, has he been making love to you ? Oh, dear, what would Nan think ? Nan's own son to do such a thing. Oh, Grania, and what have you been thinking of ? A, a person like that, what can anybody nice think of you if this gets known ? Oh, you don't know what you've done, you're young, but it's a deeply terrible shocking thing, my child, to let a man like that touch you, and of course if anybody gets to know you have let him then it's too dreadful, it's too dreadful then. Oh, Grania, for all our sakes, if not for your own sake, you must do the right thing now."

" Well, I won't," Grania broke off her crying to say this, and went on to it again with more lusty agony than before.

" Grania, you'll disgrace yourself. You'll disgrace us all."

Such little words. Little wooden words, tapping like weak hammers against a wall of impenetrable passion and unreason.

Mrs. Fox waited. She could not yet believe in this rebellion or take in all the confession implied. There would come a break and Grania would yield.

" Well, my child ? " she said at last.

" Well, what ? "

" Are you coming with me. It's very painful for me too, you must remember."

" You ? What do you care ? You don't know a thing, or you wouldn't torment me like this."

" I wonder if Nan would be able to make you see sense."

" You're not going to tell Nan ? You're not going to be so cruel ? "

" After all, she must hear sometime."

" Why need she ? No one need if you'll let me alone."

Mrs. Fox rose resolutely to her feet and went to the door. Grania flounced up off her bed and rushed across the room. Confusion and despair were in her. She was in a place of nowhere and all were her enemies. At least she would get Nan on her side before she was set and poisoned against her.

" I'll tell Nan myself." She passed her mother and ran down the passage. A ship, a fatal ship, flying before the storm, she ran down the corridor, above the well of the staircase, past the tall doorways and the frigid plaques and mouldings and garlands between them. She bowed her poor head, she squeezed her fat young hands together. She had no helper. Soo, a black little wild pig, pursued, forgotten, desolate but attentive, till the stars should change and her moment of love come again.

XXIX

WHEN she got to the nursery Aunt Gipsy was settling her hat at the glass over the mantelpiece, preparatory for departure.

"——, well," she said to me, Nan. " No, of course it's not every one could wear that colour, Mrs. Bohane, but—— Oh, Miss Grania, child, what is it ? " Nan came forward like a tower, like a cave of refuge from the other room

" I know Miss Grania's upset for my sake." She surrounded her in an invaluable protection, she built a wall about her in a moment's time " Gipsy, dear, I think maybe I'll follow you a bit later to Mountain Brig. You start away now, and I'm sure Mrs Fox will send me in the car. Good-bye now, Gipsy, I'll be after you. You know your way down to the side door ? Good-bye." Gipsy was pushed out of the room. The door was closed behind her.

" Now, child, now lamb, here's Nannie's poor baby. I know you're upset child. Tell us all about it now, and you and I will find a way out. Never fear but you and I will scheme out something. God help you it's a drink you want to pull you together. A glass of Miss Pigeon's port wine and Nan will have one too for company."

What is there about a cupboard, a high cupboard leaning backwards a little into its corner ? It seems as though privacies have wings that smell of jam and apples and flutter out a little way when the smoothed key turns and the door opens. For a fleeting second Grania was back in littleness again as Nan stood, Queen before her cupboard, reaching up strongly to take the bottle from its high shelf. Once it had been sugar biscuits on that shelf, now it was port. Nan produced the needful on all occasions, it was there beneath her hand and without effort, she was the truest and strongest person ever known. She was the core of life itself.

The two wine glasses were set down on the cloth and filled ceremoniously, unhurriedly, as if there was all time for a drink and a discussion. The effect was calming and widening to the mind. It made stranded objects float again as though a tide lifted them. This busyness with bottle and cupboard was far more effective than the drink itself. Nan took off her blue hat too and ran her fingers through her stiff grey waves and sat back in a low chair near Grania's.

" Now, Miss Grania, drink that up and have another. That's right dear, now don't you feel different ? I do myself, it's been a shock to me too, yes, of course, to hear that my poor Foley had got himself into any kind of trouble. It's a mistake of course and everything will be cleared up before to-morrow I don't doubt, but it's a nasty mistake and it gives you a nasty turn as a nasty thing will, my goodness, but we'll get over it and it will get forgotten, child, and you mustn't fret yourself. Though poor Nan is terribly touched, imagine, that you should worry for her, and Foley will be so upset when he hears he had one of the Miss Fox's in tears, child, hush, now, hush birdie, hush."

" Nan, Nan——"

" Yes, dear, yes, tell Nan what it is."

" Oh, Nan, mother says I'm to go to the barracks and tell them where Foley was this morning."

" And how would you know that ? "

" Because I was with him, Nan."

" You were with him, Miss Grania ? "

" Didn't Mrs. Bohane tell you we went schooling ? "

" Well, as it happens, I knew it, dear."

" Well, why shouldn't I ? "

" Why not, indeed ? Foley would be only delighted to be of any use or help to you or Miss Sylvia."

" Oh, Nan, don't talk like that, don't talk as if he was a servant. Don't you understand I love Foley, Nan. I love him terribly."

" In love with my Foley, child ? Love is a big word,

Miss Grania, from you to him. It's a big rock of a word."

" You aren't going to join against us too, Nan ? "

" No, no, God forbid, but tell me everything now, Miss Grania, don't keep anything back or how can I help you, child ? "

" You will help me, Nan, won't you ? "

" Oh, you can trust Nan, can't you ? "

" Oh, Nan, I need somebody to trust, I need somebody."

" Why, dear ? Why ? "

" Nan, don't be angry with Foley, it's just as much my fault. It's more my fault."

" What, Grania, tell me all the trouble dear."

" I'm so frightened I've started a baby, Nan, and what am I to do ? Is there anything we can do Nan ? "

" You—Oh, God above ! "

A look of such desperation broke across Nan's face as was near madness. Was this the end of her sacrifice to the God of Aragon ? Was the high giving of her life to be twisted to nothingness in an hour ? A Fox daughter in vulgar trouble with a servant's child. In just such trouble as the poor country girls who worked in the house had been in with the bad Fox's of all times, and they had been despised and aborted, their babies, dead or dying thrown to the river, unless they were lucky like Nan's own mother and found some man to put shoes on a Fox's pleasure. All these things have happened, all these things were true and strong in the past. They have happened again and again. Cruelty and pain and tears and death had been common mates to childbirth at Aragon. The family and the house had kept their horrid ministers for such times, women like old Anne. There had always been somebody like that old Anne, tolerant, understanding, skilled and merciless.

Nan sat back in her chair biting her lip and considering.

" Oh, Nan, they wouldn't do anything to Foley no matter what he's done if they knew about me would they ? "

"No one must know about this. No one at all. My God to disgrace the house and the family. What are you thinking of? Is it nothing to you that you are a Miss Fox of Aragon?"

Grania felt suddenly intensely more frightened than she had been. The passion in Nan's voice, the fact that she herself had put into words and made real, and a matter to be dealt with, what up to now had been only a fear made a dark frightening grove of the present, a close little wood of fears.

Nan asked her some questions in a coarse brisk way, and though she answered them truthfully Grania suddenly felt guarded and sulky, a way she had never felt with Nan before. She was in a very dark country, she was swayed by fear. She was uncertain and weak. She could not hold on to the only real importance, to Foley's danger, she tried again.

"Nan, it doesn't matter about me, I'm not frightened. It's Foley, Nan, are they going to do anything to Foley? Oh, can't we make a plan? It may be good, it may help if I'm like this, they can't do anything to Foley if they know. You must see he's the only thing that matters."

"No, you're the only thing that matters, Miss Grania."

"You don't mean what you are saying, Nan. Foley your own son. Don't you mind what happens to him? Oh, do help me, do help me. No one will help me."

"God will help us all child."

"What's the use of that?"

"Now, Miss Grania, crying won't help." In the midst of all this terror the phrase from childhood came as clear and unhelpful as it had ever sounded. Crying won't help, nor words, nor wishes, nor passionate rebellion won't help. Tears and cruel despairs are beyond the scope of sensible dealing. Besides, crying does help, and there are happenings which are beyond any sensible dealings, and demand a wild acceptance and extravagance in their treatment.

Grania knew that this was such an hour. She knew that the time for sane consideration was not now. She must race ahead and beat the full tide of disaster that was swelling behind her. She must reach a strange shore and find her feet there and run before the coming waves. Clear childish terror filled her and a true instinct to tell no more. Not a word to any one.

Nan was sitting very still in her chair, thinking and calculating. The glass of port she had poured out for herself stood untouched, deeply smooth and red on the table beside her. She was breathing quickly and Grania was not sure whether she was praying. She did not like the look of Nan at all. All the dear spoiling easiness of contact with her was gone. Nan had become in a moment a coarse strong person who would fight you and defeat you on all counts unless you cheated her, unless perhaps you gave in and agreed. Nan to whom she had gone for help in her despair was against her. Nan was going to do things to her. She was thinking far more about this poor baby than she was thinking about Foley or what was likely to happen to Foley. Grania felt sluttish and ashamed about the baby now. Before she had thought of it as a calamity not as a furtive shaming little happening, to be dealt with in furtive and cruel ways. The world had been clouded by fear, but it had been a big and terrifying thunder cloud, a dramatic and shattering fear, and in an hour she had seen how she could turn it to Foley's account. Yes, and keep him through it too, for that idea had not been forgotten in her heroics. Ah, what a word to give to the intense and moving passion of so young and unknowing a creature. Every thought Grania had was real and genuine, real down to her silly young bones, untainted by the cynical mistrust with which age and experience and a better wit might have tortured itself.

Nan was still thinking, she sat quietly pulling down her upper lip, and then letting it go again, and catching severely at her lower lip with her teeth, or pulling in her cheeks and biting at their insides as she reviewed the problems of the hour and the possibilities of their solving.

At last she got up saying briskly, with rather an affected matter of factness :

" Well, I must get to the chemist before he shuts and then I'll fix you up all right, dear. Oh, it's quite simple, you just leave it to Nan. Thank goodness you came to me at the very right moment. Your troubles will soon be over, dear, and no more bother to any one. But wait till I see Foley, just let Foley wait till he sees me. I'll go to Mountain Brig and hear what I can hear from Micky before I go near the barracks. Mickey's a good boy and a sensible boy, yes, I'll go and see Mickey. I might not get back till later, now so don't go and do anything foolish till I get back, and then we'll see."

" What shall we see, Nan ? Foley dead and me having an abortion ? "

" Miss Grania, what a word for a lady to use."

" You'd do it, Nan, but you wouldn't say it. It's true. That's what you want to do to me, but I'm not going to let you, do you understand Nan ? I won't touch any of your medicine. I won't let you touch me. Do you think I'm a child that I don't know what you want to do to me ? You're not going to do it to me, you don't know about anything that matters."

" You're not yourself, dear. How could you be, poor child." Nan's tone was professionally soothing and equally infuriating to Grania.

" I am myself. I know what I've done, and I know what I'm going to do. I'm——"

The door opened and Miss Pigeon came gently in.

" I'm in good time for bed aren't I, Nan ? " she asked anxiously.

" Yes, indeed, Miss Pigeon." Nan went over and shut the door quietly behind her.

" Yes, indeed. I'll just go in and turn your bed down. Perhaps you would manage to get yourself to bed to-night, Miss, and I'll excuse your hair brushing and prayers." She went into the other room without any hurry and quietly slipped the bolt over into it's socket as she closed the door between her old nurseries, dividing the day from the night.

"Well, Grania," Aunt Pidgie said, "you've been crying, you shouldn't cry you know, it's no use. I found that out a long time ago. Nobody knows and nobody minds, not a bit."

Grania got up and kissed Aunt Pidgie a little patronisingly as one did. Her troubles were so little and unreal.

"Good night, Aunt Pidgie, dear. I must go. You'll have supper soon, won't you?"

"Perhaps I shall, perhaps I shan't."

"Oh, of course you will." Grania turned the door handle.

"It's locked," Aunt Pidgie said.

"I saw her lock it."

Grania did not answer. She flew across to the dividing door.

"It's bolted," Aunt Pidgie said, "I heard her bolt it."

"But we're locked in," Grania said stupidly, and then in a risen voice again, "we're locked in."

"Oh, that's nothing," Aunt Pidgie sat down and began to take her boots off. "Wait till you've been locked in on a dark night in December, and no supper, and no hot bottle and no fire and then you'll know it."

"Aunt Pidgie, you oughtn't to say such things."

"Well now, she's got you too, so you may as well know what's in store, my dear. Aunt Pidgie can tell you a thing or two." Aunt Pidgie peered into one of the boots she had taken off in a very knowing way before she set it down beside its fellow. "And a nice pair you are," she said, looking at them vindictively. She raised her head and shook it at Grania. "Ah, it's no good struggling with that door. It's no good calling out. No one can hear you in the nursery. Believe me, no one can hear what goes on in the nursery."

Grania suddenly felt herself to be in a very strange and awful little world, a complete and finished world of small fears and great loneliness, Aunt Pidgie's world.

Aunt Pidgie's accepted world. Suddenly, through all her own storm of trouble, it came to her that the fears might not be so very small, that the terror was perhaps as great as the loneliness.

What happens when crying stops? A sort of dreadful clarity, a seeing power is born for a minute's life. A life as brief as the ease that follows tears and the anæsthesia of tears. Grania looked at Aunt Pidgie and saw how thin and pale Aunt Pidgie was and wondered if there was any reason for it. Could it be connected with the coarseness and hardness which she had never seen in Nan before this evening? She looked at Aunt Pidgie's boots and at Aunt Pidgie's tiny flat feet set side by side in their thin black cotton stockings, they were as thin and dark as little fins and an extraordinary feeling came to her that she would like to sit down and pick up Aunt Pidgie's poor little narrow feet and hold them in her hands as if they were Soo's feet or a baby's feet.

" Come away from the door, dear." Aunt Pidgie spoke like one old lag to another, telling the ins and outs of a prison familiar to her. " Come away from the door," she beckoned. " Come here, come, dear."

Grania went over, " Nearer, where's your ear, child ? " In a whisper Aunt Pidgie shouted, so that her breath was red-hot in Grania's ear, " *Don't say anything yet, she's sure to be listening. She'd like to catch us out and punish us. Don't give her the chance.*"

Grania whispered back, " All right, I won't."

Then she had an idea. She went to the cupboard and reached high for Nan's bottle of port. Nan had not touched the glass she had poured out for herself. It still stood on the table—egg-shaped, ruby, smooth and intoxicating.

" Have some," Grania whispered, holding it out towards Aunt Pidgie. Aunt Pidgie had. She raised her glass and looked through wine to the window and freedom.

" May she die," she said suddenly. Grania's expression must have shown some silly christian demur, because Aunt

Pidgie raised her glass again, "Yes, and rot," she amended. She tossed back the wine and licked her old warm lips. It seemed to Grania that she saw an undreamed of Aunt Pidgie. An Aunt Pidgie who had been young and devilish and known such weakness of passion as Grania knew, such helplessness, ah, but never known the joy of yielding. And all her daring now was to match a blue bow with eyes no longer blue at all.

Grania refilled Aunt Pidgie's glass and then her own. Between tears and port she was already rather intoxicated.

"I'll drink to my love," she spoke grandly. Then, feeling rather silly, she caught Soo up and said, "Then we'll drink to Soo. Won't we drink to the Sweetie then?"

What an evening! Foley in danger of death. Sylvia's man dead by now most likely. Lying on his back in the dark young heather. Nan gone like an evil old power to wheedle aborting drugs from some good little Catholic chemist, and herself locked in the nursery and getting drunk with Aunt Pidgie, where the evening sun missed the windows, and the rocking-horse, emblem of childhood's jolly hours, wore a bored and vindictive air, a long coffin-headed look, a curling grin, as he pranced timelessly on his rockers.

After the third glass of port went down, Grania slid to the floor beside Aunt Pidgie and picked up one of the mole-like little feet.

"Oo," said Aunt Pidgie, "Oo, oo, that's my bad foot."

"What's the matter with it, Aunt Pidgie?"

"She says it is nonsense. But I say it's a nail in my boot."

"Is there a nail in your boot?"

"There's always a nail in my boot. There's been a nail in my boot for as long as I can remember."

Grania picked up the boots, the kind a boy of ten might wear to go to the national school. She slid her narrow, fat, spoiled hand down and along, exploring with cushioned fingers.

" Oh, Aunt Pidgie, it's a dagger." She took her hand
out slowly. " Do you know what we'll do, Aunt Pidgie ? "

Aunt Pidgie took a sip of port. " No, What ? "

" We'll burn these boots."

" And while you're at it you may as well pop my last
winter's combinations on the fire, too, dear. They're like
sitting in a gorse bush. Really they are."

" Where are they ? "

" Second long drawer."

Grania made her blaze, and they giggled together and
put on some wood to make the boots burn better. Grania's
cheeks were glowing and her head singing. Matters
seemed less desperate than they had done an hour ago.
Still, she could not lose sight of their urgency.

" Do you think we'd better shout for somebody to come
and let us out ? She must have gone by now."

" Don't shout for anybody." Aunt Pidgie began
fumbling and rumbling about in her pocket hole. " Don't
shout for anybody at all. Wait and see what I've got in
my sporran. Now, what do you think of that ? " She
produced a key and pointed it triumphantly towards the
door. " I've kept this key for two years," she said, " and
she never knew I had it. Fancy that."

" Does it fit the lock, Aunt Pidgie ? " You have to
remember that a key was a key to Aunt Pidgie, and any
key might serve as an emblem for opening locks that she
would never dare to put it in.

" Does it fit ? Of course it does. Why, what do you
think I'd do the times I have to get out to meet my
Diblins ? What about the nights there's leprosy in my
bed, and I have to make a nest up the stairs ? What about
the nights when I'm a Birdie ? What do you think I'd
do then if I can't let myself out for a fly when she's
locked the door and gone away ? "

" What *do* you do, Aunt Pidgie ? "

" Oh, dear, I stay in my bed," Aunt Pidgie's eyes
filled with tears—" but I *could* get out, I could get out."
It was like a child beating its fists.

Grania stretched up an arm and took one of Aunt Pidgie's hands.

" What would she do to you if you did get out, Aunt Pidgie ? What would happen if she found out ? "

" Oh, nothing, nothing, nothing. She's always so kind to me, my dear, so thoughtful, so careful." The desperate twittering words came as a little dam to block the truth that Aunt Pidgie had let flow. Again a dismayed child's hands against a loosed force of water.

Grania said, " Well, I won't tell her anything you've told me, if you won't tell anything about me."

" Oh, I won't tell. I'm a cagey birdie, I'm mum."

" What do you hate most, Aunt Pidgie ? "

" Cold water on my back. Castor oil. My boots. No supper days. No hot bottle nights."

Grania stared at her. She had seen enough to open up a perfectly horrid little vista of neglects and tortures.

" But what do you like best ? "

" My Diblins. Hot bacon. Frazer. My warm bed. My sporran. Wednesday."

" Wednesday ? "

" I see the Sunday papers on Wednesday, when they've finished with them in the servant's hall."

" Oh, Aunt Pidgie ! "

" It's very nice. There's a very good serial running in the *Graphic* just now—a real good crimer. Frazer reads it too. Then there are the beauty notes. Very good too, very helpful, I find. My face would have been lined long ago but for them. You should read them, dear. And the delicious recipes for food. If you are ever thinking of getting married, Grania, be sure you have a cook who can do a nice steak and mushrooms. That and a bottle of red wine, and then a little bit of Camembert. Yes, and a good bacon and eggs is as nice as anything else."

" I will, Aunt Pidgie, I will, and you can come and live with us and have it every day for lunch," Grania promised with generous abandon.

" Ah, no, dear," Aunt Pidgie sighed, " she'd never let
me. I couldn't expect it. And then I wouldn't have the
right clothes. And how could I leave my Diblins, I ask
you ? "

" You could leave messages for your Diblins in all their
places, and they could follow after you."

" Then there's T. Runk."

" T. who ? "

" T. Runk, the God of Travel who lives in the attics
with the empty suit cases."

" But he'd come too. A journey is just his affair, Aunt
Pidgie. You couldn't start without him."

" I'd like to go to a little house by the sea, and grow
big juicy pink dhalias in the garden, and have fried fish
for my supper."

" Would you like a pebble pattern on the gate posts,
Aunt Pidgie ? "

" Yes, I would, and two glass balls, two great big
balls."

" And you could always wear sandshoes."

" And I would feed the seagulls ? "

" Of course."

" Oh, Grania, I'd promise truly never, never to rob a
birdie's nest again. Oh, I do hate to do it. But I have to,
you know. Sometimes it's got to be done."

" Why, Aunt Pidgie ? "

" Oh, my dear, I do get such a pain sometimes. She
says it's only wind, but when I get a little more to eat,
it goes away and I can get to sleep."

" Are you hungry now ? "

" No, I had a big slice of cake for my tea."

" Well, we might have some more." Grania went to
the cupboard.

" Well, why not, we've burned our boots, haven't we ? "
Aunt Pidgie hazarded this as a joke. She said it in a
" Have you heard this one " sort of voice, and planted
her little stockinged feet firmly before her on the hearth-
rug. " Hurrah," she said suddenly, " Hip Hip, Hurrah ! "

"You and I are mates, Aunt Pidgie. Have another glass with your cake."

"I certainly will," Aunt Pidgie sipped and put back her head and shut up her eyes after each mouthful.

"Why are you doing that, Aunt Pidgie?" Grania asked.

"I'm a Birdie. I'm a real Birdie."

Then Grania realised that she had made Aunt Pidgie exceedingly drunk.

"You're not really a Birdie, you're Aunt Pidgie. Aren't you, Aunt Pidgie?"

"Twee, Twee - Twee - Twee - Twee," Aunt Pidgie answered.

"And I'm none too sober myself," Grania reflected hazily. She ate a large slice of cake and watched Aunt Pidgie dipping her beak in the wineglass and throwing back her head to drink. What was she to do with her? Intoxicated and alone among the burned boots and combinations and empty bottles and sacked cupboards, retribution might fall heavily on Aunt Pidgie when Nan returned and Grania would not be there to stave it off. Full of wine and courage now, she was determined to be far away from Aragon before Nan came back to her kingdom.

XXX

" IT WAS the little dog, Mrs. O'Neill, they were on the look out for, and it was that made a fixture of Mr. Foley's arrest. I believe, whatever connection they had between all." Micky Brown and Nan were talking in the saddle-room at Mountain Brig. Micky was doing up his tack as if nothing had happened during the day, and as he talked to Nan he worked up and down the length of an unbuckled rein with a piece of soapy sponge.

Nan seemed as much at home with Micky in the saddle-room as she was in her own nursery. She had a way of going to the core of things that made her easy anywhere and in any circumstances. She was sitting on a backless wooden chair with the window behind her, and as she talked to Micky it ran through her mind how much she and Foley had spent doing up this saddle-room—the nice panelling, the stove, the big window, the rows of fixtures for saddles and bridles, all good, and plenty of room for everything. The whole room was an expression of Nan's fundamental concern with real things. Although she had no knowledge of horses she had an understanding of work concerning them, and she knew the value to the eye of a well-appointed, well-kept saddle room. She would have none of those dark, cramped damp little holes, with ill-kept tack hanging on nails and broken pegs, and never sufficient space to put anything away, nor light enough to see if leather was clean or dirty. Nan and Foley spared and skimped nothing on the stabling at Mountain Brig. And she had been right—how right she had been. The good ample air of the yard, the light roomy boxes had a psychological effect on many a buyer. They paid more than they meant to for bad horses as well as good in that atmosphere of space and plenty and cleanliness. Even the roses on the walls outside had a trimmed up, clipped-out sort of look about them. And Nan had made all this from a dirty mountain farm, a yard where, when she first came there, they laid chopped furze from the kitchen door all across the yard in winter time, so that you could walk over the slush and carts could travel their loads without going deep into the ground. And here Nan had bred a son like Foley, handsome and hardy, from her union with a consumptive mountain farmer with little education or ability. It was all Nan's work, and done as it were with one hand while her heart beat and her whole being lived for Aragon alone.

"A dog, Micky," she said. "What dog?"

Micky went on with his account.

"Well, I should say, a bitch, Mrs. O'Neill. A little smoothy white terrier with one tan ear and a lot of old foxbites on her. Oh, a proper little article and as wicked as a bee."

"One tan ear, you said, Micky?"

"Yes, missus."

"Did you ever see her before to remember her?"

"Well, I wouldn't say it to one only yourself, but I did."

"Where, Micky?"

"With Captain Purvis."

"Did you know she was here to-day?"

"I did not. Mr. Foley had her snuggled down in the little potato house. It was when she heard the other gentlemen talking that she gave tongue, you bet."

"Ah." When Nan said "Ah," she breathed deeply outwards, and it was as if she expelled all that was bad and untrue from her and left room for facts, and power to work on them. Room for her strength to grasp and turn things to her liking. She was like a tree; you knew that her unseen roots had more than the spread and strength of branches.

"That's enough," she said at last. "He knows more than he should know. He's deeper into this business than I like, deeper far. Micky, I'm afraid the young boss is in an ugly spot."

"The young boss"—they had not called Foley that since he was twelve years old. It seemed as though because he was in trouble Nan thought of him in a past tense of youth and helplessness. She was both angry and deeply concerned.

"Micky," she said, "do you know any more? For God's sake if you do, boy, let me in on it now. To-morrow might be too late for all concerned."

Micky said, "I went through the car after they took the boss off."

"What did you find?"

"Under the seat in the back there was an old envelope with Captain Purvis' name on it and Askemore Caves scraped on it with the nail of a person's hand-like."

"They were in the car so?"

"They were in the car so."

"My God above, he had a bigger hand in this than I thought."

"Or I, Missus."

Nan thought for a time. "Micky, child," she said gently at last, "would I chance going out to the caves myself and see what I'd see."

"Merciful heaven, Mrs. O'Neill, what good would you do?"

"I wouldn't say that till I'd get there."

"You're late to help them."

"It's early to say that till I get there."

"Then what do you think they did with them all day?"

"They might wait till evening when no one would be around."

Neither Nan nor Micky would say the words shoot or execute. Nan said: "If anything happens them, it might go badly with Foley."

Micky said, "Do you think the boys would give a curse what happened Mr. Foley? When their job is done, they're off, and that's the holy all about it. Don't meddle with them, Missus, you'll do no good."

"Ah," Nan said again, breathing and thinking, "maybe so. Maybe not. I'll see you again, Micky," she said, getting up. "I must go and have a look at the poor child within. She got a terrible knocking about. Is the horse anything the worse of it?"

"He hit himself a bit of a belt, but it is a thing of nothing. He's hardly lame on it."

"That's good, I'm glad to hear that." She spoke with much satisfaction as if there was nothing else left to trouble about. So she could detach matters and consider them separately. Now it was Doatie's turn. She got up and shook out her skirt before walking over the yard towards the house, her eye alert for any change or disorder and her tongue ready to comment tartly or to praise. Nan did not live in the present minute so much as in the present second.

Gipsy met her in the kitchen. She would not have thought of going across the yard to speak to Nan. The yard was not her province and she was a one for the conventions no matter what happened. The conventions and a nice new hat and you were all right. Now she had a cup of tea ready. A cup of tea was always right, it was always the thing. And a nice bit of sliced bread and fresh butter. It was not as much as two hours since they had had tea at Aragon. But then it had been a very up-setting sort of day and you couldn't go far wrong with a cup of tea.

"How nice, Gipsy," Nan said while her eye swept the kitchen. A warm heavy smell came from a pot of potatoes boiling for the chickens. Nan appreciated it at its good worth. She stood for a moment as Grania had stood in the morning light, but in no such transparent stillness of speculation and hope. And the evening light was deeper and heavier against the white walls, sinking sullenly into their thickness, melting towards darkness in the breadth of the open fireplace, waiting for the day's end. Grania had stood and trembled for the future, to-night the struggle of past years surged to Nan's memory, years past with all the old harshness unforgotten. There was nothing pretty to remember about these years she had spent here and away from Aragon. In these years she had pulled the place little by little and one thing after another from its unkept ragged status of mountain farm, from its chill and snivelling and unnecessary state of weakness and dirtiness, disorder and seeming poverty, to the tidy sound affair it was now. One thing after another she had managed and arranged and kept going—the chickens out of the kitchen, that had been her first battle when she came here from the state and luxury of Aragon. After that the stream which, in winter time, spread over the yard, a boggy and desolate lake where there was a hollow to hold water, and an endless sluice of dirty water-courses where steep channels could carry it away. Nan's mind went back to age-long tiresome arguments with her delicate thriftless husband. He had never said " no " to any scheme of hers, but he had never put forward hand or foot to help in its accomplishment. Next week, it had always been, or, when the turnips are thinned, or, when the corn is carried, the dung spread. Nan had found this uncertain obstructionism exhausting and hateful, but she met and defeated it with unfailing cheerful will and strength. She would look at the delicate man and tell herself to a nicety how soon he would be dead. She was very good to him because she saw an end to it . . . then there had been the complacent satisfaction of the years when Foley grew up, herself over again for strength and good tidy living, they could put their heads together, they could work out schemes and see things in a definite orderly outline as they would be next year or next week. Foley had been in every way the son she had wanted, bred to her own mind and liking, inheriting her own breadth and virility of mind and body, her own looks and strong ability and charm of manner. Foley had had all she could give him, and made very good use of it until now.

Nan had not stood half a minute in the kitchen, yet the whole consciousness of the situation past and present had flowed through her mind. The sense of things past is never so serenely, cruelly sure as when one returns to a place once more familiar than old sheets at a week's end, returns with a changed mind, with trouble at heart and no clear plan for the near future. Nan stood in the sad remembered evening light and wondered suddenly how it was that she had lived through the first long light springtime of her marriage.

" Well," she said, turning from the doorway, with a firm nurse's smile fixed on her face, " may I go up and see poor Doatie ? "

" Oh, certainly, Nan, certainly, and oh, when I think, you could be looking at her in the Habit (and I was looking at such a nice one for a young girl to-day, Nan, imagine) and the candles lit, and all white flowers, of course, wouldn't it look lovely ? Oh, but I mean things are never so bad but they could be worse, are they ? "

" Gipsy, there are people in this world, and things are *never* bad enough to please them."

Nan walked unhurriedly out of the kitchen with this shot, leaving Gipsy uncertain whether or not to take it as a personal insult, constituting a new breach in the amity so lately re-established. On the whole she was pretty sure she had been insulted again.

Upstairs Nan found Doatie flushed and in pain, vague and sick from concussion one moment, and the next in floods of tears.

" Well, dear, well," she took a hard hot little hand in hers and sat down beside the bed, nodding affably across the world of sickness to the young nurse.

It was characteristic of Foley that he should have succeeded in procuring her presence here despite the changes and chances of his day.

" Well, poor little Doatie-girl. Don't be worrying your head about anything. The horse is all right, the dirty brute, and so will you be soon, love."

" Oh, Aunt Dymphnia, what's happened to Foley? "

" He had to go and see a horse in Kilkenny, dear."

"Oh, no, Aunt Dymphnia. It's something else. Mother won't say but she has the head nodded off herself with mystery and secrets about Foley all day."

"Ah, child, don't trouble yourself, Foley's all right. I do assure you. It's the crack you gave your poor head has you bothered."

"Aunt Dymphnia, I'd like to speak to you, please, if nurse wouldn't mind."

The nurses, old and young, exhanged nods and glances and the young one slipped out of the room.

"What's on your mind, child? Just tell me and don't be talking any more then."

"Is Foley gone off with Miss Grania, Aunt Dymphnia?"

"Is Foley—fiddlesticks! Now, what in God's wide earthly world put such an idea in your head?"

"Are you sure, Aunt Dymphnia? Are you certain?"

"Doatie," said Dymphnia with awful certitude, "Foley will never while he lives go off with Miss Grania. Now do you believe me? I promise it, child."

"Yes, Aunt Dymphnia." Doatie rolled her head deeper into her pillow. The outline of her little body went slack under the blankets, her eyes closed. This dreadful day of fear and grief and pain was yielding towards evening. She believed Aunt Dymphnia. Aunt Dymphnia was never wrong. She was strong and frightening and hard but she was not afraid to tell you the truth. Foley would not go off with Miss Grania. He would come back to her and she would tell him she was afraid. Tell him everything. There would be understanding for her and forgiveness. Doatie worn out with pain dropped into sleep, happy in her belief that life could not change, content as the sick can be looking to that strange future when they shall be well. Then the most ordinary things shall be shining and glamorous and bridges fling themselves between possible and impossible. To-night in the nowhere of sickness Doatie was at peace.

XXXI

NAN had no definite plan in her mind when Micky dropped her on the lonely road with dark mountain rising above it and dark mountain falling below. She knew the way well from here to the Askemore Caves. How many children's picnic parties had she not conducted there in years past. And Nan never forgot the road to any place.

"Thank you for bringing me this far, Micky," she said in her easy voice. She stood in the road looking at Micky's strained frightened face with understanding and respect for his trouble. She was sensible of his danger, although she might not believe it to be so great as he did himself.

"Remember, Micky, if you're asked any questions, it was on my information you brought me here. You don't know anything, mind. Home now as quick as you can. And thank you, child, you're a real good boy, and I'll not forget it to you."

"Mrs. O'Neill, you're doing a terrible foolish thing," Micky said it for the last time, and Nan smiled at him, she was still smiling her nurse's smile when he had turned the car round and driven away.

But when the car had gone out of sight she rested her face from smiling. She stood looking round her with her face in dark unsmiling repose. She looked to left and right of her, to the mountain rising on her right hand to the mouse-soft evening sky, and dropping on her left hand to the depth of a little river before it started its upward slope again.

"A long, lonely road," Nan said to herself. "A long, lonely road and no gate on it. That would give you an idea how lonely it is." Nan's road was the green ghost of an old coach road through the mountains. Part of the stone-built stable where they had changed coach horses still stood up darkly against the stones and heather, its usefulness and importance dead and long forgotten, its reality slowly sucked back into the wildness that it had once broken and disturbed with so much transient bustle.

Perhaps it was part of Nan's inheritance from the Fox's that she should have an instinct for wild places, an eye for a road and a memory for a turning not frequent in women who lead indoor lives ; such a feeling comes either through natural necessity or through generations when the occupations of idle years have bred gentlemanly familiarity with wild places ; shooting grouse in these mountains, hunting in the valleys, and home at night for indoor sports in the bad old house below.

As Nan walked stoutly forward along the faint road, the sound of water was loud below her in the evening. She was not thinking of what she might find or what she might do in a little while. The idea of danger for herself in this unplanned undertaking did not present itself to her at all, and indeed it did not seem as though danger could overtake the bold strong woman in her good navy blue suit and thick pearly silk blouse. Her neat dark blue hat had a little pad of pheasants' feathers tucked inside its ribbon band, and turned up at the back off her coiled neat hair and strong neck. She wore gloves too, yellow chamois gloves with one button, washed soft as velvet by herself. She was no imitation lady, Nan. She was a person to whom, in her own right, order and beauty and an earned and duly valued luxury belonged. Her cruelty belonged to this same streak of luxury. A curious and ugly freak in her soundness and strength. Her ability to dwell on Aragon's beauty was a part of the same. She could feed a strange part of herself as she stood before some portrait of a forebear, some young man with dreamy eyes, lace at his woman's hands, jewels on his fingers, something in her agreed with any excess they had known in their time, agreed with and commended the unknown pleasure.

As Nan walked stoutly along the mountain road her

thoughts were all below at Aragon. When she was away her mind would go back there and pass through stone-pillared gates and walk the avenues or explore the groves. Her mind was often in the groves, beech woods and the blowing air between their stems, and the round bare ground beneath them. Ash groves : women's long round limbs in form of trees, pale images, powerless and rooted in their soft decaying selves, clothed and held in the close dark stink of nettles and briars, chalk-white in such darkness. Fir woods with their close little paths gay and provoking at first to lead you into their own quietness, threatening, unhappy, and still as a tank of water. Her mind was familiar in these places.

Nan knew her way well along this road—picnics at the caves had been one of the regular summer treats of the young at Aragon. Although the last of such picnics was years ago now she could have told which hazel tree in the little thicket round the caves bore the best nuts, where the richest blackberries ripened, and, given a torch to guide herself by, there was not an inch of those rather awful caves through which she would not have remembered the way with bold accuracy. As she walked on towards that place where last she had sat in sun and shelter spreading bramble jelly on buttered scones and colouring the sugared milk in pink mugs with tea (tea for outings and holidays) the mountainy air blew a little colder on Nan's warm healthy cheek. It was always cold, she remembered, round this corner of the mountain. The wind came in cutting draughts down the heather, through the sheep's bent horns, whistle round and sharp. Here she had always said, " Put your coats on," to her children. It was the best part of another mile to the upstanding rocks and the caves beneath from here. Now the roadway bent downhill. Near below five poplars grew in a group planted in a watery hollow. Pencil tall, valley green, they looked as exotic as palms in a Scotch garden. You could see the plains of two counties below. This evening they seemed as shining and as soft as if a green oil was poured

between the distances, softening honey-coloured distances
and puce under a sky of orchid green. The lands below
had no connection with the austerity of the mountain
places where Nan walked. She passed the gap by the
road where water always lay and the children had dabbled
and rattled sticks. A little stream had been led about and
about by queer devices. Up here men's hands alone were
used for all engineering. Awkward ideas were followed out
with pious care, walls built with earnest meticulous
method, stones fitted in as carefully as bones in a fish,
and the method of wall building varied every mile or so
with the inherited ideas of the builder. Mountain sheep
bounced on and off impossible obstacles and made away
into the heather with a rattle of little hoofs. Black cattle
ran along the fence tops as actively and cunningly as dogs.
Short grass came up to meet the heather and dark gorse
with hardly a flower on it grew in patches through the
grass fields beyond, but the nearest farmhouse was a mile
away at least as Nan rounded a shoulder of the hill and
turned off the road on to a less used path that went close
round the mountain foot. Before her now were tall rocks
like pillars, and deep in their faces, five stone steps
leading down to it, was the little iron gate set before the
narrow cave mouth and locked against adventurous
children.

It was only when Nan set foot on the top step that
she knew clearly what she was going to do. She went
down the steps in a gay brisk manner, her between nursery
and bathroom walk, quick and preoccupied, and she
shook the little iron gate in a determined rattle with her
gloved hands.

" Hullo there ! " she called.

" Hullo there ! Just a minute. Just a word with you.
It's important. I'm from friends."

She knew in the hush that followed she had been heard.
She knew it before she heard the tread of boots on broken
steps below. She knew how a whisper would echo down
there, magnified by some trickery of echo, how often on

the picnic afternoons had they played at that game, and now she waited for an answer.

" Put your hands up," a voice came. She saw the white glimmer of a face in the dark below, streaked by the iron bars of the little gate, and up went her hands, the palm flesh coming in comfortable little hills through the buttoned glove opening. She looked faintly absurd standing there facing death with her neat gloved hands flung up against the mountain side. She looked so unlike violent death, that indeed the possibility of such a happening was compelled to retreat before so strong and well-dressed a woman.

" Come along," Nan called as she might have coaxed one of her children, " I'm quite alone and I've got a message for you."

" Who is it ? "

" Who is it ? "

" Foley O'Neill's mother it is."

The bottom of the gate grated on the stone beneath it and a pale young man, masked and with a gun in his hand, stood a moment in the opening before he advanced towards Nan, motioning her back up the steps until they stood on the level together. There she appeared immeasurably greater than he who was young, tired and sick with dread at the thought of that hour of execution when night should fall on the heather.

" You'll find the message in my coat pocket, child," Nan said gently, her hands still above her head. " No, the right-hand pocket," and in the moment when they stood so near she raised her powerful knee and dealt him a low blow like the kick of a horse.

" I learnt that trick off a medical student." Nan stooped down and picked up his gun that had rattled on to the stones as he doubled up in pain. " Take your time, my boy," she said kindly. " I know how this works too, imagine. Sure, you hadn't it cocked at all." She stood there covering him while his pain lessened.

" Now, then," she put the gun to the back of his neck,

" I don't care how many of you is down below, you'll be the first to get an ugly dirty death."

" I mightn't be the last, you bloody old chancer," the boy was crying with pain and exhaustion and rage.

" No rude talk now. Take me in to where you have the prisoners and if we aren't there in five minutes' time, mind, you get the contents of this," she gave him a dreadful poke with the gun, " and I'll find them myself. Believe it or not I know these caves backwards, and you wouldn't spend five minutes getting any place in them. Better now. On please."

She followed him down the crooked flight of stairs that plunged towards darkness Strong and brisk on her feet. His torch flashed out, a thin fan of light. Nan had only one hand to help herself to lean against the sweaty rock walls. Sometimes she had to step from rock to rock with a black depth under her feet " Go slow, boy," she warned him pleasantly, " or the gun might go off on me and we don't want a nasty accident, do we, imagine ! "

Round them the rocks mouthed and gaped their strange formations like growths ; half-known half-guessed stalactites reached down and more awful stalactites reached up. Yellow greasy rocks below mounting bluntly towards rocks that dripped like candle-grease of a thousand years above. Narrow, dark throats of rock opened into huge bellies where echoes played and rattled about together.

These caves had been a favourite resort of picnickers from the time of their discovery in Victorian days when the passages and rock formations had been named with heavy appropriateness The voices of many guides had uttered those names, leaving that place-tamed feeling in the sombre air, domesticating the ugliness, as though it had been painted on a souvenir mug, or a German waterfall, complete with pine trees, dashing its way across a painted china plate. Such is the influence of guides' voices naming for years a pendulous mass : " The Golden Fleece." An upthrust of smooth stone : " The Ladies' Saddle." Or again : " The Monkey's Head," " The

Horses' Teeth," "The Elephant's Foot," and, rather a show-piece, "The Organ."

Nan could name them each as she passed. Her accurate mind going strongly back to the picnic days when the children had stood enthralled by the rock shapes so remarkably true to their names, when they had hopped and floundered on uncertain feet from chamber to chamber, from the House of Commons to the still nastier House of Lords, walking upright where Nan had to bend low under the toothed ceilings, slopping delightfully through puddles fed constantly by the drip from the roof.

Nan called the names out now as she passed the objects by, her voice as easy as though, when this exploration was over, she would sit on a rug in the sun and spread again the butter and bramble jelly on brown scones.

Everything Nan undertook she achieved with the ease of a full river between its banks, even in the course of achievement she moved freely and uncramped, her flowing style in life unimpeded, unlet, unhindered by any circumstance whatsoever. Now Nan scarcely even felt elation when she heard the muted hollow sound of voices in front of them.

"Stop," she whispered to her guide, "and shout out for every man to put his hands up."

"The boys is gone," he answered, "They're out settling a grave. There's only the prisoners and myself here."

"Shut up, and shout out," she ordered sharply. In the dark he felt her poking at him with the gun, an alarming fumble. "I have it now," she grunted easily. "Shout out, child, shout out, or——"

"Hands up, boys, we're surrounded," he screamed into the dark and the echo bounded off the "Ladies' Saddle" and "Seal's Head" and went crashing into the unseen domes of the House of Lords.

A faint cheer (which would not have disgraced one of R. M. Ballantyne's own heroes) answered this announcement.

" Ah," said Nan. " In the Chamber of Horrors, are they ? Isn't that very good ? Now I might as well get you out of my way, mightn't I ? But I won't, child. Be good now and you'll be all right."

The two boys were sitting quietly on two stalactites, rather like picnickers of old, except that their hands and feet were tied. They were not gagged, as their captors were undramatic and rather sympathetic men, who had no wish to make this short imprisonment more tiresome and incommodious than necessary. They would gladly have played cards with their prisoners or done any little thing to while away time before nightfall and execution, but they had to get the graves dug.

" Good-evening, Captain Purvis. Good-evening, Mr. Craye." Nan said pleasantly. " Isn't this an unfortunate business, imagine ! Do you remember me, of course you don't. It's Nan from Aragon, Foley O'Neill's mother." Even now she took time for an introduction, and saw nothing strange in their polite How do you do's from the darkness.

" Unfasten the Captain," she said to her guide, much in the same voice in which she might have set a nursery maid some bit of business.

" I have no knife," he answered surlily.

" I thought of that," she said. " Take my nail scissors and hurry."

It was all rather like a picnic. A get—your—socks—on, don't—delay, now—then—where's—our—jersey, sort of rhythm about it.

The two soldiers stood up unsteadily, twisting their hands gently round their numb wrists. They tied their guard up without any rancour or bad feeling, asking him if he was quite comfy, and saying " good-bye " before they turned to follow Nan back through the labyrinth where she found her way as easily as if she followed a thread.

Nan kept warning them as if they were children of this or that obstacle as they went along. Where the roof sagged low, where the path dropped steeply. The air was bad and no one wanted to speak for the effort was heavy and the necessity for haste was great.

Among the hazel bushes, grey as cats at evening, Nan handed over the revolver as if it had been a jammed scone.

"Take the awful thing," she said. "I couldn't shoot it off if you paid me, and hook it for the barracks like blazes. You'll get through if you're lucky, and mind when you get there and see no harm comes to my Foley. Give nobody away, remember that, please. I've taken a bit of a chance for you, and that's what I ask you. Keep quiet. Foley has to get his living in this country and so do I. Go separate ways down the mountain, and go, excuse me, like hell."

"We can't leave you up here alone, Mrs. O'Neill," they protested.

"Now, whatever chance I have alone I have none with you two near me." She clapped hands as though she was starting them in a race, and they went off without any kind of farewells or thanks, simply doing as they were told.

Nan saw them go and waved one of her gloved hands as they disappeared from her sight. Then she went down the steps to the iron gate again as she had a sudden idea that matters might be still further delayed if she locked it and threw away the key. This she did with neatness and dispatch. She was coming up the steps dusting her gloves together when Killer Denny and his mate came round the corner of the hazels. They carried a spade with which they had been digging a shallow grave at a peat cutting a mile away. The mountain people who had seen them had kept away knowing that death and trouble were near.

"Oh, good-evening," Nan said pleasantly, "Can you tell me, I wonder, is there any one could show me over the caves? I hear they're very interesting and I'd love to see them, imagine."

"The caves are not on show," Killer Denny answered, "Who are you, and what's your name?"

Nan thought a moment. If she told a lie she might get a start down the road, but they could catch up with her without any trouble. They could overtake her before she had gone a mile.

"My name is O'Neill," she told them. "I'm Foley O'Neill's mother, and I'm here to ask you to let those two officers go free for the military are holding my boy as hostage for them."

"He yapped, I suppose, or you wouldn't be here. I'm sorry, Missus, but I can do nothing for you. It's hard on your son, for God knows it was little he did to assist us." Denny spoke in the harsh voice of a person repelling a professional beggar, but Nan ignored the rudeness as if it was unheard and kept pleasantly on.

"Isn't it a wonder to you then that he hadn't the soldiers here hours ago? Maybe he can hold his tongue if he can do nothing else, eh? Wouldn't you agree?"

She was burning to know how large a part Foley had played in the capture. She had so strong and natural a curiosity that she would have chanced anything now, to satisfy herself exactly.

"Oh, a very heroic silence," Denny jeered, "and he cock-certain they were dead in the heather since twelve o'clock this morning. Why would he put himself wrong with the I.R.A. for two cold corpses, eh? He is selling horses long enough, now see, to cod the military over any two little things like that and no trouble to him."

"And they're not dead?" Nan rapped it out with swift certainty. "They're not dead, aren't they?"

"Who told you so?"

"Oh, child, it's plain in what you say."

"Well, see now, listen, Missus. You can do no good here and you might do a lot of harm. So off you go and keep quiet or it'll come harder on your gentleman son. When his English friends are done with him the I.R.A. might be knocking at his door, now see, and while we're at it, how did you know to come here to-night, for all he couldn't split?"

Nan put her hand in her pocket and took out the scrap of paper with Askemore scrawled on it.

" As good jailers as you are, boys, one of your prisoners left that after him in Foley's car ; it takes a nosey old Nannie to stick her nose into the like o' that, eh ? To turn up the floor mats, and lift out the cushions, what ? She nosed out something, imagine ! So take advice, let yous be quits."

In excitement Nan's speech plunged towards the idiom of her youth, her beautiful voice rang now against the hollow hill behind her, it sounded roundly in the birdless mountain evening.

Killer Denny was a really hard and wicked little man. Of the three he only had no dread of this hour of execution. He had spent years in America, he had never known a lucky day there, and he was tough with a toughness from the underworld of big and cruel towns. There was a greater hatred in him for these things that Nan stood for and Aragon stood for than there was love for Ireland or hatred for the English enemy.

The other two boys knew fear and prayer and were sustained through ordeal by a terrible martyr's spirit of patriotism, but to Denny the Irish war was only a business, a dangerous, exciting and highly remunerative business. He was the mercenary soldier of all time, the same tough guy who did the job on the princes in the tower. That and something more, something worse, for he had a little education and a bitter grudge against the world for the great hardships he had known, the hunger, and the coldness of charity.

The boy with him had not spoken. Now he said, nervously, " We should hurry, captain, we should hurry."

" What hurry are you in ? " Denny stooped to light a cigarette with provoking deliberation. He liked playing on any one's nerves. " Didn't you hear Mrs. O'Neill say her heroic son would never split to the British that he drove ourselves and two of his late customers as far as the seven crosses this morning. Ah, boy, he mightn't die for Ireland in the style you or I would, but he knows bloody well he should keep his mouth shut. It's waiting for him on all sides, now see, if he don't sing dumb."

" We should hurry, Captain, we should hurry," the boy repeated, his face was desperately pinched and nervous, framed in the upturned collar of his trench coat.

" What a hurry you're in for your first execution, aren't you ? "

" Oh, Jesu ! "

" Jesu ! "

Nan and the boy breathed it out together.

Killer Denny showed his small regular teeth in a smile. " All the talk that goes on about Ireland and her holy wars," he said, " but someone has to do her dirty work, now see, for all the prayers and priests never got her very far. Well, come on now, I'll not delay the little matter any longer."

The boy turned round with a green face. He was suddenly sick, retching and heaving, his hands to his head.

" Let me off it, Captain, for Christ's sake," he gasped. " A fight is O.K., yes, but a bloody murder on a nice evening spare us. O Lord, oh holy Jesu have mercy on the poor beggars. Oh, Jesu, did you hear one give me a winner for Thursday ? And I'm to turn round and pump lead through him. God knows I'm a poor shot, I wouldn't know where I'd hit him." His voice rose to a scream. " You wouldn't know how long a chap would be dying, he mightn't be rightly dead and we throwing the sods in on his poor bloody eyes."

Nan too turned on the killer.

" How long, I wonder, before yourself's corpsed in a wicked ending and your toes cocked in the grave and not a word more about you, God damn you, that had no pity for another."

" What's your interesting proposition ? " The Killer was delighted by their hysteria. " That we should let these two prisoners go so that they can identify any one

of the three of us at leisure ? " He spat. " You and your
talk about fair fighting," he spat again. " How many of
us are there in this country and how do you think we're
to take on the whole British Army, can you give me an
idea ? " He sank his head and spoke low to Nan. " You
and yours on any side of the blankets—Oh, I know your
noble ancestry, Missus—is backing the British against
your own. Mind you, your connection with the Fox
family was well looked into before gentleman O'Neill was
ordered to do a bit for Ireland beyond a drink or a bed
for a boy that might need it."

" What was he to do ? " Nan fired out the question.

" Oh, a little liaison work, will we call it, between the
big house where he's so popular with his lady cousins,
and their friends at the barracks. But, as it happens, we
didn't need his help this time. The two fools we were
after as good as asked us to take care of them, without
any assistance from Aragon or its bastards."

Nan swung back her hand and arm and hit him a
savage blow across the face.

" You rat," she said. " You Yankee rat, keep the name
of Aragon out of your dirty mouth. Even to name it, oh."
Her face was white and her eyes blazing. " Bastard I am,
and thankful for the blood and breed that sets me the
world away from scum like your wicked little self."

They were a strange group on the side of the hill. Nan,
immeasurably beautiful in her rage and pride, facing like
a tigress the little gunman who cleared his eyes of the
stinging tears her blow had brought to them, and the
boy who knelt among the stones now, gabbling prayers
and shivering in the sheltered still air. Round them the
leaf-like pallor of the evening light sank in faint levels
towards night. Then, shattering the hush that followed
on Nan's blow, coming before the pause of surprise could
break or lessen, a voice was shouting through the echoing
dark below.

" Captain Denny, Captain Denny," it cried. " They're
gone. They're gone, Captain, they're gone," the voice

grew nearer, changed from echo to voice. Soon there was the sound of stumbling hurrying feet, uncertain in the dark with the echo fumbling after them, a rush of feet up the last broken stair, and a white face behind the iron gate, and incoherent speech while hands gripped the bars and shook at them, and the two men outside listened stunned to the broken story. Nan helpless to fly, stood silently, a figure of immense triumph between them. The last of the evening sun flung her shadow, compact and orderly, up against the rock face.

" They couldn't even tie me up," the boy inside the gate was panting, " I got myself free."

" As bad as they were they were able for you," Denny snarled.

" Only for her and her trickery we had them yet. Oh, she beats all for devilment."

Nan laughed a splendid joyful laugh.

" There's no great difference between Ireland's soldiers and boys in the nursery when it comes to managing either," she said. " And now if I was you chaps I'd hop it quick for your prisoners are tidy runners, and they have a nice start of you, and they might be back with a reinforcement, imagine, to turn the tables, who knows ? "

The Killer caught Nan by the arm.

" And you, Missus," he put his face near hers, " do you think you'll get out of this hole alive, do you ? Do you ? You won't strike me three times, I'm telling you."

The praying boy said again, " We should hurry, Captain, we should hurry," but his voice was glad now, not anguished.

" I'd count my life well given," Nan said, though the first shadow of fear crossed her face and for the first moment she looked lost in their power.

" You would, would you ? " The Killer said quietly, " I believe you, Missus. Well, I'll do better than shoot you. I'll do better for you than an easy death in the heather. March now to the house you're so proud of, and see what I have in store for you."

" Hey, hey," shouted the boy who was behind the bars,
" let a fella out, will you, am I to stop here like a chained
dog, eh ? "

" Let yourself out."

" I have no key."

" And where would we get a key. Break the lock at
your leisure."

" 'Tis the lock of a tower, 'tis the lock of a tower," the
boy cried, " Jesus, Mary and Joseph save. Jesus, Mary
and Joseph have mercy. . . ."

His voice pierced the silent mountain air as his hands
rattled at the gate.

Nan said reasonably :

" We wouldn't spoil five minutes letting him out. See
there where I threw the key in the young brackens."

Her level sense held them. The three bent their eyes
to the ground searching among the little bits of gorse and
the springing heather and bracken. It was like a game
of hunt the thimble, or looking for a chocolate Easter egg
hidden in the daffodil leaves. The praying boy crossed
himself and sent up a little petition to Saint Anthony.

" Saint Anthony is very good," Nan said with satisfaction
when the key was found. The boy nodded complacently.
" I'm always praying to him." He spoke in the voice of
one who says, " He ought to be used to me."

They opened the gate in the rock face, locked it again
and threw the key farther away. Then they hurried Nan
off down the road on the way to her execution.

XXXII

FOLEY was being put through his third examination since he had been brought a prisoner to the military barracks that afternoon.

The first conversation had been a tell-us-old-chap affair with one of the young officers whom he knew well. That is to say, he had sold him one very good horse and talked him into buying two moderate horses, and afterwards assisted him to pass them on. So, though they might be said to know each other pretty well, yet here they could find no common ground at all. It was a futile and embarrassing business.

" Look here, O'Neill, I know you'd want to help us get our chaps out of trouble. They're your friends too, dammit old boy, and you're far too stout a chap to lie up with the shinners."

Foley replied, " If I knew anything any good to you or them I'd have said it hours ago. I don't. Your chaps are finished, I'm sorry to say, and I'm not going to inform on the other crowd."

" But look here, O'Neill, you can't admit you know as much as that and lie low about the fellows who've murdered Michael and Tony. There are limits."

" There's no limit to the difficulties you soldiers can put the likes of myself in this country into."

" All we want is a straight answer to a straight question, and every minute lost getting it is a chance lost for Michael and Tony. After all, O'Neill, you've ridden hunts with them, you've sold bad horses to them."

" And good."

" And good certainly. We've always treated you as one of ourselves here, and now we're in a jam you're going to turn it all up and act, you'll forgive me, pretty yellow. Poor show, you know."

" See here," Foley frowned in an effort to get through

all the good fellowship implied in the earnest stilted speech, " I've got to live in this country and earn my living in it and work hard for my living. You chaps are only fighting in it."

" And if we could count on a decent bit of co-operation from you people living here, there'd be damn' little fighting left for us to do."

" Ah," Foley said. " Well, make the country safe for co-operation then. See to it that those who give you information aren't taken out of their own lonely beds and shot a week after."

" That's what you're afraid of, is it ? "

" Yes," Foley said, " I am afraid of it."

" Well, for a chap who can ride a hunt or a race like yourself it's a poor show."

" Ah, talk sense, man."

" Sense ? When Michael and Tony may be getting it any minute. For the last time, O'Neill, will you tell me what you know about this business, or will you not ? "

" I will not."

" I see. I'll have to tell the Colonel I was wrong about you. I really thought you'd the guts to lie up for a gallop of this sort with the right chaps. I'm not a great judge but, by God, O'Neill, I'm disappointed in the form you've shown. It's a rotten show."

" Well, there's the position," Foley said hopelessly.

" I'm afraid you aren't quite at the end of this business, you know, old chap. You may find it healthier to talk to me now of your own free will."

" I'll talk to no one."

" You may find you'll have to."

" I may find this, and I may find that. I'll deal with what I find when I find it. If you and your Majors and your Colonels have no more common sense in fighting the war in this country than the lot of you have in making, breaking or buying horses in this country, God help England and her army."

Now this was an insult, and Foley was very mistaken

to have made it. To connive at the shooting of one's pals and at the escape of their murderers was one thing, but to follow that up by insulting the horsey side of The Regiment was another. It was worse than a sneer at their women kind, or at least quite as bad. It got under the skin of vanity and simple pride. Coming from Foley who had always made it his business to ask opinions of horses from the soldiers, and rarely, if ever, to give his own, the bitter truthful jeer was the more venomously barbed.

The boy said, "Thanks for your opinion of us," and got up. His face was white with temper. He would not try another yard in the matter. Foley could hardly have taken a more conclusive way of putting every officer in the barracks against himself.

XXXIII

WHEN the boy had left him, Foley sat thinking and measuring things out in his mind. To himself his position was clear enough.

This morning he had been more than unwillingly involved in the death of two officers, two men who by their personal carelessness, in a country with which they were supposedly at war, could put himself and others like him in a stick as cleft and awkward as could be found. It was entirely out of his power to save them, and to the best of his belief they were dead men an hour from the time he had left them on the mountain road with their captors. To him there had been no reason for, and every reason against, his going to the barracks and informing as to where and with whom they had last been seen. Foley had perceived no chance at all for them and so had set his mind on the next problem of his day, finding a nurse for Doatie.

He had chosen the best looking of the two girls available at the County Hospital, and flirted with her on the way

out to Mountain Brig. He could not help himself. Everything in him and about him was a challenge to the female.
He could not look without a caress in his eyes, he could
not touch a girl's elbow without impelling her to know
his interest, he could not speak except on a tender
bantering note, as if his voice would play with her
stranger's hand, or pinch a neck, frigid still to him.
Foley was the " Oh—you—are—awful " boy of all time
and all class. The Fox licence in his blood was coarsened
and made more natural by the peasant side of his breeding.
At the same time this peasant side of his nature had a
revolted primness, a chill recoil from his own acts and
ventures in love. It was bred in him as strong as his
good looks and came through as many generations of
austere mountain ancestry as Nan's Fox strain came
through generations of mannered bad living.

It was the O'Neill side of Foley that went out to
Doatie and the pure (because untouched by him) quality
of her childish passion and obedience towards him. In
the back of the car now there were paper bags of fruit
and sweets he had taken pains to choose for her. Beside
him the nurse he had found for her eyed him roguishly.
Through her alert talk of racing, she was a bookmaker's
handsome daughter, and with every response she made
to his challenge he thought the less of her (that was his
way), and drove faster to get her to Doatie, his wounded
child.

There was an exalted cruel streak in Foley which was
fully conscious of Doatie's present fear of horses and
rejoiced that she should subdue and hide it from him . . .
rejoiced that for him she had known terror and been
hurt. . . .

In Aragon's basements there was a passage that ran
its length to reach one room only, a room distant from
any other, a room whose lonely window looked straight
out over the river, deaf sailing ships might pass below it
but no other traffic. This room was unused for many
years. There had been an effort made once to turn it

into a butler's bedroom, but butlers less austere than
Frazer could not enjoy a night's quiet sleep in airs so
shaken and petrified by long past doings. The walls of
this room had been papered over in blue and white, but
where the paper had peeled in the damp air from the near
river, you could see underneath one of old chinese design,
a most peculiar design, perhaps rightly hidden and in
parts purposely defaced. About this room there remained
still an air of past luxuries. White and gold pelmets over
the windows, an Italian decoration on the ceiling, a thin
marble mantel and steel basket grate—a strange room to
find in the basements of Aragon where the hordes of
servants had slept in dirt and confusion. Once the room
had been hung with mirrors. Other curious contrivances
were set in the walls. There was still an old ottoman
covered in faded *petit-point*, white rose wreaths on a
shadowy blue background. And it was locked. It was
fifty years now since any one had opened it and closed it,
sick and shuddering at a half-understanding of delicate
ivory-headed cutting whips and other fine and very
curious instruments.

" It must be burnt," Mrs. Fox had exclaimed. " It must
be burnt immediately." She had hurried wildly away
from it, nor ever solved the problem of who to entrust
with its destruction, or how, most delicately, she could
convey to Mr. Fox her horrid knowledge of such a wicked
boxful. Somehow she could never speak of it, for it was
his grandfather who had used such dreadful tools, who
had built this far-off room for his pleasures. She would
tremble. *It was Mr. Fox's own grandfather* . . . and
Foley's great-great-grandfather. No wonder a little
cruelty made his blood quicken, made the idea of sacrifice
and pain pleasant to him, and Grania's youthful un-
instructed passion a little less than necessary, a little more
than he wanted. Had it been given him without the
implied difficulty of her different birth he would have
most likely passed her safely by, but the challenge of the
whole thing had been irresistible.

He thought, with some relief, as he sat in the bleak
guardroom, that this affair at least would put an end to
all that. If he had been an unlikely suitor before to-day,
he was an impossible one to-night. Foley was so without
imagination that his mind could fling a bridge across
any hell and see Grania in an unimaginable placid older
life, in which he would be forgotten as though their
encounter had never been. He saw the truth. But he
was unseeing of the pain that must go before such a
terrible forgetfulness—a pain so beyond any help but
his, that the placid future was hardly reason enough for
its endurance.

But Foley lived in the present and in some untouched
future, he did not live in that nervous place just beyond
the present, he had no ecstatic to-morrows or sad fainting
yesterdays, his life was in Now and in Then, and to-night
in his Now, Grania was only by the way. His concern
was for himself alone. He knew he was in a certain degree
of danger, but he would rather stand in a grave degree
of danger from the British enemy than in an uncertain
disfavour with Ireland's soldiers. So he was implacable
in his resolve for silence.

A Major came next to interrogate him. There was
nothing friendly about this interview. The Major had
entertained no great fancy for Foley at any time in his
popular career. The Major was a keen hard soldier, and
a hard and brilliant man to hounds, and knowledgeable
enough about horses to have avoided buying any from or
through Foley. He did not share in the younger soldiers'
respect and enthusiasm for Foley's horsemanship, or liking
for him as a person. He was a jealous man to hounds
and very serious in his pursuit of the chase. It troubled
him unduly that Foley should so often have the best of a
hunt, and should achieve it with such seeming ease. Where
the Major set his teeth and sweated blood, and put
himself and his horse quite frequently in hideous and
spectacular danger, Foley would slip over the country
with an effortless appearance of ease, a boldness so quick

and artful that it hardly seemed bold. The Major had never got the better of Foley in a hunt or a race although they had had some contests of wits and endurance in both. He valued his only superiority to Foley in any way that was important to him, and as he was a very simple social snob, he was careful to foster the gap that so divided them. He found Foley's widespread popularity most distasteful, in fact it was hateful to him.

He looked on Foley's present position without understanding of any kind, indeed with some satisfaction. Bitterly and deeply as he felt about the almost certain deaths (murders rather, all English soldiers killed in the Irish war were murdered) of his two most able young officers, it was with a deep sense of bringing many things he hated to justice and to light that he confronted Foley this evening.

" Good-evening," he said coldly, doubtful rather whether he should recognise Foley as anything except a traitor and murderer. But this was not a formal military inquiry, nor was guilt actually proved satisfactorily, except to the Major himself. However.

" Good-evening," he had said it, and Foley had nodded and murmured a polite abstracted reply. Not the attitude for any man in so grave a situation as that in which Foley was placed. Not the right attitude at all.

The Major put a pad on which he had pencilled notes in front of him on the table.

" I gather from Mr. Young that you prefer to keep any information as to the probable murders of Captain Purvis and Mr. Craye to yourself, Mister O'Neill." There was a great deal of emphasis on the Captains and the Misters. " Is this the case ? "

" Yes, Major."

" You admit you have some knowledge of their whereabouts ? "

" I don't admit anything."

" Yet you say you prefer to keep what you know to yourself ? "

" I explained my position to Mr. Young, Major. I have not got anything more to say."

" I think, Mr. O'Neill, that we must try to persuade you to say just a little more. Just a short explanation perhaps, of your morning's activities. And please remember I can check up on most of them. Do you, for instance, know a public-house called the Wren's Nest ? "

" Yes, I think every one knows the Wren's Nest."

" It's a cosy little bar, isn't it ? And very popular with some of the gentlemen on the run in this country."

" It's not a spot I'm often in, Major."

" You don't go to Bungaron much, then ? "

" Oh, you mean the Wren's Nest on the Quay ? "

" Ah, and why should you think I meant any other Wren's Nest ? Why, Sir ? Why do you immediately think of another pub called the Wren's Nest ? "

" There is a Wren's Nest on the mountain road behind our house, Major, I often pass it. I don't think I know the Bungaron one as well as you do, Sir. But I've heard it is a nice place."

There was a quiet insolence in Foley's speech that enraged the Major. Foley had fallen into and out of his elaborately arranged pitfall, and then cheeked him quite as if he was not on suspicion of a horrible charge of murder.

" Perhaps, Mr. O'Neill, you can tell me why you visited your favoured Nest at 10.30 this morning ? "

" I called in to get a glass of beer."

" You were on your way—where ? "

" I was on my way to Bungaron to get hold of a nurse."

" And do you generally go to Bungaron by that road ? "

" Not generally. It's out of the way."

" Then why did you choose it this morning ? "

" I had a reason."

" Why did you choose it this morning ? "

Foley thought sulkily for a moment. It was not from any motive of chivalry that he kept quiet about Grania. It simply seemed easier not to drag her into it too.

" That's my business," he said. Then he smiled. " It's part of what I won't tell." Nothing could have been worse for him than this piece of ill-timed levity. But he could not help having a mild dig at so much round about pomposity.

" I see. So you have reasons which you will not state for going twenty miles instead of ten to get a nurse this morning. I imagine someone in your house must be rather ill, Mr. O'Neill, if you have to get the services of a nurse ? "

" Yes, my cousin had a bad fall this morning."

" Ah, ah. Then you must have had a very excellent reason for your delay in fetching the nurse ? "

" It's a perfectly simple reason, Sir, but it's my own business."

" Quite. Quite. Well, perhaps later on you will explain that part of your business to us. There's a good deal about your business, Mr. O'Neill—let's leave your horse business out of it, shall we ? " (His tone dragged the horse business to the forefront of the matter.) " That is a bit shaky, a bit mean, a bit difficult to understand by simple chaps like us soldiers, Mr. O'Neill. It seems to me that it is not only in the way of your business that you know how to put your friends through it."

There was a refinement of passionate dislike in his voice. He paused a minute and bent his head, writing on the paper in front of him. The dreary room was growing darker with the slow stretching dusk of the spring evening. The sound of a car stopping outside in the barrack square came through the slightly opened window. The Major raised his head and looked long and thoughtfully at Foley.

" Where did you find Captain Purvis' dog ? " he asked quietly.

" I didn't find any dog," Foley answered slowly.

" You deny that Captain Purvis' dog was in your possession, do you ? You deny any knowledge of Captain Purvis' dog ? "

" Yes, I deny any knowledge of Captain Purvis' dog."
Foley suspended his voice—he had more to say. The
Major waited now he had him. He had him now. " But
perhaps you mean Captain Purvis' little bitch, Judy ?
Would you know a little dog from a little bitch, Major ?
Maybe you know more about dogs than you do about
horses, only it sounds funny calling Captain Purvis' bitch,
Judy, a dog—I thought everybody knew Judy." Foley
lit a cigarette with an air of amused disquiet. Fancy any
one being so silly, in every line of his easiness.

The Major's eyes snapped. His temper snapped too.

" Insolence isn't going to help you much, Mr. O'Neill,
I'm afraid, although it may be a certain relief to your
feelings, and if you have got any, they may need relief,
or I imagine they would, under the circumstances.

Foley murmured.

" I've got very tender feelings."

" Look here." The Major stood up. If he had not
been so aware of being an officer and a gentleman he
would have screamed at Foley. " That's enough. We
know you were involved in the murders of Captain Purvis
and Mr. Craye this morning. We know you were in the
pub with their murderers. We know you drove them to
their deaths. We know that you gave us no information
which might have prevented their deaths. And we know
that you refuse any information that may lead to the
capture of their murderers."

Foley said, " You could frighten any story you wanted
out of the cripple, you know."

" Not a story that hangs together quite so convincingly
as this one, I'm afraid. Perhaps you don't realise that a
fellow who plays traitor, as you have done, can put
himself in a very dangerous position, in a very dirty
position. Do you realise, or do you not, that you may
have to answer for this with your life ? Even the British
Government is getting a bit fed up with chaps like you,
and justice can be done quickly under martial law, you
know."

Foley was not looking at the Major, he was staring across the room over the Major's trim shoulder to the open doorway where Grania stood, and there was a look both stricken and exalted about her. It gave age to her fat youth, it hollowed awkward shadows in her sweet and silly face. Somewhere all exuberance had been shed, she had gone from young girl back to bluntly determined child, or, perhaps, to savage extreme, womanhood.

Behind her in the doorway her mother fussed and whispered to the Colonel. The Colonel fussed and whispered back, unsoldierly, embarrassed. He was a nice man.

Foley stood up, but did not come forward. Grania smiled at him quickly, but he did not smile back.

Mrs. Fox put her arm through Grania's and said :

" How do you do, Major Radley. My daughter has some information she is anxious to give you about, er, O'Neill's movements this morning."

Foley looked at Grania across a width of amazed dislike. What was she going to say ? What could she say ? What now ? What next ?

Addressing herself to the Major, Grania said, in a weak clear voice, the voice of youth that can only say the thing it means, to whom the truth is of violent disproportionate importance.

" I heard you. But you can't do anything to Foley. None of you can. You are our friends, and you can't, because the thing is——" She stopped and looked from the Major to the Colonel, and then, with as much defiance as though it was her mother's doing, at Mrs. Fox, " the thing I've got to say is, that Foley and I are going to have a baby."

There was a shocking silence. Mrs. Fox did not look more appalled than Foley. The Colonel, alarmed now, as well as embarrassed, turned his back on the party and gazed out of the windows. The Major looked down at his notes and fiddled with a pencil.

Grania stood, shaking and swaying a little, gazing with

deep alarmed eyes at Foley, she was gazing over a coldness as of water, a coldness that slowly became real and deep to her, more real even than his danger.

"Oh, Foley," she went across to him. "I had to say it, Foley. It's true and true, and what would I do if they killed you? What would I do then? I ask you, I ask everybody."

Mrs. Fox followed her across the room and stood between her and Foley, a fierce if rather a belated chaperon. Every feeling she had, of pride, of restraint, of decency, of rectitude, was outraged beyond a raw and quivering limit, and beyond this again a passion of maternal protectiveness, quickened to an awful strength within her.

"Darling," she said, and love and bitter chastisement were mingled in the word. "Come away with me, come away at once."

She was the other world to Foley, her neat profile with its expensive veil, twisted into a little ball under her firm, plump chin, and tied in a neat bow at the back of an expensive toque, a brown fur stole round her neck, a bunch of scentless purple auriculas pinned in it. He saw her hands in neat expensive gloves, and her feet in neat expensive shoes. The rest of her he did not see. But he passionately approved her, and as passionately revolted from Grania's generous lawlessness. The Fox man in him found in Grania what Fox's approved only in their mistresses and detested in their wives.

"Shut up," Foley said to Grania. "Shut your mouth, will you, will you, you dirty little tart."

Grania did not spring back from him, nor cower away. She was not defeated by this angry coarseness. Something in her was well matched to it. While the others in the room drew in a breath of shocked indecision, she turned from him to them, saying :

"You hear what he says about me? You see it's true what I told you. Now will you save him for me?"

Mrs. Fox was in tears.

"Colonel, I apologise," she said again and again. "I

apologise. I had no idea the crazy child. . . . Oh, she
just told me she would tell you, would tell you where
the man had been this morning. It's all too shameful, too
terrible. . . . I apologise. I'm sorry."

The Colonel was murmuring and helping her into one
of the shiny leather seated chairs with wooden arms. Mrs.
Fox was so little, her neat shoes swung off the floor as she
sat, and she buried her neatly toqued head in her scented
white handkerchief—Parma violet. In emotion and
excitement she exhaled the scent of Rimmel's Toilet
Vinegar and Parma Violets, rather delicious.

So far, the Colonel had not addressed his prisoner. He
had only played with the blind tassel, and consoled Mrs.
Fox as gently as he could. He turned to Foley now, and
it was not to say, "You are a cad, Sir," but to say :

"O'Neill, I think you find yourself in a very cruel
position."

Foley said :

"I do, Sir."

Grania clasped her hands towards Foley. Major
Radley rattled among his notes, and Mrs. Fox did her very
utmost to subdue her crying.

The Colonel then said :

"I know you were implicated in the capture of our
two boys this morning. I should guess against your will.
I'm sure of it, in fact. However, it's not impossible for
you to make amends for that terrible business if you will
give us all the information in your power that will lead
to the capture of their murderers. Will you do this ?
In asking you I am not unaware of the grievous danger
I ask you to put yourself in, because I know you are far
from a cowardly fellow.

"Oh, Foley, do tell him, please, tell him," Grania
pleaded, and Foley could have struck her. He said :

"If I tell you anything of any help to you I'm bloody
well finished in this country. I've kept out of doing
I.R.A. work, beyond a meal and a bed for a boy on the
run."

"Harbouring gunmen," the Major interrupted, "we thought you did a bit of that too."

Foley paused. Then he said with the simple ignorant bitterness of a peasant :

"The ruin of Ireland, Major, is chaps like you and Cromwell."

The major, whose ancestors had fought with Charles, sniggered silently, and put the remark away in his mind to use as an Irish story. For years after the British Army had left Ireland he carried his own punishment about with him in the shape of Irish stories, stories that caused any whose interest he sought to shun and fly from him.

"I suppose Cromwell has got to come into it somewhere," he said now, "but I don't think we can blame him altogether for this situation." Something in the way in which he avoided looking at Grania made her even more the situation than the murdered and their murderers.

Foley got up and stepped forward :

"If I chose to take what's coming to me, and keep my mouth shut, it's none of your damn' nosey business."

"Keep yourself quiet, boy," the Colonel said easily. "We don't want any rough stuff. You know that yourself. No help to anything."

Mrs. Fox said :

"I think we'd better be going. We cannot do any more. Come Grania."

Grania said :

"You go. I'm staying till I know what happens to Foley."

The Colonel said :

"Nothing will happen to any of us to-night, child."

"For God's sake, Grania, go home." Foley was white and tired. "Go home like a good little one."

Blind with tears, Grania stood up. By so much as she had given, by just so much was she apart from Foley now. It was not her poor body, that had taken far more than she gave or knew how to give, but worship and faith were broken and slighted in this her fight for his life. The young do expect to get as good as they give to those they love, and the first disillusionment is ashes and bitter water to drink.

It was then that the two boys, Michael Purvis and Tony Craye, came in, quietly and without drama.

" Well, you two have given us a nice bit of bother to-day, haven't you ? " the Colonel said with gentle sourness. They grinned uneasily.

" Now you'll be able to spare Mr. O'Neill the ordeal of informing on the soldiers of his country," the Major said. There was disappointment in his voice. " And you'll also be able to tell us how he assisted in your little affair to-day."

" Foley ? Never saw Foley all day," Purvis said. " But he's for it all right, I'm afraid. You know who got us out ? "

" Foley's mother, Nan, Mrs. O'Neill." The other boy hurried out the names that would explain her to all.

" What ? " Foley was profoundly upset. What had she been doing ?

" Made fools of the lot of them. Put our jailer in his place, and talked to us as if we were back in the nursery."

" What are you talking about ? " The Colonel leaned across the table towards them, " let's get it straight."

" Well, it was like this, Sir, she just walked in, disarmed the guard and let us out."

" Walked in where ? "

" That's just what we can't say, Sir."

" We promised we'd keep quiet about it, or every one would be in trouble."

" More people keeping quiet ? " The Major's voice was chill.

" If it's not putting it too strongly, Sir——"

" It sounds silly, I know——"

" But she absolutely saved our lives, Sir."

" And asked us to lay off making any bother for the

other side. Said they'd have it in for Foley, you see, if we did."

"So we can't talk. Really we can't, can we? You know, she was damn' wonderful."

"Most marvellous woman I've ever seen. It was a hell of a show."

"Oh, awfully good show. We were for it, you know."

"Absolutely for it."

The babble of excited relief showed plainly enough the nervous tension they had been through.

"Nan could do anything," Mrs. Fox said with desperate quiet conviction, "anything in the world I think. But where is she now?"

"Putting Miss Pigeon to bed, I should think. She shooed us off—said she'd be better off alone."

The Colonel said, "She seems to have managed a good deal, while we chaps sat twiddling our thumbs."

"There wasn't a thing you could do, Sir."

"And all we could get out of Foley was Judy."

Foley said, "I made sure you two would be cooling on the hill-side before twelve o'clock this morning."

"So did we."

"It was terribly decent of you to keep Judy."

The Major looked at his watch. "As this has turned from an inquiry into a party of mutual congratulation, I think, if I may, Sir, I'll go and have my bath."

"Sorry to spoil your crack at the Shinners, Sir."

"Very sorry, Sir."

The Major said, "I'll overlook it for once. But next time you are nearly murdered, go through with it, won't you? Don't disappoint your superior officers."

When he had gone, the Colonel said:

"Now then, what about Foley? This isn't official. But I think he'd be better out of Ireland. What do you think yourself?"

Foley thought. "Yes," he said, "the boys won't forget it to my mother. They'll have it in for her all right over this day's work. They're bound to example her."

" And you are their obvious victim, unless we make a
political prisoner of you."

" That's right."

" You'd do better to take a chance out of this country
for a couple of years. Till things get forgotten."

A couple of years—the words were cold stones dropping
through cold water to Grania's heart.

Foley said, slowly, " I've got every penny I own in the
horses and the little place." His voice made it sound very
pat and cosy, comfortable and profitable.

The boy who came from Norfolk spoke :

" It would be rather an investment for us, Foley," he
said, " to help you set up an establishment on the other
side—the same sort of thing."

" I will help, too," Mrs. Fox said eagerly, " for Nan's
sake."

Grania squeezed her fat cold hands together in her lap.
What about my sake ? What about Grania's sake ? The
words racked her but she did not speak. No. She looked
down sulkily at one hand squeezing agonisingly at the
other.

The boys took it up :

" We could buy young horses over here and send them
across for you to finish and sell."

" It's easy money."

Foley thought, " Easy money for the people who sell
you the horses." He was puzzled and furious, angry with
his mother for this uncalled for heroism which had so
undone his silence. Angry from the centre of his vanity
with Grania who had so shamed him and herself. Angry
and hurt that outside circumstances should uproot his
life, the hard but pleasant life that he had made, the life
that suited him so well. His horses, his trade, his hunting,
his girls. He felt desperately lonely at the thought of
starting again in a strange world of men and horses, none
of his own used ways about him. Hardy as he was, Foley
had a sort of passion for the things he knew. His own
things. The familiar ways of Mountain Brig, Aunt Gipsy

knew how long he liked his egg boiled, the saddle-room
he and Micky had made, where he could put a hand
without thought on any piece of tack he wanted. The
stove that boiled the linseed, a cross little affair, but he
and Micky knew how to humour it exactly. He was proud
of his dining-room, with his cups and the photographs of
himself and his horses, and the pictures of the Pope. He
had all his mother's strong liking for things and her
ability to take care of what she had, to hold things fast
and keep them in good order. His bantams too, those
game little cocks, no one had a breed of bantams to touch
Foley's. Sometimes Aunt Gipsy would roast one for his
supper, a better bird than a partridge. Somehow the
bantams were uppermost in Foley's mind as he said :

"Ah, I'll chance things here, I think. I don't think
I'll run. Thank you very much all the same."

Mrs. Fox said with blue-lipped calm, " If what Grania
has just told us all is unfortunately true, don't you owe
it to her not to take any risk with your life which you
can help ? "

The Colonel said, and for the first time he spoke
coldly, " I more than agree with Mrs. Fox—the sooner
you get out of this country the better."

Grania looked across at him, dumb and stupefied. All
she was she would have given for a secret kept, for a body
freed by any drastic drug of Nan's. She would not speak
again.

"You should go to-night," one of the boys said.
" Have you got the ready ? We can lend it to you."

Foley muttered, " I couldn't get a boat to-night."

" The timber ship," Grania said, " she went down the
river at tea time, you'd catch her in Bungaron. I'll drive
you down. If you won't let me——" she turned at her
mother's immediate protest, " I'll do something awful,
I really will."

Mrs. Fox wavered and abandoned her principles, the
look of Grania frightened her.

XXXIV

THE ROAD to Bungaron followed the river, ran beside the river through the wooded valley. It passed Aragon on the opposite bank of the river, its walls dropping to the drop beneath them, rising from the trees and river below to the trees and hill above. The river light was bottle-green in the windows, the little stone foxes, their bushes straight out behind, flew motionlessly through the swimming dusk. The river tide was still high as they drove along, Grania and Foley. It carried the lower branches of the willows, dragging blue leaves in its green bosomy floods.

Grania drove the big car very badly. It was a mark of her severance from Foley that she should drive at all, not leave all that to him while she leaned and chattered by his side. Now she reached for her clutch and rammed in the awkward gears that caught and tore their teeth, one in the other. Sometimes tears fled down her cheeks and sometimes not. So close to each other in the near dark, they were each minute of silence farther away, the distance lengthening inevitably between them.

Only seven miles now, Grania thought, as they passed the different places that marked distances for her in a road she had always known. The road to the sea and Christmas trees ; to the dancing class, and to tennis parties and balls. Now the road to cold without end, to ceaseless desire, the road into this new pain of loss which was too great to be borne. Grania's love had been much beyond any strength of pride or spirit, and now that she had lost these things, nothing was left her, no place of cool strength that was her own. No room for the vanity that the young should have. All had been lost in her great silly act of love. Not for years was Grania to feel anything but the hot shock of shame in thinking of her confession that evening. Not till she was established

in a life of love and success, which the same round
generosity and abandon of her nature brought her equally
with this disaster, was she able to look back with understanding and pride, not with shame and pity, to the child
she had been then ; the shamed and crying child driving
along the familiar road, driving her love out of her life,
in six miles, five miles now, while the soft airs of the spring
evening stirred and crept round them ; the indifferent
primroses spread themselves like light growing in a room,
pale wedges and pools up and down the dark rocky banks
of the road, and the river water flowed past, the same cold,
milky green as the willow branches it dragged down
hopelessly to its breast ; the luminous strong-smelling pads
of the elder flowers ; grew along the road, and white
hemlock in the ditches was only less mooney and solid.
The water birds were uttering lonely independent cries,
and soon the foxes would be barking through the night
woods, and Foley, like any other travelling fox, would be
gone. But only in her very death, Grania thought, could
her longing and hope for him be quieted.

Ah, if hope could die more quickly ! Many brave and
affecting little speeches got as far as Grania's lips that
evening, speeches to which he could not but respond as
he ought with protestations of faithful and enduring love ;
with plans and promises of gold rings and little houses.
But the words died before they were spoken, so remote he
looked, so tough, so far removed from love's pity or the
touching reach of words.

Now they had left the darkness of demesne woods
behind, and the river grew wider and more still as it
reached towards sea water. The fields beside it grew
smaller and their high flowering banks taller, as the sea
was closer ; and far beyond the thought of the little
striving fields of men, the river turns lay under the
mountains. The intervening land was hidden. The
mountains spread their quartered spaces bare against the
sky. In the evening they were white and grey and deeper
grey, no pretty blue shadows, only height and depth and

the quietness of the sky, great height and distance falling
to the water and splitting the sky into deep V's of evening
light. Little white houses glimmered in the dusk, a light
burning in some and others dark. Red brown fishing nets
were hung on poles outside the houses to dry ; heavy
swags and garlands against the pale water, water so full
and still that a gull flying slowly over seemed to be
dipping the points of its wings in its own shadows, it kept
so low across the river.

It was Foley who spoke at last, and said :

" Was that true, what you said at the barracks, or did
you say it because you thought it would get me off ? "

It was not the words but the light, unkind tone of his
voice that found in Grania some still unwounded place,
some last small place, and so hurt it that pride and anger
were born of it together, and she turned on him and cried :

" No, it wasn't true. Thank God it wasn't true. I'm
all right, and even if I wasn't I never want to see you
again. I'm glad you have got to go. You're bad. You're
like Nan. You're cruel."

" Oh, don't start that stuff," he spoke with that savage
sourness through which men seek to avoid a scene, and
through which they precipitate the disaster of untold
grievance upon themselves for ever. " If you're all right,
you're all right, aren't you ? Be glad you're not mixed
up in my life any more. It wouldn't suit you, believe me.
We've had lots of fun, hadn't we ? You'll remember that
part and forget about me in no time."

Nothing could have been more light and cruel than his
careless, vulgar reassurance. His assumption that the
affair between them had been as slight to her as to him.
It was as if her heart was a little old basket he held in
his hand and squeezed its dry frail sides together and
threw away the carefully made thing for the dusty winds
to play with and rattle through its ribs.

Now they were near to the sea. The land-locked sea
welled inwards up the river across the narrow Bay of
Bungaron, the fields on the opposite headland maintaining

their pattern as far as you could see in the dusk. A small town was built low under the headland, pink houses and white cottages and queer stiff Georgian shops and houses. There was a high stone-built quay where the sailing ship waited, its masts and rigging wild as a dream against the low-built town and ribbed mountains above. Now, in the evening it was as easy to look at the bright sea as it is to look up a church.

" You don't mind about any one, do you ? " She stopped the car by the sea wall and turned to him. " What about your mother ? Not even a question. What about the two boys ? You knew all about them, but you wouldn't take a chance, would you ? Not a chance to save them."

" And I wasn't any too grateful for your own heroic act to-night, was I ? " He could tease her still.

" I did that," Grania said, " for a reason you'll never know anything about."

" What reason, child ? "

" For love," she said, in an ordinary voice, because it was so true. " And here we are at Bungaron, so get out."

" Are you taking me to the boat ? "

" No, I don't want to be seen with you very much, you can walk. It's no distance."

" You're very cross, aren't you ? "

" Not cross, really," she put the back of her hand to her eyes, and up against her silvery hair in a complete gesture of sadness, " only frightened that people can be so different from what you think."

" Well," he got out of the car, " don't let us part bad friends. Ah, Grania, don't let's." He bent towards her, any resistance calling to him, as always, to be defeated and subdued to himself.

" You wouldn't know when I'd come back to you, and then you'd be sorry you'd been so mean, wouldn't you ? "

The voice that had shaken her and enchanted her, the strong sweet common voice speaking half-words of love, implying anything, promising nothing, charmed Grania once again. And when he saw he had won, Foley turned light again.

"Of course, you're right," he said, "forget me as quick as ever you can." He kissed her cheek, not her mouth, and leaned away from her again. He stood beside the car for a moment, patted her hand through the open window, lit a cigarette, and went off down the road, the sea on the left, the mountains on his right. Foley had not got the niggling short-stepped walk of so many horsy men, he strode out like his mother, carrying his strong beautiful figure along with unaffected swagger and endless challenge.

Grania watched the sway of his shoulders and head. He was a sailor in a foreign seaport town who left her. It was a man as strange and unpitying as that. That moment passed too, and a wild panic for herself, herself only, took its place.

"Listen! Wait, wait," she called in a passion of lonely fear, "where shall I find you?"

But he walked on to the turn. He had not heard her.

Grania sat on in the car after he had gone out of her sight. She could not take in that this was an end. He would come back along the road. He would say, come with me, Grania, and they would be on the ship together, going down the last of the river to the night and the sea. How unspeakable the joy of it would be. She put her hand in her teeth and bit on it to hold herself quiet. Then sorrow, going to her stomach, as it will, she leaned out of the car, pale, and vomiting dryly and hopelessly, hands clasped against a sweating forehead. She felt very cold. She could not make herself leave the chill sea wall where little never-breaking waves sucked and lipped at the stones—there was a star out now, she could see it high over the ship's lonely rigging, high above the mountains and the town. It must be nine o'clock and more. The headlands were faded out, ruled no more one behind another, the mountains were theatrical, violet cardboard now, and the town, which had been so grey and white and quiet in the dusk, became garish and too much of a thing with clusters of lights, and light's long shiverings in the water. Again the desperate thought of being deserted in a gay foreign town was with Grania. But she did not know what it was to feel quite alone until she saw the sailing ship leave the quay and go down the river on the turn of the night's tide.

There are no words to describe the anguish which may possess the young in such straits of emotion, in such utter loss as this—there are no words for a finality of height or depth, and there is a region of sadness which it is a little death to know, a gap, and blank of terror. But in this place mercifully there is no real abiding. It cannot hold the very young. They escape and recover. But at that time nothing except a strong and natural fear of death kept Grania from wading through the surging weeds into the tide of the sea and the river current, and swimming with them after Foley's ship until she should be drowned.

XXXV

SHE was not really so near doing this as she thought. She was too young and fat and frightened for the moment of insanity to have grip enough on her despair for such an ending. She could only turn the big car round and drive her breaking heart home to bed. She did not even drive as recklessly as the occasion demanded. Indeed she could not see well enough for reckless driving because of her tears. So she went slowly and waveringly along, and the sea road and its little fields gave place again to the river road, with its dark trees and pale primroses and demesne gates with high stone pillars and gravelled sweeps. This was the gentry's valley. The river was lower now. Its mud banks wet, dark, pearly, the water and the willows parted till to-morrow, the green pallor of the spring night growing narrower every five nimutes in the emptying river until it was only long and smooth as an old candle. All the faint spring yellow of the woods was olive dark now, and tall houses showed through their trees as white as geese, with here and there a light among the lines of dark windows to show there was life and business still to do. These houses were built too high above the river for their lights to reach the water   Great clumps and masses of rhododendron and laurel and oak trees, bare of-leaves still, grew down the steep banks between the houses and the river.

Grania drove past these houses that she knew, feeling as if each held her enemies : hostile mothers, cool daughters, sons to ignore her politely, arrogantly avoiding the embarrassment of her company. She knew the formality of the society in which she lived, knew and respected it enough to fear its ostracism. Even to-night in all the great despair of her loss she could imagine the little slights and little politenesses by which these faint houses would put and keep her in her outcast place. After

all, this was Grania's only world, and a world she would
have met with glad defiance if Foley's love had been
behind her, but robbed of any love or help from him she
cringed at its strictures and feared its displeasure. All the
cold august Geogian houses down the length of the river
valley seemed to turn their long goose faces from her as
she passed.

Shall I have to go away, I wonder, Grania thought
desperately, for she loved Aragon. Abroad, no Soo to
comfort ? Will Nan be able to . . . ? Nan had been right.
Merciless and quick. But to end it, that was the thing.
Be free of him. Be free of this warm strong pain in the
breasts, of this fear that was certainty, and certainty that
was not sure, but dreaded and longed and feared most
of all. It had not been fear when she had thought she
could use her pregnancy for him. Then she had been glad.
Not even ashamed. A little rapturous in fact, to own it.
Now she flinched from the vain fool she had been an
hour ago, crazed and blinded by the thought that he
loved her.

Another two miles and she would be home again. She
would have to face her mother and Nan and Sylvia. Ah,
Sylvia. If she had thought of Sylvia when she was down
by the sea she might really have climbed the wall and felt
the cold water flowing bigger and higher until she could
not save herself. But it was only now that the thought
of Sylvia, cool and polished, and odious, overcame her to
distraction. In the thought of Sylvia her despair quickened. It was like a hot wire in her wound, a bee sting
on her lip, a nettle in her armpits, the thought of Sylvia,
calm, vile inquisitress !

From the peak of her grief Grania slipped suddenly
into a kind exhaustion, an exhaustion founded on a pain
in her back that called only for bed, for bed and a hot
water bottle in knitted bag, for the kind of pause that is
extinction. She thought with passion of her bed, of Nan
magnificently caring for her because now she would be
obeyed. Ah, the comfort of being ill with Nan. Nan did

not fuss and pet you. She upheld you with her strength and skill, her good taste in food and flowers. The finest bed linen in her cupboards was brought out of its scented dark for the invalid. Sickness was dramatised and cossetted with an artist's instinct so long as Nan was all powerful with the patient, the giver or withholder of all good things—oh, she could have her way with Grania now, she could do what she liked, so long only as she would be kind—the memory of all her resolves for Aunt Pidgie, resolves taken when she was drunk, faded from Grania's mind. Probably, almost certainly, Aunt Pidgie had exaggerated ; certainly she had been blind drunk when Grania had left the nursery, full of wine herself, and had turned the key in the door to lock Aunt Pidgie in, so that she might go blameless and unpunished on Nan's return. Aunt Pidgie did tell such awful stories. The black men who tried to get in at her windows. The Diblins who gave her shells in the woods. T-runk, the god of travel in the attic. The leprosy which infested her sheets at the full moon. . . . No, you could not pay serious attention to anything Aunt Pidgie said about Nan. Grania blamed herself uncomfortably for having listened and encouraged, and wondered with dismay how she was to explain away the burning of the boots and the winter combinations. She could not let Aunt Pidgie take the blame, not all the blame, although it was absurd to suppose that Nan could really punish her. The nearer she came to Aragon and to Nan, her only supporter, her strength still, her help to come, the more Grania wavered towards Aunt Pidgie's cause. The strength of the truth she had known this evening in the nursery became fantasy, love and pity for Aunt Pidgie were succeeded by the exasperated indulgence which she usually inspired. Now, against Grania's own overpowering sea of trouble Aunt Pidgie's case seemed a slight matter, not the horrifying tragedy it had been when Grania promised her the house by the sea with pebbles on the gateposts, and beefsteaks for her dinner, and fine leather shoes, and lambswool of the softest to wear next her skin. Now she found herself planning to buy Aunt Pidgie a handsome present of soft shoes and fine wool combinations and so settle the question. She would forget this wild talk they had had together soon enough. Perhaps the combinations only, not the shoes. She would speak to her mother about shoes, in fact she could not quite see why her mother should not buy both shoes and combinations, Grania could choose them . . . if Nan would not be too much offended by such interference. . . .

Grania was nearly opposite to Aragon now on the other side of the river, the lovely house would soon dawn upon her sight, spread above the sunken wax river, the mountains low beyond its high standing, and the sky hollow over house and lands. Grania was always sensible of the dramatic, vision like quality to this aspect of Aragon. Even to-night she waited the moment when the pale walls would rear up against the sky and she would see the muffs and capes of cherry blossom lace dark trees to the river edge with the faint accustomed stir in her mind.

When she rounded the high wooded corner she saw Aragon on fire. Its height and beauty dwarfed and crippled by the height of flames, flames that burst out from the windows and wound their tongues like awful roses through the stone balustrade along the roof and leapt about against the faint sky and sank from it again, the soft, unpitying sky. Under the house the little foxes and the formal stone urns were terribly lit, ghastly disinterest surrounding their remote stoney formality. The foxes would be there and the urns would hold their scorched flowers to-morrow. White magnolias and cherry blossom stood out like paper between the firelight and the dark of trees and hill. The roaring of a mountain side of gorse on fire rose and crashed louder on the air carrying the peculiar deathly smell of fire. Such wind as there was bellied the fire outwards towards the river below and the strip of deep water would redden and grow dark again

as the fire blew or straightened like ribbon to the sky.
The wet mud banks glowed and gleamed hideously and
sucked up the true and the reflected showers of flame and
spark that fell to them.

The shock of fire, a shock beyond any other struck at
Grania. She screamed and stopped herself angrily and then
she screamed again and all feeling of her sorrow fell from
her, for she remembered Aunt Pidgie was locked in the
nursery and none but she and Nan knew this, Aunt Pidgie
and Soo. The key of the door was in Grania's room. Aunt
Pidgie's secret key, hidden so that Nan might not guess
how Grania had escaped and perhaps blame Aunt Pidgie
for her going. The house was so changed in its consuming
fire and smoke that Grania could not tell whether or not
the nursery windows showed flame too. Surely someone
had got Aunt Pidgie and Soo out in time. Surely they had
got the door open. Grania's heart sank terribly as she
thought of those heavy mahogany doors, smooth and
beautifully fitting, and who was to know that the key
was hidden in the shell box on Grania's dressing-table?
Despairing and terrified Grania set the car going as
fast as she could, faster than she had ever driven or dared
to think of driving. She dashed up to the corners, and
this road had as many turns as a snail shell, and trod on
the brakes as she reached them, skating round and on
again. The powerful awkward old car charged along like
a heavy, angry bull. Grania found a new kind of nerve,
born of terror and uncaring despair, and it gave her a
desperate grand pleasure to drive in this way, wielding
a power that frightened her, tearing through the evening
with crashing brakes and screaming horn (when she found
a hand to blow it) but the steering took most of her time
and all her strength. It was three miles and more to get
round and over the bridge, across the river to Aragon,
and Grania went, bundling madly along, for more than
two of them with success, punctuated by hairbreadth
escape and wicked venturing. A dog was her undoing.
She could not kill a dog no matter what was happening

to Aunt Pidgie, and the greyhound puppy that ran out of a farm gate on her left and the slight bend which the road took to her right, combined to send the car skidding and hurtling and diving into a deep ditch where she stood quivering on her radiator for a moment before sinking backwards, like the outraged gentlewoman she was, instead of pitching over into the field beyond, as she might well have done.

Grania got out and ran to the cottage from which the greyhound had come. She hammered at the door and shouted, but no one answered her. Her hopes of a borrowed bicycle faded. As the mountain people had kept to their houses to-day, so did these people who had seen the great burning of Aragon.

Grania left the house after a minute and went running down the road, running and sobbing for breath, pausing and running on again. The evening was like one of those dreams of vast stations, trains that will not be caught, foggy disaster and endless forgetting. Yet as she reached the high pillars of Aragon's gates and ran between the two cut stone foxes and entered the grove of lime trees that bordered this avenue, part of Grania's dream changed to the exquisite relief of waking, for now she knew that she was not going to have any baby, had she guessed, never been going to have any baby at all.

XXXVI

THEY gagged Nan on the mountain that evening, pulling the scarf from her neck to bandage the gag into her mouth ; they tied her hands together and marched her along between them, the killer and the boy she had outwitted.

Nan was a strong walker, but now her heart was beating and choking her and she could not breathe properly with the gag in her mouth. Soon she was dragging and stumbling between them along the rough mountain track, frightened and breathless now, all her bravery dead, and only a terrible fluttering failing sensation of fear possessing her. If she could breathe she could bear anything, she felt, and her eyes moved in a pitiful distorted way in her head as she tried to express without hands or voice how much she longed to be freed from her gag. She staggered and barged into her captors, trying to make them understand that she could go no further. But they only laughed at her and barged back in return, and the Killer showed her a pin he would prick her with if she did not hurry herself. A piece of heather as sharp as a thorn got into Nan's shoe and tortured each step she made. She walked lame but they only laughed at her tricks and jogged her on again. Oddly enough, the thought of Miss Pigeon and the nail in her shoe did not cross Nan's memory then. Not so strange is reality perhaps because if Nan's imagination had ever touched Miss Pigeon she could never have used her so unkindly for so many years. Nan had not seen herself as cruel. Frazer's indictment of her this evening had come as a shock, an enraging shock to her, but now all past feeling was lost in her present pain and fear.

The endless soft evening melted round them as they walked over the mountainy highland. Below the country lay, particular as an old map, as artificial and unreal.

The loops of its deep river were unwound and laid out flat and silver, its woods and mansions dwarfed blobs, its fields meaningless tatty little patterns. Nan saw that they were making towards Aragon, dwarfed on its river height below, and she grew more frightened and breathless with every painful step she took. Her heavy heart beat against her side and leaped towards her stuffed mouth. Everything she passed added to her pain. The shrill lettuce gleam of moss growing in a wet spot among the heather, birds' wings in the evening, the dodging of the horned blackfaced sheep, the yellow of the gorse, the rain-whitened lichen on the stones of a wall, they bundled her over it, hurting her knees and grazing her hands. All these ordinary mountain sights assailed her spirit with the awful importance assumed by objects which may never be seen again. It does not make the object valuable, this vision through fear, but it squares it out and fixes its place in the tortured mind. Here are things which can never suffer, contrasting with an hour of waiting and fear.

They reached the shelter of the woods of hazel and little native oaks that grew between the heathery upper country and the carefully planted woodlands nearer Aragon. Rides and cross paths had been cut for the woodcock shooting, the stems of the oaks and hazels were crooked and pale, and darkness itself was enveloped in the mosses and old leaves and distances under and between them. Now and again heights of wet-faced rose among the trees paler than the stems of birches, blotted with the lime green of lichen. Hazel trees and alders, dark as plums, grew in thickets, meeting each the others branches across the deep narrow glen river that ran down towards Aragon. It was a place intended for any dark and nasty deed, and Nan pulled back in terrified strength as she entered its shelter.

" What ails you now ? they laughed at her. " Tired ? You were not too tired to walk the mountains and loose our prisoners, no ? Well, you can go a bit further now and see what traitors get."

" Who opened the hen-house door, eh ? "

" Oh, it's a dose, I tell you it's a dose."

" Oh, not a nice dose at all, that traitors get."

They dragged at her arms, but she was a big woman, and she sank like a bag of meal, her head, in its smart hat, dropping forward, her chin, in the crisp white V of her shirt front, her knees gave way and she knelt between them on the rutted path through the wood.

" Ah," said the boy who had prayed, " you were too rough on her, Captain. Jesus, she couldn't stick it. This is too much of a dose she got. Give her a chance now. Take out the gag. We'll get no good of her this way."

They took the gag out of her mouth. " Let ye sing dumb now," they warned her. " One yelp and back it goes."

Nan gasped with relief, stretching her stiff jaw, wetting her dry blistered lips with her tongue, taking a terrible moment of ease while she could, whispering her thanks in humbleness and despair. Her grandeur was gone, melted from her bones like style off a sick bloodhound. She would have done anything for mercy now.

" I'll not speak," she whispered. " Look boys, away with ye now, and I'll send fifty golden sovereigns from my savings to any safe address you'll give me."

They laughed at her. " Oh, that's an easy one, Missus. Try another way."

" I swear before God," she said.

" Do you remember, Missus," the Killer said in a dreamy voice—they were smoking, and the smoke from their cigarettes went up faint and easy among the little trees. " Do you remember the dirty little boy you caught in the brush room, and he doubled in two and vomiting with an inward pain, poor little sod, and you with a nurse's veil on your head and a starched apron, hunting him out to clean the boots, do you remember ? Ah, these were the days ! "

Nan remembered. She remembered her easy conviction that the pantry boy, like all pantry boys, was deceiving her, playing sick and shirking work. But there had been a sequel that had given her a twinge of conscience then and a pang of fear now.

"Ah," Denny said, his eyes boring into her, "two months after he got the sack for drinking cream from the dining-room jug, and a week after that again the Nuns were knocking hell out of him, his poor little belly stuck full oozing tubes in Bungaron Hospital. He pulled out of it, he pulled out of it, though. They kept the life in him—wasn't it a great pity, see now, Missus, they to keep the life in him for this evening's wicked work?"

She put her face down in her strong hands, and tears came running down through the fingers.

"What do you want with me?" she said in a low voice. "Whatever it is do it quickly."

"After that the poor little beggar got another nice job in a gentleman's house." Denny the killer went smoothly on with his story. "Ah, if he had got in there he might be a bully butler to-day, see, and never troubling Ireland's cause, but what happened the job? Some party made it her sacred bloody business to warn the lady engaging him, to watch the dining-room cream jug, yes, and count the dried fruit in their boxes, yes, and the candy, coffee and sugar, how are you, so in the wind up he never got the job, only a hungry, weary, knockabout life kept him small and a bad stomach kept him cross, and at eighteen years he was a starving dirty little rat South of the Slot in Chicago, him that might have been bowing behind his buttons in gentry service, a stout, well-grown, harmless fool, only for you, now see."

Nan flung out her arms in the dark woods of her dear Aragon, the dark and unfriendly woods, the cold frivolous birches, little sour oaks and pale ash trees ; the groves she loved leaned from her, apart in their own cold way of living. Their light airs and mists would accept her dead and rotted body in wavering unconcern.

"I did you wrong," she said. "I did you wrong. Forgive me."

He rose to his feet, and his mates rose uncertainly too. They seemed to make awkward copies of his every gesture. They looked around them, peering through the trees.

" These trees are very small," said one.

" She's a big woman," said the other.

" It will soon be dark now," the Captain said. He looked down at his hands and rubbed them together.

XXXVII

AUNT PIDGIE woke out of her drunken stupor at ten minutes past nine. She came of a family that had always been able to hold its liquor like Fox's and gentlemen. Now, although a little dim and dazed, she felt perfectly well, and rather strengthened than otherwise by her unaccustomed outbreak. She peered at the clock on the mantelshelf for some moments before she took in that the time was advanced so far beyond her usual supper hour. What a silly little doze, she scolded herself severely, denying to herself that she had been asleep since seven o'clock, what a naughty little doze. Her eye travelled from the clock to the table where the sight of the port bottle and the half-eaten cake filled her with foreboding. I'm afraid I have been rather a naughty thing. She moistened her lips and swallowed some spittle in anticipation of possible punishments. Would it be a cold bath? No hotty? No supper? Or no cake for a week? The memory of the burnt boots suddenly assailed her. She feared very much it might be all of them, and all for a week.

So far there had been no supper, and although it was past bed-time, no Nan. Perhaps this was some new kind of punishment. Aunt Pigeon went over to the window, discovering as she moved a slight pain in her head and dizziness. She leant her hot forehead to the pane and gazed up the river and down the river between the iron

nursery bars. She felt vague and lonely. Almost she would
have welcomed Nan's angry footsteps outside the nursery
door. Then she found herself trying to remember what
Grania had told her to say in explanation of her own
disappearance; anyhow, she decided, I'll say she drank
up the port. She breathed into her hands trying to cup
and sniff her breath. No, perhaps I'd better not say
that. Just a little drop, Nannie, half a glass to warm my
tummy. After that I felt so queer I dropped my boots
in the fire. She shook her head rather hopelessly. I
know I'll make a mess of it somehow. I know I will.

Aunt Pidgie felt more and more depressed and agitated
as she gazed down on the slowly sinking river, on the
cherry blossom pluming the steep banks, white as owls'
feathers in the evening, at the dark foxes running their
endless chase at proper intervals on the stone balustrade
where it parted for shallow descending steps. On many,
many brimming summer nights Aunt Pidgie had gazed
out on this prospect, on stone and falling distance, trees
meeting water and water that had its ending in the sky, so
deeply were the mountains clefted down to the river bed.

Aunt Pidgie hated the beauty and isolation of the
prospect with all her heart. She would look out on the
wildness and beauty she had always known, with her
heart mourning for that dream cottage with its trim
garden path and gate posts stuck with pebbles and sea
shells and blue sea-smoothed pieces of glass bottles—the
cottage where she could be her own mistress and lie half
the morning in a hot bath if it pleased her. She would
set places for her Diblins at the table, the table that would
groan under its burden of beefsteak and macaroons, fried
eggs and bacon and mushrooms, home-made lemonade,
strong tea and crème-de-menthe, boiled brown eggs and
butter and toast. The wildest fancies pleased her as to
life in the little house while she gazed, as she was gazing
now, at the green sky and the evening star. In the
summer months she felt the smack of little waves on
pebbly shore, and saw the clearest mark in the world—

bird's feet on sand. She thought of the chains of rock
pools that held whopping monster shrimps, the colour of
sand and water ; lustrous rough-bearded and prong-eyed
shrimps. She could see the blue plate that would hold
them at tea-time, their once transparent bodies blushing
now a succulent pink. She imagined visits that would be
paid her by the children and their mother—not long
visits, rarely or ever would she have a guest to sleep in
the spare bedroom. She would like to keep that nice. A
white quilt on the bed, and red velvet with a bobbled fringe
tacked to the mantelpiece, and all along it would stand
her shell boxes. She looked forward to collecting cowrie
shells in the summer and sticking them neatly on to little
boxes during the long winter evenings, evenings when she
would sit at ease by her fire, piling it up with coal and
pieces of driftwood that burnt with blue and salty flames.
The mornings she would spend gathering wood along the
shore, after a nice hot breakfast, with a good hot lunch
in prospect.

Aunt Pidgie saw herself hard at work or hard at play,
eating a lot and sleeping deeply. In her dream she was
strong enough to undertake anything. Her dream had
no relation with an old lady, but with a strong-bodied,
strong-minded individual. Now, these tea-times when the
girls and their mother paid her a visit, it would be : You
sit here, my dear, and you sit here. No sugar ? Really !
The doctors say it is most strengthening, they have
ordered me three lumps in every cup. And how long do
you like your egg boiled ? Brown bread and butter with
your shrimps ? Try some of Mary's chocolate cake—
quite one of her best, and I have a lark's nest to show
you in the field after tea. Perhaps you would like a
lobster to take back to Aragon. . . . Nan, she never
allowed herself to see in the house, not even for the
pleasure of putting her bang in her place. No, that
shadow was kept without the gate. That dreadful
strength never dwarfed the cottage. That terrible common
sense never got near enough to block a fancy. And now

she leaned her tired mad head against the window and sighed all alone to her fancies and to the single star. Presently she wondered dreamily if she should not go to bed, wondered if another slice out of the ginger cake would add much to the total of her punishments, but in a sad fuss and reaction from her earlier daring, decided against its consumption.

She left off staring at the cake and went across to the door into her bedroom. Locked still ! She was locked up —locked up and forgotten. It had happened before and would befall her again, but always a terrifying sense of being a prisoner, and a hungry prisoner too, assailed her with this punishment. It nearly always came on her unexpectedly. She would not know the exact minute when Nan locked the door and left her. But she would find out, running from one door to the other. Sitting down and resolving to be calm. Getting up again to make sure she had not been a silly and failed to turn the handle properly. Hop, hop, from place to place, like a newly-caged bird. Tap on the window in case it might arrest some person's attention below. Not that she would have dreamed of asking anybody to come up and let her out. She only wanted the feeling that someone knew where she was, it was a link with outer things, this waving and pretending, it postponed the time that certainly came during these punishments when she sat by herself softly screaming—but softly, very softly, that Nan might not hear if she was outside the door ; a rasping sigh and a bat-like squeak, her face covered by her hands to shut out the all-aloneness, and a voice as papery and thin as the old moon that might be white as a bone in the sky. The thin voice and the thin moon. But the moon sailed free and cold, and Aunt Pidgie was caught and kept till death should be her rescuer.

Usually if these corrections were enforced in the evening hours she could at least go to bed—supperless, hot bottleless, but still curled, head and toes under the blankets, you could at any rate fancy yourself to be a birdie in its nest on four eggs. To-night, even this pretence was denied her. She sat in her low chair, drawn up to where the fire had burned, her black-stockinged feet out before her, and waited. It did not strike her that Nan had been ignorant of any of her crimes when the doors were locked. She only supposed that Nan knew. Nan always knew.

Outside the evening grew deeper, the river darker, and as the tide lessened, more full of the sounds of its flowing. There was too much beauty round Aragon, and too much beauty is dangerous. A complete thing is near its ending. The white brooms in the garden, even such slight mountainy things, had grown to a false fat stature, sleek as white, overfed cats in their ordered groupings. Behind the brooms rose the trimmed plumes of lilacs, grossly unbearably sweet at night. A magnolia's horned and flowerless bones were crucified against a shallow alcove in a wall alcoved for no reason but to complete an alcove at the house's farther extreme.

Rising above the river bank and the stone flights of fox-watched steps, the house with its balustraded height and outflung walls, had the attitude of a bird on its wings over water. It had the lonely quality of bird flight—only stone and water-fowl have this isolation from lush surroundings. As a wild duck might rise uncaring, from a pool of lily flowers, so Aragon was detached from the gardens and the evenings ; there was no meeting place where the house yielded at all to their awful sweetness. Not on this night did Aragon yield, nor on those other nights to come when the breath of lilacs and azaleas was to billow in at glassless windows and blow through again to the farther side of the house ; not when birds, growing used to desolation, were to fly through the roofless hall, from the river side to the red castles of rhododendrons on the hill behind would Aragon yield familiarly to desolation.

There was a time to come when seeded ash saplings would crack the cut stone steps apart, and elders flourish horridly in the round embrace of the drawing-room wall, out-curved above the river, high windows dark in it as holes burnt in a blanket. Stone by parted stone, Aragon would fight her way against desolation and holding to her life be rescued.

Some houses become ruins with meek despair, fallen masonry and rubbish is rounded over by the sod, quiet and solid as a grave. Cattle wander in and out from deserted pleasure grounds, seeking shade on hot summer days, and shelter on stormy nights—then the walls of a ruined house are useful and at rest again, no longer the racked ghosts of a dwelling-house. It is well, too, when white grass and brambles choke the exotic shrubs and wreathe and crush their bones, ending a sordid and indifferent struggle to survive.

But Aragon had been so long lived in and the gardens so well cared, that the lilacs passed only slowly from double to single, flowering more meanly each succeeding spring, pale suckers struggling from their roots. The sleek brooms withered sooner into rusty cages. Only the magnolias, breaking free from their crucifixion, propped crooked elbows to the ground and flowered with extravagant perversity. And the rhododendrons, towering magnificent above the desolation, thrust down roots into their own rotting leaves and grew from themselves. Azaleas that flowered here once, exquisite and artificial, were to fade from flame and scarlet to honey and paler honey, and succumb at last to nettles and brambles, like so many meek hungry gentlewomen, to the strong obliteration of charity. But the house, with its five cracked plaster nymphs and little stone foxes, was to endure, purged by fire and rain and sun and frosts, of its evil and its ghosts, good and bad, until the day came for Aragon to be built again by young Fox's.

Pale and hungry was Aunt Pidgie on that last night, as she sat on and waited. She was so far removed from the busyness of the house that she could not even hear the sounds of night-time maids, drawing blinds and bringing cans of hot water to the bedrooms, where they would turn down the beds swiftly and neatly and pop delicious hot-water bottles in bags of wool or quilted satin between the chill linen sheets. Aunt Pidgie could hear nothing, and this evening no one came out of the house to sit on the low wall and look dangerously down into the river. Careful, careful, Aunt Pidgie often longed to call to the girls and their beaux when she saw them do this. But she never liked to, for fear they might think she was spying on them from her window. Though after all, if they leant back even *that* much. . . . Everyone forgot the poor Aragon bride who had once gone crashing and hurtling down through the tree tops to her death. It was her widower who had built the little wall before he had married again. It was not quite high enough to be much use, but why hide so lovely a prospect because of one stupid little bride? Taught her a good lesson, I expect, Aunt Pidgie would say in her fiercer moments. Or again as she looked out and down by herself, she would shrink and tremble to think of the poor bride breaking through the branches, bouncing off the ground and ending with a great splash in the river. Her Brussels lace veil caught in the top of a tree, and two garden boys (clumsy fellows) broke a leg and an arm apiece in their efforts to fetch down an object which must so grieve the master. But he had grieved for her deeply in spite of this sad reminder being detached. He gave two black swans to the river, planted a double white cherry on the bank, and married again within the year, for he could not bear to live alone with such a memory.

Aunt Pidgie knew any number of little stories like this, both sad and gay, connected with Aragon and the Fox's who had lived there. She often ran over the dramas in her own mind standing on the spot, or as near to the spot as she judged safe, or could guess where they had been enacted. To-night when she was very weary of her chair she crossed again to the window and looked out across

the empty terrace and down to where the Bride's Tree
glimmered like old snow in the dark. I wish someone
would come. I wish someone would come, she said. Her
voice was like one mosquito in the summer dark. As she
gazed, a curious procession came into her view—a
procession that filed down the shallow terrace flight and
halted at the river wall, halting with their backs to the
river below and their hands held high over their heads.
It was the servants, Frazer, the cook and kitchen maid
(always changing, Aunt Pidgie could never know her
rightly) and Kathleen and Rosie, the two housemaids.
Behind them came Sylvia in her smoke-pale evening
dress, with a paler ribbon tied high above her little waist,
and her arms up too, pretty graceful little beast, and that
horrid dog of hers after her as usual. Last there came a
man in a belted coat, a dark hat pulled down over his
eyes, and something wrong with his face ; it was
bandaged, and he had something in his hand. Aunt Pidgie
looked out as at a little play, peering from her bad seat
in the gallery, and saw that it was a gun he had in his
hand. The group stood quite silent and still on the
gravel. Frazer's shirt was a milky gleaming petal between
his dark coat fronts ; the maids' aprons frothed and
swirled about them in the light evening air—what were
they all doing. Suddenly it came clearly to Aunt Pidgie's
slight, slow brain—this was a hold-up. The man in the
overcoat was a masked gunman, and what, it flashed
through her mind, would he do to Sylvia before all was
over ? Aunt Pidgie was glad of her locked doors now—
no nasty men would get into her room, whatever they
did to Sylvia. She and Soo had only to keep quiet to
come through the ordeal unnoticed and unmolested.
Whatever happened, keep quiet, keep quiet till Nan
came back.

Peering round the edge of her curtain, Aunt Pidgie saw
every lifted hand pointing towards her window. Like a
chorus on a stage, the line took a forward step and
pointed violently at her windows. Oh dear, dear, the

mean cowardly things to give her away like that. Even
Frazer had pointed. Was she to join that group who
would no doubt be shot one by one and their bodies hurled
backwards like the Aragon brides down through the trees
to the river. Ah, Aunt Pidgie shivered. She would not
join that doomed party if she could help it. She looked
wildly about her, wondering where she could hide.
Suppose they broke the lock to drag her out ! As the
thought struck her she heard heavy steps running up the
stairs, and a strange voice shouting, " Any one there ?
Any one there ? " and fists smashed on doors and rattled
at handles.

A violent trembling took Aunt Pidgie. She sat down
in her little chair. Signed to Soo to jump on to her knee,
pulled her skirt over her head so that they were both in
a private cage within this house of terror, and stopping
her ears violently with her fingers—I'm a Birdie, I'm a
Birdie, I'm a Birdie, she said to herself over and over
again. So she did not hear her door rattled and shaken,
or the voice that called, " Speak up now. Speak up if
you're in there. We're firing the house. Fire ! Fire !
Fire ! "

The voices went shouting past her unheard. I'm a
Birdie, a Birdie, a Birdie, she repeated, hearing only the
blood in her stoppered ears, and the clatter made by the
" D " in Birdie against the roof of her mouth. She did
not hear Killer Denny shouting to hurry and get on with
the work, the old B. was safe enough or she'd have
squealed out long ago. Blind and deaf, she sat on, busily
being a Birdie until Soo, suddenly restless and frightened,
struggled out of her dark nest and went, whining and
sniffling, to the door.

Then Aunt Pidgie threw back her skirt and raised her
head and sniffed a curious smell, a smell of burning, and
heard a crackling rustling noise, the sort of noise, she
thought, a big bonfire might make. She stole over to the
window and peeped out. Smoke was pouring out of the
windows below her, blowing up against the glass of her

own so that she could hardly see, but it puffed between the close white iron bars and blurred the glass.

She gazed out stupidly, smelling the queer, dangerous, hungry smell of fire, hearing its hidden roar and crackle. At last, seeing a little curl of flame in the smoke far below, she knew what had happened.

She sprang about and rushed to the door, shaking its handle and piping out in that lone mosquito voice : " Fire ! Fire ! Fire ! Help. Help. Fire ! Fire ! " But only silence poured back to her. Not even the roar of flames could be heard from this side of the room. Back to the window again ; she pushed up the heavy sash and pressed her head between the upright bars, calling : " Frazer, Frazer, Frazer."

She heard Frazer shouting in answer, and through the clouds of smoke she saw the white-aproned maids sinking to their knees in prayer, sinking down in the stones with their eyes hidden in their hands. She saw Frazer and Sylvia and their guard running towards the house—they shouted :

" All right, Aunt Pidgie."

" We'll get you, Miss——"

Then she turned round and saw Soo beside her, licking her lips uneasily, licking her thin black lips and coughing a little. Poor Soo, little French tart in sore trouble, though her exquisite waist looked an inch smaller from anxiety and her dark brown eyes popped out of her head a little as the best French girls' do at times. Aunt Pidgie picked her up. As she held her strong anxious little body between her hands, that basket of strong ribs, that round and thrusting head, she felt like a young person in her determination that Soo should not burn. Her brain, for once concentrated and alert, worked at lightning speed. She sat down and took off her black stockings. She tied them round Soo, making a harness of stockings. Then she went to the drawer where the ball of string was kept, and knotted and double-knotted the end of the string in the harness. Soo mimbled and curtseyed and licked her lips. "Now," said Aunt Pidgie, and lifted her up on the window-sill.

"Hallo, hallo," she coughed and coughed again, for she was speaking into a cloud of smoke. The figures at prayer still on the terrace below looked far away, tears poured down Aunt Pidgie's face, and Soo's eyes looked watery enough as she shrank and cringed in her harness on the sill.

"Cook," Aunt Pidgie screamed. "Damn you, come here, Cook!"

They heard her and advanced, overcoming with difficulty that horror of the doomed which so often besets the living. They advanced, crying, towards her window.

"It's Soo," Aunt Pidgie shouted. "Do you hear me? Come nearer, you fools, it's Soo."

"Yes, Miss; yes, Miss," they said, standing exactly where they were.

"Come near."

"Yes, Miss."

"It's Soo," she screamed out again through the smoke. Without looking at Soo, or she could never have done it, she pushed her over the edge of the window-sill, and started to unwind the ball of string, tautened to snapping point by the struggling nine pounds of weight dependent on it.

It was the kitchen maid, the youngest and least intelligent in household matters, who grasped what was to be done and rushed into the smoke. "I have her, Miss, I have her," she shrieked.

Aunt Pidgie felt the string slacken in her hands. Alone now, she threw the ball out of the window, and stood still trembling with fear, "Fraser, Frazer," she whimpered. "Nan, oh Nan, come back." She stood still, rubbing her thin withered fingers where Soo's weight on the string had bruised into their slight flesh. Her back was turned stupidly to the open window where the smoke gushed in. Her eyes were fixed on the locked door.

XXXVIII

IT never occurred to Sylvia not to dress for dinner that evening when she feared her love lay newly murdered up in the heather. At 7.30 she took her bath with its accustomed drops of rose-geranium and washed herself with as much meticulous concentration as usual. She had felt cold as lead when she lay down in the hot water. When she got out and dried herself she was still cold and shivered as she walked across the passage, past all the tall mahogany doors, to her bedroom—her bedroom that had no more colour in it than the whites and greys and near-greens of river weeds, with all the distinction of such water flowers. Sylvia sat in front of her clear glass with its old nibbled frame of worn gilt and its pale golden bird posing in a leaf circle. In the glass she saw tears pouring down her clean chill cheeks, she saw a girl weeping in despair and hardly knew it was herself. She could know her love dead ; her glass-cold little heart be shivered in pieces, but the pieces were still glass. Shock acts strangely. With Sylvia it delayed her yielding to despair although it left her without a movement towards hope. She was shut in a neat square box of despair and being Sylvia she moved with her usual grace and precision in this small dark place. She blew her nose and stuffed back the awful tears, but they flew up through her head again. She despised her own crying. I'll be good, I'll be good, she strained against the cruel evening air. Is it over ? Yes. Yes. The tears went back. Four or six defeated her will and raced down her face and fell on her bare knees that were laced together, twisted up for strength to resist this crying. This was sorrow. Not to think of him. She didn't think of him. She thought backwards very quickly about a woman's face in church. What was she wearing ? Make a list, don't lose hold. Hat, blouse, coat, skirt, shoes . . . don't lose hold. . . .

She brushed her hair back and back from the little peaks in which it grew down her forehead and above her ears. She would not look in the glass at her shaking mouth. She turned her back on the glass and put on her clean fine underclothes, her grey dress with its faint high-tied ribbon, her short string of river pearls. She picked up her work-bag and went down to the drawing-room to wait alone for dinner. As she waited she stitched at the flowers in her tapestry. It was as if she made a neat little wreath for a grave.

Frazer came in at five minutes to eight, he shut the door quietly and crossed over to where she was sitting.

" Will you have dinner at eight, Miss, or will you wait for Mrs. Fox and Miss Grania ? " He always spoke with the soft distinctness of a good servant, but this evening he breathed the words gently, as if he would rebuke his own voice for speaking at all, and if speak he must, the air should hardly be stirred by him.

" I won't wait beyond 8.15."

Sylvia's voice sounded improperly natural, " They may be very late."

" Very good, Miss."

She was left alone again, the perfect figure in such a room, as right as any of the marble reliefs that stooped with their garlands of pointed leaves in the plaques on the mantelpiece. Her strong small neck was bowed, her hands busy and steady as on the day before, when she had finished her swan's wing, and eaten her dinner with so much pleasure and good appetite.

To-night, as yesterday, the river and the April light were joined and took the indoor air together, sharpening the red in the coats of dead dull Fox soldiers and hunting men, dwelling and drowning in the pale round carpet, turning the white glaze on china milk-soft and luxurious to the eye, swelling light romantic and untruthful through the room. The air was burdened with ragged water scents. Broken river smells lifted the lilac on their strength as scent is built, so that lilac, doubly, terribly sweet filled the room too, and the rich heart-breaking songs of birds

Sylvia sat on, her hands moving busily at her work. She thought with passionate liking of the silent grave herons, glad that she could not even see that lonely flight from their nest in a flat-topped cedar to the river below, they had no connection with sweet scents or rapturous songs. She could think of them.

The gong sounded and Frazer opened the drawing-room door and stood inside it with a murmur, dinner was served.

Dinner was eaten, soup, fish, cold lamb, a tiny savoury. Sylvia would show no silly signs of heartbreak through plates of untouched food. She ate steadily and went back to the drawing-room for her coffee, then the paper. After dinner she always read the paper. To-night, beyond any other night, there must be no change. The *Morning Post* of the day before was lying folded on the table by the sofa where it was always put. The fire, ten minutes lighted, gave out no heat. The curtains were not drawn and only one lamp near the fire was burning. Sylvia picked up the paper and sat down beside the light. She began to read the leading article, a furious indictment of England's weakness in the conduct of this Irish war. She read on in bitter agreement with all the *Morning Post* proposed to do to Rebels and Gunmen, read on until the door opened and she looked up to take her coffee from Frazer.

It was Killer Denny who stood there with his two boys, one on either side of him, and all three had guns in their hands.

" Good-evening," Sylvia leaned out of her chair towards the fireplace.

" Don't touch that bell."

" What do you want ? " Sylvia asked as steadily as possible, for there is something unutterably alarming about three masked men with guns in their hands standing suddenly in your drawing-room on a spring evening. None the less so because you have just been reading that their country is at war with the government under which you live. None the less surprising because to-day they had killed your lover that to-night they should stand in your house with guns in their hands.

Sylvia was frightened, and because she was frightened she spoke boldly and rudely.

" Get out," she said. " Get out of this house at once." How silly, how shrill.

Killer Denny laughed quite naturally.

" It's you who'll do the getting out, now see," he said going up to her, " and quick mind you, unless you want to burn along with your ancestral bloody home, now see." He went to the fireplace. " Not much heat out of that," he said, " We'll soon have a better blaze."

He stood over Sylvia. He did not touch her. He did not put out a hand towards her. He looked at her out of his bold little dark eyes, bright as a rat's through his mask, and he turned his head on his strong neck and spat on the carpet.

" I've wanted to do that," he said, " for a long time." When he had done it he was ashamed. It looked awful. It is one thing to burn a beautiful house, it is another thing to spit on its floor.

Sylvia was recovering some of her horrid poise.

" A childish thing to do," she said, pulling her skirt closer to herself, " childish and dirty, don't you think so, hardly what one expects from an officer of the I.R.A."

He turned to his two men, " Go and get the servants out, boys," he said, " and quick. Bring the lot in here."

" There's a very old lady upstairs," Sylvia said, " may I go up and explain this little party to her? She may be rather alarmed, you know."

" One of the servants can get her out. You stay where you are. We don't want any help from you."

Sylvia sat back in her chair—was it any good arguing? was it any good doing anything? What did one save when houses were burnt? Silver? Jewellery? Papers?

" Could I collect a few personal belongings," she said, frigidly, pompously.

" No."

Suddenly she stood up, thin and straight in her grey dress as smoke in a frost.

" It's outrageous, it's awful, what good will you do to anybody by burning Aragon ? " She looked wildly around the room. At the mantelpiece. At the dark glass. At the honey-coloured shells curling in the inlay of dark thin tables. At the china she had always seen, the gay-flowered coats of groups of Worcester and Chelsea. Suddenly she felt again the ache to touch that bright china gives to children, she cried out in their defence :

" You can't do it. Why are you doing this ? "

Killer Denny followed her eyes to the Chelsea group.

" I had a great admiration for that ornament when I was a little fellow," he said softly. " Mrs. O'Neill got me one day with it in my hand, she took it from me and she beat hell out of me."

He picked it up again, a boy in a mulberry coat with a hen in a basket under his arm. He looked at the pretty silly thing and then dropped it on the flat stone before the fireplace, it broke, but not much, because it was tough and light.

" You'll have to try again," Sylvia said.

He picked it up and held it in his hands, fitting the broken bits together.

" Nothing I do," he said oddly, " would divide me from that little boy."

" I don't remember you."

" One dirty pantry boy is very like another." He put the broken figure back on the mantelpiece as the boys came in driving the whispering, terrified servants before them. Even in such a pass they felt very uncomfortable in the drawing-room. The housemaid thought the cook would take offence because she was pushed in before her, and the tweenie was miserably conscious that even such a disaster as this promised to be could not save her from a

row because she had no cap on her head. Frazer was quite
undone, pale and shaking and terrified for his northern
blood.

" Out there, now." Denny pointed through the window
to the wall above the river, " and if there's a word or a
stir out of one of them, fire, boys." It sounded very
alarming.

" Can't we save anything," Sylvia asked.

" Christ, God," he swore, " how much more time are
we to waste ? Till the soldiers are here, I suppose ? Quick
now, out with them."

" But Aunt Pidgie," Sylvia cried wildly, " she is not
here, let me get her."

" Get out. I'll see to her, we don't want to burn old
ladies, but we will if we're short of time Out now the
lot of you and keep quiet."

Sylvia wanted to get a coat from the hall, but the boy
in charge, the boy who had been captured by Nan, was
too uncertain of himself to allow any leniency. Sylvia
recognised early that he was far more likely to shoot one
of them for disobedience than was his tough superior.
He had the shaky manner in bullying that turns quickly
to extremities for its support. It was better to hurry out
into the garden, out into the chill evening and stand
against a wall to watch the house burn.

Every few minutes she would say to the boy. " What
about the old lady? Why don't they bring her out?"
And he would answer in the voice of an official in the
customs :

" Captain Cussens will deal with that matter."

She broke out of the line once crying desperately that
she must find Aunt Pidgie, but she was halted, ordered
back with such temper that she knew the foolishness
of persistence. The wind that blew under the maids'
aprons nipped her bare arms and roughed her neat
hair. " Mayn't we put our hands down ? " Sylvia asked
then, " we haven't any arms and it is so tiring."

" Captain Cussens orders," he answered, so they continued to stand like people in a game painted on a box lid, backs to the river, palms up towards the house.

Sylvia began to cry when she saw no sign of Aunt Pidgie being brought out. It was so terrifying not to know about her. By accident she might burn. No one's evil intention, but fluster and hurry and excitement would leave her helpless and unaccessible with Aragon burning round her. The burning house cutting off the way to the nursery, there would be no way of getting her out through the barred windows. Sylvia clapped her hands, and shouted, "Aunt Pidgie!" "Aunt Pidgie!" the cook shouted. The other servants were too timid. Afraid a little of their own voices or far more of their guard. Frazer grew pale and looked like a little frightened man, all butlerhood cast aside. "Miss Sylvia, Miss Sylvia," he whispered, "do you want to get us all butchered?"

"If there's another word out of any of you," the guard said, "I'll fire."

Sylvia was silenced. Indeed it was as well, for Miss Pidgie was sitting now with her ears stopped, so that she could not have heard a sound from the garden far below. She did not even hear the boys when they knocked at the door, calling and shaking the handle. She did not hear the steps going away or the shouts. It was Soo and the smoke that brought her to the window twenty minutes later.

"She's there, she's in there still," Sylvia cried.

"Oh, my God, she's done for," Frazer said. "There's flames from the landing window, there's flames from the linen-room."

"Ah, the poor little old dickens," the boy said, horror in the light curious words.

It was then that Aunt Pidgie saw the three break from the line, Sylvia, Frazer and the boy with the gun. They ran towards the house calling confused reassuring words while the maids left behind sank down on their knees on the stones.

XXXIX

BURNING curtains are madly beautiful, but there is something terrible about the sight of a flaming bed, as shocking as though a good comfortable hen was on fire. It is an unbearable sight, one would as soon look at a fat cosy bishop on his pyre.

It was through the open doors of the bedroom (left open to fan draughts) that Sylvia saw the fat beds blazing. Smoke poured out on to the stairs blinding and choking her. On the stairway going up to the nursery linen and blankets and pink eiderdowns had been pulled out and blazed in heaps and wreaths.

Frazer stood appalled. " We'll never get her," he said ; it was like someone in a hunt saying : You can't go there. You can't get through there, wire, it's wired.

Sylvia said, " It's only the linen burning, get some water, get the minimax." Fraser and the boy stood coughing and doing nothing.

The two who had done the burning came running up the stairs. They had the savage desperate look of boys who had committed some outrage beyond their own believing, an outrage that has got beyond them and taken on a strength of its own.

" Outside," they shouted, " what the hell are you doing here ? " The boy said, " The old lady is above yet."

" Come away, come away," Frazer said. " Do you want to be listening to her in her death ? "

" There's no one in the house," Denny said. " God damn, didn't we try every door."

" She's there, she was at the window." Sylvia tore past him to the corner at the end of the corridor where a fire extinguisher was hung. As in all large houses there were perhaps three at extreme distance throughout the house, refilled last not less than ten years past.

"Get water, show them where to get water," she shouted to Frazer He put his hands over his eyes and ran coughing down the stairs and out of the house.

"Well, the old rat," Denny looked down into the hall below, "would you believe that, eh? Would you trust the sight of your sacred eyes?"

The boys had run down the corridor after Sylvia. They came back with cans of water in their hands like housemaids at their ordinary evening business.

"Yes, do, boys, and then fire down a spit and make a job of it." He took the minimax from Sylvia. "Go and put a coat on you," he said. "One spark and you're up in a blaze, now see. Give that here, and you chaps lift a carpet out of that room at the end, it's not burning."

He cracked the knob of the extinguisher and sprayed the burning blankets on the stairs. They threw the carpet down and stamped out the curling flames He shut the door of the burning linen-room and ran shouting up towards the nurseries.

"Keep the fire off the stairs, boys," he called down behind him.

Sylvia came flying up from the hall, coated obedient to his order, she ran past the two on the stairs, past the awful roaring sound of the burning linen-room. He stood above her in the dark passage, white-faced, coughing, he had pulled off his mask and his hat, he was stooping down trying to get his breath.

"Aunt Pidgie, are you there?" Sylvia called at the nursery door. She twisted the handle. "Open the door, Aunt Pidgie, quickly. It's all right. It's Sylvia. It's Sylvia, do you hear me?"

"Nan locked me up," Aunt Pidgie spoke in a clear, trembling voice. "All the doors are locked, Sylvia. I can't get out There's no way out, Sylvia."

"What does she say?" Killer Denny was whispering at Sylvia's shoulder, they were alone together with the terror and horror of Aunt Pidgie's certain death around them.

" Captain, Captain, this stair won't last," the boys'
voices came calling.

" She's locked in."

The Killer pulled Sylvia gently away from the door
and crashed his shoulder against it trying to burst it
open. Then he said, " tell her to go back from it. I'll
try to shoot the lock off."

" Aunt Pidgie, do you hear me ? Go into the night
nursery."

" The door's bolted," came Aunt Pidgie's clear hopeless
little voice again

" Get away from this door, go over to the window.
Get into the cupboard, Aunt Pidgie. We've got to shoot
off the lock."

He was profiled against the door, arm out, head sunk.
Sylvia was close as a plaque to the wall behind him. He
fired, once, twice. The shot crashed and echoed in the
narrow place. The smell bit its way through the other
smoke. He tried the door again. The wood was bruised
and splintered but the beautifully made lock held firm.
In the succeeding silence Aunt Pidgie's gnat's voice
spoke.

" It's all right, Sylvia. Frazer says the soldiers are
coming, he sees the lorries on the road across the river."

" Do you hear that ? " Sylvia whispered to the Killer,
he was squeezing a splinter out of the ball of his thumb.
He nodded and ran to the stairs.

Tears poured down Sylvia's face as she wrenched at the
handle and flung herself on the door, she would have
broken every bone in her body to get in. She was alone
now. She knew that it was madness to stay here. She
was doing no good. In a few minutes she herself would be
more hopelessly trapped than Aunt Pidgie.

Sylvia was not in the least fond of Aunt Pidgie. She
would have done this for her own dog as readily. With
the same vain protectiveness of the strong towards the
weak. All that was tough and cold and fair in her, all
indeed that was least pleasant went to the sacrifice.

" Would Nan's big scissors help ? " came Aunt Pidgie's voice again in most sensible suggestion.

" Yes, yes, shove it under the door."

Sweat and tears running down her cheeks, Sylvia was struggling to drive the scissors through the splintered wood and somehow catch the lock when a hand was put on her arm and she looked up through her fallen hair and saw Denny.

" You came back. But you'll be caught."

He gave her a direct look. A look that crossed fire and death and their opposite ways of living. A look straight from a tough guy to a tough girl. There was a streak of divine humour in the soft way he said :

" Ah, no. You'll get me off, now see, won't you ? "

" I will," Sylvia said, and the promise was given. She would do as much for his safety now as for Aunt Pidgie or for her dog's safety.

Then it was again, " Stand back, Aunt Pidgie, say when you're in the cupboard."

" One, two three. Fire."

Aunt Pidgie's voice came brave and oddly strong before the crash and echo of the gun. It was like a child playing soldiers afraid to be afraid of the bang.

This time more of the wood was shattered away. Denny picked cleverly and slowly at the bared lock. It was as if he had an afternoon before him to do a neat carpenter's job. His hands were as leisurely and as sure. Sylvia found herself forgetting the fire that was raging under them. He said to her, " Go and keep water on the stairs where the boys were, if you can, and look out for yourself. The wall of that linen-room will go any minute."

The hot crackle of fire was coming between the door he had shut and the jambs, the wall was like a plate out of the oven. Sylvia picked up the jugs the boys had left down when they had gone and ran down the passage to the bathroom, they had shut the bedroom doors, smoke came out flat underneath them and rose up in puffs. It poured up from the hall, the heat was terrifying, and what had she heard about putting wet cloths on your mouth in a fire ? She had no cloths. She came heavily back with her jugs of water, sobbing out her coughs. She flung the water weakly, and it seemed to her pitiably, at the sizzling blistered door of the linen-room. She could hardly see as she set back down the wide end landing again towards the bathroom.

When she got back the door had fallen inwards. She looked into a hellish bowl of flame, of insupportable, impossible, raging flame. It was blown outwards to the stairs, through the door, like rain flat before a storm of wind. Sylvia put up her hands to save her face from the intense awful heat. She screamed upwards to the man she could not see :

" Come down, come down. It's too late, do you hear, come down." There was no answer. She made an effort she did not know she had in her. She staggered up the six steps to where the fire would come through on to the stairs, and she poured her two cans of water on the steps, and screamed out again.

Then she saw him. He came down the dark corridor, and he carried in his arms a bundle as small as a six-year-old child, covered in a blanket. Aunt Pidgie's head against his shoulder showed out round through the blanket, like the drawing of some holy child underneath the mother's shawl. He stood for a moment at the head of that flight of stairs with the fire he had lighted belching towards it, then he tightened his grip on Aunt Pidgie and ran down into the smoke and flames.

Who can measure how intense the shock of burning is ? He was trembling and crying and holding the wrist of his burnt hand while Sylvia squeezed the flame and scorch out of his clothes. Aunt Pidgie, out from under her blanket, was shaking but unsinged and obedient to orders.

They ran all three hand in hand down the wide stair-case. " Can we get through the kitchen way ? " Sylvia asked. He nodded, coughing. They pushed through the heavy swing door that divided the hall from the back passages and suddenly the quiet was like that of a cold still well. The quiet of a dripping tunnel with a burning hot road at either end. The musty smell of back passages, plate powder and damp and firelessness, the smell of old pocket linings and empty wine cases was soothing to their throats. They felt real again. He said suddenly, and all the time they were running, " I could do with a drink."

" Yes," Sylvia said, " so could I." In Frazer's pantry they found a bottle of whisky, the rows of clean tumblers in the cupboard looked sane and peaceful. It was worth waiting to get this, they needed this.

Sylvia said, " We must keep Aunt Pidgie with us and they'll think we're all trapped up there. They'll be getting ladders "

He said, " But no one knows I'm with you."

" Listen, I'm not bargaining." Sylvia turned the cold tap into their whisky. " But what have you done with Captain Purvis and Mr. Craye ? "

" My God," he said, " and I'd forgotten her, too."

" Who ? "

They drank, gulping in haste and looking at each other, a new distrust growing between them.

" I'd like a drop too," said Aunt Pidgie.

" Yes, perhaps you do need it." Sylvia measured it out like medicine.

" Ah, for God's sake, give her a drink," he laughed.

" Who have you forgotten ? "

" Listen, child, when I'm gone, away with you down the mountain avenue, and you'll find what I've forgotten."

He would not say any more. She realised it was because he was afraid she would not help him. Sylvia grew a little afraid too. What would she find.

" What about the two officers ? " she whispered.

" Safe back in barracks, when they should be cooling in the heather."

They were growing apart, the bond of death and fear loosened.

" Thank God ! "

" What about me now ? " He looked at her closely,
he did not trust her as he had done when she said, " I
will " in the darkness and the smoke.

Sylvia said, " I'll get you out," she looked at Aunt
Pidgie who had shrunk in importance now, shrunk back
into the poor little old nuisance she really was. What a
situation Aunt Pidgie had put her in.

" You'd want to hurry yourself," he said roughly.

Sylvia said, " Out through the stable yard would be
the best."

They were running again, Aunt Pidgie bundled along
between them. In the yard she grew suddenly very
weighty on their arms, her legs did not seem able to keep
up with them. Once they pulled her back on to her feet
which trailed behind like a dead duck's.

" Aunt Pidgie, are you all right ? "

Aunt Pidgie shook her head peacefully. " Put me on
my nest," she said, " I'm a clocker. I'm broodie."

" What are you talking about ? "

" I'm a broodie birdie."

Denny looked across her at Sylvia, there was laughter
in his eyes, " Blind," he said.

Sylvia said, " We'll shut her in a loose box. She'll be
all right." They opened one of the painted wooden stable
doors and put her in. There was a heap of straw in one
corner. There Aunt Pidgie nested contentedly.

" Don't move till I get back, Aunt Pidgie."

" It takes twenty-one days," Aunt Pidgie murmured,
closing her eyes.

As she settled down they saw that her feet were bare.
They had hurried her down the flagged passages and
across the gravel on her bare feet and she had not said a
word in complaint.

Sylvia felt a sudden pride in Aunt Pidgie. Again to-
night those tortured little feet had their strange effect on
cruel youth.

" Oh, Aunt Pidgie, your poor feet."

Aunt Pidgie curled them away beneath her, " Chook, chook," she murmured drowsily. " Chook, chook, chook."

Sylvia saw the soldiers first. They came through the back door. They had rifles in their hands and they looked as foreign as men in uniforms always do.

" Get back, quick," she said, " get back with Aunt Pidgie," she spoke without turning her head, and as' she spoke a flood of determination to save him rose in her, the hunted creature must be saved. Danger is sacred ; she was glad that her word bound her.

The soldiers, five of them, came running across the yard towards her.

" Any shinners 'ere, Miss ? "

" They've cleared off." How unsteady a lie makes the coldest voice.

" We've got orders to search the stables and out-offices."

" For heaven's sake go up to the yard and get the long ladder, there's an old lady trapped upstairs."

" Sorry, Miss, the poor old lady's done for. Terrible thing."

" Butler says, floor went five minutes ago."

" Quite a tragedy, Miss."

" Yes, shocking, and the other old girl gone west on the drive. We were upset."

" Who do you mean, not Nan ? "

" That's it. That's what the young lady called her."

Sylvia leaned against the high door of the loose box where killer Denny crouched against the wall, his empty gun in his hand, and Aunt Pidgie stirred in her nest.

" Right," she said, raising her head, " get on with it, boys. Don't mind me. Careful of the chestnut mare at the end, she's a bit free with her heels. And leave this box alone, my young horse is here, he's half-cracked with the smoke and the smell."

" Better get the 'orses out, I'd say."

" The wind's all the other way. Send the stable boys

down like good chaps when you're through. The horses will go handier with them."

" Right, Miss, we'll carry on."

They went down the line of boxes.

Sylvia went in to Denny.

" Woa, boy, steady, little man." She spoke idiotic words of horse comfort and love, while Denny watched her with fierce bright eyes, the look of the cornered wolf was on him.

" Right, Miss," they called, coming back.

" O.K."

" Thank you."

" The beggars weren't going to 'ang around, were they ? Do the dirty and run, that's them——"

" Quiet, old chap ; quiet, little fellow," Sylvia soothed the air.

Their voices faded across the yard. " Quick," she beckoned Denny. She went up the pigeon hole ladder to the lofts before him, her long dress catching and tearing as she climbed. They were up in the green, powdery dark of the lofts together. Sylvia went running ahead between the heaps of hay and straw, the carefully turned piles of oats, dark and blond. She knew the lofts in the particular way remembered from childhood. Knew the holes in the boards and the windows where the stable lads always undid the wire so that they could drop down on to the dung-heap below and short cut it into the village.

Yes, it was open. She knew it would be open. These things are unchanging.

" I'll be all right, now," he said.

Suddenly she put out her hand.

" Thank you," she said, "and good luck."

He held her hand in the smooth, dry grip of unnervous people.

" I didn't do Nan in," he said, " I don't know what's happened to her."

" Hurry ! Hurry ! " Sylvia felt that even Nan's death was less important than his escape.

But when he went, dropping off the window-sill and disappearing into the night, she felt the hour empty, she was drained of all purpose. She was left with a sense of horror at what she had done and a sense of triumph in having done it. She had let a dangerous man go free, because he had chanced his life to save a cracked little old woman. He had nearly murdered her lover to-day and to-night she had his life in her hands and she had held it safe for him. Who would understand, no one, no one, least of all her lover. She sat in the dark, forgetting Aragon, forgetting Nan, crying over her secret she must never tell. Crying because her heart had shrunk so that there was not even room in it for relief and joy that her lover was safe. Because of what she had done, she had lessened her love to herself. Because of this past hour of peril with a tough stranger her importances were changed. She had played traitor to them and in their betrayal she had known an hour of truth. For that hour she had been closer, more obedient to one from whom by every law of her nature she was divided, than she had ever been to any man or woman in her life. And now the hour and the man were lost to her. Before she became once more the Sylvia of tennis parties and white hunting ties and blue habits, the Sylvia meet and right for her Norfolk lover (heir to a respectable old baronetcy) she must know tears for all that was lost to her. A bitter unreasoning grief that left her exhausted and unstrung.

XL

THE evening light was still steady under the level bottom
branches of the pale limes where the three boys hurried
now out of the woods and across the field to the long and
empty avenue. Nan could expect nothing from them
now, the desperation of hurry was on them. Whatever
they were going to do to her their minds were beyond it,
and on their next business. Her feet felt the smooth
avenue under them, the avenue she had walked up and
down so often with the beautiful blue pram, and God
help the nursery maid who did not keep it as Nan required.
Ah, the blue pram with its goffered white pillows and its
soft wool rug and its lusty baby. Lovely example of Nan's
sacred pride in health, example for all to see of her
professional skill. Those golden busy days, she thought
of them this evening as clearly as if they were last week's
memories, far more clearly ; but then her feet never
walked the full nice round of the avenue's surface without
her mind carrying back to those years, so why not
to-night ?

Where the limes ended and the rhododendron and
laurel at the outskirts of the pleasure grounds arched their
branches out over the avenue, the house could be seen.
Not all of it, but a stretch of stone, pale as a face, broken
across by trees and the spread of mown grass. There the
boys stopped and one of them jumped up the low wall to
the level where the dark laurels grew, he bent down a
strong limb of laurels towards the avenue below ; the rank
sweet smell of its dusty white flowers was bruised and
shaken out. A pigeon clattered away into the still
evening. The moderate white iron gate between Nan and
Aragon looked easy and domestic as it had done when
she took the pram back through it at tea-times. When the
bough was bent down to the avenue, Killer Denny took

a little rope out of his pocket and the boys crossed themselves.

Nan knelt on the gravel. Then she sat, awkwardly as a child, flat on the smooth avenue, and held the ground and the grass at the side of the avenue with her fingers gripping, her nails sunk into the very body of Aragon. She watched as the Killer tried the noose in the rope to see how did it run. It ran smoothly and freely, as tidy as could be. The other boy caught the strong laurel and held it down. His face was whiter than its dusty flowers. The smooth pointed leaves smelt of almonds, sharp and cleanly different from the flower smell.

They stood Nan up under the bough and slipped the rope over her gay hat and pulled it round her neck. It was too dark to see her desperate eyes among the laurel leaves. Suddenly she lurched and leaned against their hands, and rocked heavily to the ground unconscious.

" Quick, man," said Denny, " we have the guts frightened out of her, she'll do." He fastened the rope so that it could slip no tighter, and knotted the free end to the bent bough. " She may rattle and choke like a fish on a string, but she won't hang," he said.

" I think we should make a job of it, Denny," said the more frightened of the two boys, the one who had prayed for her release from death on the mountain, " if we get caught she'll be a terrible witness."

Denny spat, a big spit down on the avenue. " There's enough to recognise you now, boy, without calling on her testimony. So mind yourself and don't get caught."

They left Nan half-hanging, half-sprawling in the avenue and went on up to the house.

When Nan got back her consciousness she was in such extremity as cannot be found either in life or death. She was exhausted, so exhausted that her mind was almost free from the heavy business of her body. But her mind was, for the time, wrecked by the mental fear and torture it had been through. She was like a person waking after an operation. She felt her way back to the business of pain, the life under ether retreated from her. Again she would not know whether she had suffered or been glad. Now, as ideas came back to her brokenly she hardly knew if she was hanged till she had died before Aragon, or if she was still alive. Her hands were still fastened, stiff and numb behind her back, the gag was in her mouth, if she turned the rope chucked in her neck. She could not say a prayer. Only she fixed her terrible eyes on the house and drank some consolation from its walls and windows, she thought of the beds inside. She would be laid in one of them if she did not die. She trembled to think of their kindness and beauty. She thought of her staircase, of its wide shallow steps, ease in their climbing. " If I am alive," she thought, " they will carry me up the front staircase, it will be the easiest, and put me in my good bed. I shall need care if I am alive."

Now she knew she lived. She was fully aware of the pain and the hideous discomfort that wrenched at her till there was not a nerve in her body that did not scream out for a second's ease. Only a second, free from this torture. Her eyes and her nose were running with the dusty powdery strength of the laurel flowers, pulled down like a wreath round her face. Nothing could deepen this hour's pain.

As she felt this, a terrible knowledge bounded up in her, sent her heart soaring and knocking again in her body, sent sweat in rivers down between her breasts, and every hair on her body itching with terror. For she saw that Aragon was burning. They had tied her here to watch the burning. Tied her so that she might watch her own soul burning. For Aragon was her soul. For Aragon she had given her life long years before when she had denied her love. And, dying to herself, she had taken the house and its ghosts into the comfort of her strong lonely life.

Now she saw the smoke and the rosy flames from her linen-room window. My linen, my pillow cases, my sheets. Like all the furnishings of Aragon, they were hers, she had always experience a sound satisfaction in so calling things " mine." My good brocade curtains, my fine new towels. Hers to keep from sun and moth and careless hands—most truly hers who could so cherish them, playing the careful steward to their excellence.

She saw fires lighting, one after the other, down the length of bedroom windows. Flames springing up behind the dark small panes of the windows, making the rooms behind the unblinded windows suddenly visible in the growing darkness. It was a stripping aside of that hushed and curtained privacy preserved so long and carefully.

She moaned against her gag and swayed, her hands in torture to rush towards the flames and drag out such treasures as she could, to beat down the flames with the great strength and power of her mind and her body. And then beyond the thought of her consuming treasures, there came to her with horror the remembrance of Miss Grania and Miss Pidgie locked in the nurseries. She could not reassure herself. She could not even hope that they would be freed and saved. She could hold no thought beyond despair. She leaned towards the house, and in her nurse's mind she saw clearly what their burning would be like. Sobs thickened in her throat and broke against the gag. Aragon was burning. All that she had piled on all was consumed before her eyes. And with Aragon, Miss Pidgie, her charge, and Miss Grania, her last baby, would die by burning.

Nan sawed with her chin at the rope round her neck, tucking down her chin, trying to get inside the loop that held her. It was no use. She stood quiet at last, bound fast to her laurel. Her hat had gone now and her beautiful round head was flung back in its curious wreath of leaves, her eyes had in them the horror and the madness of one who has looked at the execution of a loved person.

Now, when she came, as she thought, to the end of despair, a quietness drew closer and closer around her, a calm of different things, and at her side she felt the height of the one she called " the Child," close at her side, but she had no hand to put down to the level of its hand, no voice to whisper a word towards it. Others were with her too, Fox's who had loved Aragon with the same madness as Nan. Dull, good Fox's, and bad amusing Fox's, they came from the woods and from the soft kept places in the pleasure grounds where they walked among the trees and flowering shrubs they had planted in their time at Aragon. The dashing lady who had brought the first magnolia from Spain was here, and the pale, decorous Mr. Fox who had returned from an appalling honeymoon in Italy about the year 1870 with the seed of that stone pine where the herons nested now, so much more happily than he had done with his young bride.

These present shades were calm, they were so long dead that this burning of Aragon was only a chapter to them in Aragon's story. They looked at the consuming flames as they had looked at the fireworks and the bonfires which had celebrated their coming of age, their marriages and the births of their heirs. All time with them, they knew the house would rise again. A house would be built here for happy Grania's children. Grania looking back to the lusty foolish child she had been, and a little proud of the brave child she had been, would live here with her children, and the garden of Aragon flower after its desolation, and Fox's go fishing and courting and hunting from Aragon.

This calm knowledge flowing from them was like a bed under Nan's weary broken body. It was hands in her hair. It was solace to her guilty heart, the Fox's were her holy ghosts and comforters. They were standing close about her when she heard the sound of a car far down the straight avenue, the sound of a big engine gathering speed as it came towards her. She tried to turn her head, but she could not see through the thick glossy leaves of her laurel. But as the sound drew nearer she knew it was the soldiers come to save her house. A great surge of thankfulness and relief was lifting her heart as on a splendid wave when the lorry struck her down and killed her, on the smooth well-kept avenue.

XLI

" Instantaneous," the Sergeant said to Grania, " that's some consolation, isn't it, lady ? Well, I mean you must look for the bright side, mustn't you ? But it's a tragedy and no mistake. Can't blame the driver, Miss. We all saw some parties standing round, looking at the burning like, but they cleared off as our lorry approached. A chap couldn't be expected to know a lady was tied to the bush, could he ? I mean, fair's fair, isn't it . . . ? Yes, we *was* driving fast, and fast we must drive. Can't 'ang about and give the Shinners time to crack us off, can we ? Very sorry, Lady, but fair's fair, as I said, and we're not in any too 'ealthy a spot right here this minute. We're isolated. Straight on for the mansion, I suppose . . . ? "

They drove through the gate, hitting a post as they went and cutting across a corner of mown grass, old rich turf, abruptly torn and scarred after its years of repose.

A terror of Nan's dead and battered body seized Grania. She would not stay alone with her. She ran away crying, like a child that is lost in a bad dream, down a dark side path towards the stables, away from the burning house and the dreadful Nan she had left.

Sylvia was coming up the path from the stables. They met between the great box bushes cut into castles and peacocks and arches, the bushes that always smelt of cats, a smell they had not minded once, this had been their favourite playing place as children, before their strange hate divided them. Here they met and caught each other's hands for comfort and sobbed in the dark.

" Aunt Pidgie is safe, Soo is safe."

" Michael and Tony are safe."

" Nan ? "

" Nan is dead."

They sobbed on, still holding hands. Neither told the other what lost love she mourned.

THE END

The first Virago Modern Classic was published in London in 1978, launching a list dedicated to the celebration of women writers and to the rediscovery and reprinting of their works. While the series is called "Modern Classics" it is not true that these works of fiction are universally and equally considered "great," although that is often the case. Published with new critical and biographical introductions, books appear in the series for different reasons: sometimes for their importance in literary history; sometimes because they illuminate particular aspects of women's lives, both personal and public. They may be classics of comedy or storytelling; their interest can be historical, feminist, political, or literary. In any case, in their variety and richness they promise to confuse forever the question of what women's fiction is about, while at the same time affirming a true female tradition in literature.

Initially, the Virago Modern Classics concentrated on English novels and short stories published in the early decades of the century. As the series has grown, it has broadened to include works of fiction from different centuries and from different countries, cultures, and literary traditions; there are books written by black women, by Catholic and Jewish women, by women of almost every English-speaking country, and there are several relevant novels by men.

Nearly 200 Virago Modern Classics will have been published in England by the end of 1985. During that same year, Penguin Books began to publish Virago Modern Classics in the United States, with the expectation of having some 40 titles from the series available by the end of 1986. Some of the earlier books in the series were published in the United States by The Dial Press.